FROST HEAVES

FROST
HEAVES

STORIES

T. Stores

GREEN WRITERS PRESS *Brattleboro, Vermont*

Printed in the United States

10 9 8 7 6 5 4 3 2 1

Green Writers Press is a Vermont-based publisher whose mission is to
spread a message of hope and renewal through the words and images we
publish. Throughout we will adhere to our commitment to preserving and
protecting the natural resources of the earth. To that end, a percentage of our
proceeds will be donated to environmental activist groups. Green Writers
Press gratefully acknowledges support from individual donors, friends, and
readers to help support the environment and our publishing initiative.

Giving Voice to Writers & Artists Who Will Make the World a Better Place
Green Writers Press | Brattleboro, Vermont • www.greenwriterspress.com

ISBN: 978-0-9994995-1-1

PRINTED ON PAPER WITH PULP THAT COMES FROM FSC-CERTIFIED FORESTS, MANAGED FORESTS
THAT GUARANTEE RESPONSIBLE ENVIRONMENTAL, SOCIAL, AND ECONOMIC PRACTICES BY LIGHTNING
SOURCE ALL WOOD PRODUCT COMPONENTS USED IN BLACK & WHITE, STANDARD COLOR, OR SELECT
COLOR PAPERBACK BOOKS, UTILIZING EITHER CREAM OR WHITE BOOKBLOCK PAPER, THAT ARE
MANUFACTURED SUSTAINABLE FORESTRY INITIATIVE® (SFI®) CERTIFIED SOURCING.

CONTENTS

*Dedicated to Charlie Marchant and all the storytellers
of southern Vermont.*

ACKNOWLEDGMENTS

MY CHILDHOOD IN A SOUTHERN EXTENDED family taught me that life is made of stories, but it has been in my true home of southern Vermont and with my true family of Susan, James, and Izzy, and my community of friends-who-are-family, that I have been able to write a world made of shared stories. Frost Heaves would not be possible without the story-tellers of southern Vermont—my friends and neighbors who have shared their lives and tales with me. Thank you.

Dede Cummings at Green Writers Press is a dynamo. She believed in *Frost Heaves* from the moment she read it, and I am deeply honored to be one of her family of writers. Thank you also to Jessica Zeng, who has a deft and gentle editorial touch, and to all the interns and staff at Green Writers who have had a hand in getting this book into print.

The stories in *Frost Heaves* have been long in the collecting and curing process. I owe much gratitude to those who have helped me refine them along the way, beginning with the generous and brilliant Claire Messud, who was my workshop leader at Bread Loaf, and Dorothy Allison and Rob Spillman at Squaw Valley Community of Writers. Thank you also to my colleagues at the University of Hartford, most particularly my writing support group of Beth Richards and Erin Striff, and also Bob Logan and Bill Stull, who both reassured me that the work was worthy when I needed the boost the most.

The journal publications and prizes these stories garnered over the years gave me endurance for the long haul, and I sincerely appreciate those publishers and editors who saw their value. "Big Night" was first published in *Blueline* in 2013, was a semi-finalist for the Fish Story Prize, and placed 13th in the Mainstream/Literary Short Story Category of the 80th Annual Writer's Digest Writing Competition. "Fisher" was published in *Literary Mama* in June 2011 (www.literarymama.com), was a finalist for the Fish Story Prize in 2006, and won the Angel Award in the Glass Woman Prize Competition. "Fresh Air" was published online as the Unmanned Press Story of the Month (February-March 2013). "Labyrinth" placed 9th in the 2010 Writer's Digest Short Shorts Competition. "Love/Theory 7" was first published in *Sinister Wisdom* (Winter 2014–15), and "One-Hundred Ones" first appeared in *Atticus Review* (Summer 2014). "Frost Heaves" was first published as a short story chapbook by Kore Press (December 2009) after winning the Kore Press Short Story Prize in 2009. Thank you all for believing in these stories and for helping me to share them with the world.

This book was supported by Vermont Arts Council Development Grants (through the National Endowment for the Arts), University of Hartford Cardin Faculty Research Grants, and a University of Hartford Summer Stipend.

A human being is a part of the whole, called by us "Universe," a part limited in time and space. He experiences himself, his thoughts and feelings as something separated from the rest—a kind of optical delusion of his consciousness. This delusion is a kind of prison for us, restricting us to our personal desires and to affection for a few persons nearest to us. Our task must be to free ourselves from this prison by widening our circle of compassion to embrace all living creatures and the whole of nature in its beauty. Nobody is able to achieve this completely, but the striving for such achievement is in itself a part of the liberation and a foundation for inner security.

—Albert Einstein

FROST HEAVES

MEETING

We forget her. Indeed, we are almost patholog-
ical in our forgetting, in the way we forget
that other thing—death—that is daily present
and forgotten. Perhaps it is our communal forgetting that
brings us together.

She starts awake. We thump over her head—all of us
animals who return to den each long, cold, silent season.
Now the same spring smells—thick wet snow warmed
into slush with rain, churning river cracking ice, food
scraps thawing in buckets and cans and heaps behind wire
fence, the musk of males and females humping under a
full moon, the Worm Moon—lure us all out into fecund
nights and lengthening days. Today we meet in the Union
Hall over her den.

In our forgetting, she draws her thick black and white
tail around herself and closes her eyes. She will bed here
until after the kits are born in late April, until they are
ready to follow her into the meadows at shortest night. She
herself had waked to this den a spring ago, the same den
to which her mother's mother had waked, and of all those

mothers before. The huge furnace clunks on, humming fire-warmth into our dark earth and stone den.

Henry Smalls loves the first Tuesday in March—Town Meeting Day. He has risen early, brewed up a pot of coffee, dressed in his best plaid flannel shirt and jeans, laced up his Sorel boots, and walked from his house across the Common to the white-clapboarded, green-shuttered Union Hall of Neweden. He misses his wife, who'd been the town clerk and in whose memory he's kept up his duties as the keeper of the Union Hall. He misses the way they had always made this annual trek together. Before she died, they'd felt as if they themselves had called the people together, prepared the way for Spring. But that summons, Henry knows, like the irresistible thing that took his wife before she was sixty, comes from something else, something wider and wilder and older.

This first Tuesday in March, the sun peeks over the mountain at seven, the sky clear and blue, yesterday's snow plowed from the roads and sidewalks, and, warming in the sun, whomping from the roofs to ground in huge clumps. Henry has unlocked the ten-foot high front doors, stomped the snow from his boots and turned up the thermostat, listening as the furnace in the basement clunks on.

Satisfied that the radiators will start hissing and creaking in bit, he opens the storage closet where the rock salt is stored. A faint whiff of skunk. Damn. Thought he'd got that hole in the foundation plugged last fall. Near impossible to get 'em all with a stone foundation. Still, it's a sure sign that spring's coming, he thought. When the skunks wake up and Town Meeting Day comes around.

He picks up the plastic bag of rock salt, drops it a couple of times on the granite steps to break the clumps, then scoops out the tin cup full and arcs his arm to strew the sidewalk thoroughly. The window shade flies up in Sharon's apartment, next door to his house across the Common, and he sees her looking out from her kitchen window, the morning sun glinting in her red hair. He guesses she sees him, because she raises her hand halfway, a wave, and he feels his ears go warm under the flaps of his cap. He raises his hand in a return salute. Henry hopes she'll come to the meeting. A truck pulls up to the curb and parks, one of the Selectboard come early to get things set up.

Paul Dean sits in his pickup truck at the snow-crusted curb of the Common and straightens the tie under his fleece vest. He's chosen the lavender one, a quiet little signal to his constituents that yes, indeed, those rumors about him coming out gay are true. Most folks must know by now anyway. And hell, if they don't want to vote him back on the Selectboard because of it, the heck with 'em. Vermont isn't like that though. Paul already knows they'll vote him back in. The real battle will be convincing his son, Jared, that a gay dad isn't such a big deal.

Paul sighs. Jared is about as up-tight as they come. Furious at him. Won't even return his calls. Maybe Katie— his ex—can talk some sense into him. Paul wonders if Jared—home from college on spring break—will come with her to Meeting. He hopes so. He misses his son. He's a good kid, their only child. And now they are all apart, and him dating another man, finally doing what he had always known he was supposed to do. It's like an irresistible gravity inside, something he'd not thought about, *worked* at not thinking about. Now he's never felt so comfortable in his own skin, like that other self has died, been shed like a snakeskin. Without it, though, he's never felt so sad.

No regrets. Paul straightens his shoulders and tugs on his gloves. No hiding. Jared will come around. He has to. Paul determines to put it out of his mind, not think about it. Forget it.

He grabs his brief case and opens the truck door. Better make sure the meeting agenda is all set. His stomach growls. He smiles, thinking about the man still sleeping in his bed. It had been a late night. No time for breakfast this morning, but somebody will be selling muffins in the vestibule for the school trip to Boston.

Julie Stevens rips open three packages of Styrofoam coffee cups and stacks them next to the urn alongside the bowls of stirrers and sugar packets. She opens a quart of half-and-half. The vestibule is starting to warm, muddy snow-prints melting.

Paul Dean takes a cup and puts two dollars into the cashbox. "Morning, Jules. I'll just take one of these blueberry muffins."

"Sure, Paul." Julie looks around for Wes and Ashley, her kids, who are sliding down the iron hand-rail on the front steps. "Kids," she calls, "find the tape and put up the sign."

"Aw, Mom," Wes says.

Typical, Julie thinks. Everything a resistance with a twelve-year-old. "Just do it," she says. "This is your school trip, kiddo."

People are starting to arrive, walking in batches down the sidewalks, the parking spaces around the Common and behind the Congregational Church filling. The bake sale to help fund the school trip to Boston is an annual part of Town Meeting Day. Those people will be hungry and generous. The mood is festive—schools closed, people off work, spring coming.

"Hey, Jules." Christine, the partner of the high school art teacher, Mari, places a cake box on the table next to the brownies she and the children had made the night before. "Mari made cupcakes," she says. "Of course." Julie looks up just as Mari appears and slips her arm through Chris's. Chris's expression softens and Mari meets her lover's eyes, their glance expressing something private. It's a familiar look, but Julie can't quite place it, an old memory. Something sweet. She wonders. What is that look about?

"Where's Hal?" Chris asks, looking around for Julie's husband. "Does he teach today?" Chris likes Hal, likes talking theory with him, the only other academic in town, though he is tenured at a Connecticut university and she is still a grad student at UMass.

"Teaching," Julie confirms, looking from Chris to Mari and back again, her thick dark brows narrowing, speculative.

Mari pulls at Chris's arm. "Good luck with sales," she says to Julie, and "We'd better go in before the balcony fills," to Chris. As they walk up the steps, Chris resists the urge to hold Mari's elbow. Hell, she resists the urge to scoop her lover—her wife—up and carry her to the top. "Julie suspects something," Mari whispers.

Chris laughs. "But we won't tell, right?" she says. Our secret, she thinks, for now. She squeezes Mari's arm closer. Twins. Mari is pregnant with twins. They are going to be mothers. At last. Next year, they will come to Town Meeting with babies. Chris can't believe it, but the years of trying to get pregnant seem to have vanished with this new reality. Nothing but now and future, all joy, ahead.

The scraping of chairs overhead wakes her—the one we have forgotten—again in her den. She hisses, growls. We two-leggeds are gathering, and we are loud. She is tired from night prowling and does not want to be disturbed. The kits that are growing inside her make her want to sleep until the deep snows have gone. Laughter. Voices. Thumping. We are alive and together and it is Town Meeting.

Sam Fellows waves to Mari up in the balcony. They both teach at the high school. He checks his pocket again for the speech he has prepared about the cemetery project he'll be proposing at Meeting. Where has Paul Dean got to? Sam wants to get early on the docket.

"Need help with tapping out this year?" Henry Smalls claps him on the back hard. "Been warming up real nice, I reckon," he says.

Sam grins. "Already done it yesterday," he says. "Could use help with collecting buckets this week though." He sees Jack Crossly working his way across the room toward them. "And there's just the fellow to help out with that."

Jack, who is bent half over with age, hasn't bothered to shave. "You ain't 'specting me to actually work, are you?" he says. "Old man like me."

Henry laughs. "Old bird like you works just fine," he says. "Least wise if we uncork the right fuel."

Jack scratches his whiskers and grins. "P'rhaps," he says.

Sam knows Jack will show up at the sugar shack and sit next to the warm fire, maybe stick in a log or two now and then, because that's what Crossly did every year at sugaring. He'll come for the whiskey and the talking. They all do. Henry will come over and haul some buckets. "Hope somebody like Pelletier brings his kids along to do the work," he says. "I know you fellers ain't worth much."

Jack's wife, Katherine, comes up behind him. "Ain't that the truth," she mutters, her mouth a thin, hard line. Sam remembers his cemetery project. He ought'a get up there to the Crossly place and measure out the stones there one of these days.

"Katherine." Lawrence Withers touches his wife's old friend's shoulder. He and Katherine had been kids together, gone to grade school together sixty years ago, and she'd been Alice's friend when he'd brought his young bride back to Neweden.

"Ah, Lawrence," Katherine says. She places her hand on his arm, and he feels the strength of her grip through his coat sleeve. "How are you?" Her lips soften and her smile erases ten years from her face. "How are you holding up?"

The surge of emotion closes Lawrence's throat for a moment. He's forgotten again; Alice is dead. He swallows and looks away from the maze of lines in Katherine's face to the straight rows of folding chairs, the even blocks of twelve over twelve window panes in the walls of the Union Hall. "Fine," he says, more gruffly than he intends. "Just fine."

"I miss Alice so much," Katherine says, her voice quiet. "So much."

Lawrence coughs. Sentimental talk. "Saw my first robin yesterday," he says. "Over by the orchard." He glances at her then cuts his eyes back to the windows. "Thought you'd be interested to hear spring's coming."

Katherine's fingers press into his arm again. "Have you heard from Rose?" she asks.

Lawrence frowns at the reminder of his daughter. He shrugs. "Nope," he says. "But that's how young people are these days. Flighty as wrens." He shrugs off his coat to rid his arm of her hand. His daughter is a disappointment. No need to think about that.

Pelletier narrows his eyes as his eldest, his daughter, separates herself from the family and moves up the stairs to the balcony. She's up to no good. Lucky if that one graduates. Boy crazy. Good for nothing girl. Nothing new under the sun, he thinks.

From the balcony, Krystal Leclare watches her mother snake her way through the room below, pulling Krystal's father by the hand, her brothers, Robbie and Cash, following. They are smaller from this vantage, and Krystal likes that. Pieces of the crowd—heads—bobbing and ebbing and moving toward the family below as they greet each other and make small talk. It is always this way with Mom, who knows everyone, who tries to make everything and everyone happy. Energy seems to come off her mother like ripples in a pond. And I'm the big fat whale in that ocean, Krystal thinks. Never going to be small enough to tow along. Wait 'til Mom sees the new tattoo, a black cat, her familiar. Wait'll she sees the ring Trevor has given her.

Trevor is missing, of course. Getting stoned out back, probably. She leans over the railing. "Hey Robbie," she calls down.

Her brother looks left, right.

"Up here," she calls.

Mom looks up. "Krystal!" she says, frowning.

Not ladylike, Krystal thinks. Too fucking bad, Mom. She shrugs. "Get Robbie for me," she says.

Mom grimaces and grabs Rob's arm. She says something and points up.

Robbie's face breaks into a grin. "Sis!" he yells.

Good old Rob, Krystal thinks. "Go find Trevor," she says, nodding toward the doors. "Outside." And as Robbie nods, Krys has one of her flashes. She is a witch, after all. But this one leaves her cold, frozen despite the waves of heat rising upward from the crowd on the floor of the Union Hall. She sees Robbie covered in blood. No. No. No. Forget that.

The baby inside Vicki Wells hears the world in muffled song through blood, through amniotic fluid, through the heart-song of the warm world of mother. She knows familiar low tones and the iambic pentameter of life-beat. She swishes and sleeps and flutter-kicks to the lilt of mother laugh, father rumble, world outside, inside, all one. *Due in June. So happy. So glad we moved here. If you need anything. Come to dinner soon.* A song to the baby inside, a lullaby of words she does not know, folding over and around her like the topography of hills, like the winter into spring into time. An old repeating tune, only remembered now and then.

Thump. Thump. Thump. The moderator taps the microphone. *Town Meeting of Neweden shall come to order. Please rise. I pledge allegiance to . . .*

We have forgotten her.

She growls, fully awake now. She does not want to rise, but she does so, slowly. Her head turns and she looks up, the boards inches from her head, thin streams of light, moted with dust. A boot scuffs, breaking the beam.

The microphone squeals, and the fur at her neck stiffens. She stomps her front feet, warning. This is her den. We should not forget her, but we do. We will again.

Up first, Rusty Hathaway with the roads report. Randy, come on up.

She stamps her front feet again, then begins to turn, her tail lifting like a flag.

A cough. A throat clearing. *Before we get to the budget, we got signage goin' up now. You got a frost heave, you can call—*

The spray is all she has. The spray is everything. The spray is the world, the meeting of worlds. It is the thing that makes us remember, that wakes us again. It is the smell of life, of death, of being.

Groans and shrieks and laughter and hurrying feet as we evacuate, remembering her. She will soon be alone again in her den. And we will return, again and again, having forgotten, remembering the world.

BIG NIGHT

First sex after a twenty-year dry spell makes you stupid, Sharon thought, her wellies squishing in roadside mud. Rain dripped onto her nose. The winter smell of damp wool rose from her pea coat, blooming out with her body's warmth. She shined her flashlight at a frog the size of a bon-bon, who sprang into the road and stopped dead on the centerline as if waiting for a car to squish him. She revised the thought: *sex* makes you stupid.

The April air, sweet with snow-melt and leaf-rot, rioted with peeper songs, desperate and excited: *We're awake! Let's do it!* It was Big Night, the first warm rain of spring. Thawed amphibians were on the move, returning to the vernal pools where they had hatched to mate. Thousands would be flattened crossing roads in their willy-nilly rush to sex, except those that volunteers like Sharon would assist. *Stupid.*

The song fragment running through Sharon's mind was "Let's get it on . . . ." Marvin Gaye, 1974; she'd been hot for a farm-boy turned hippie. She licked rain from her lips. *Sex.* She'd been stupid forty years ago—pregnant at eighteen.

He'd ridden his Harley off into the California sunset and she'd settled down to raise that baby to a man alone.

And the first time I have sex in twenty years—*stupid again*.

Tail lights glowed through the trees. Sharon flashed her light as Randy had demonstrated in class—Ecology 101 at the community college—then shined it on the yellow sign they'd hammered into the frost: SLOW! SALAMANDER CROSSING! The tires splatted water against her poncho. Sex has made me stupid, she thought.

Sharon's car had died on her way to the first class. It figured. First thing she'd done for herself in thirty years. The practical old Taurus coughed and bucked. The roadside was banked with snow, so she maneuvered into a turn-out.

Damn it. She hadn't wanted to take the stupid class, but her friends at Neweden High, where she was a secretary, had been reminding her every semester when registration time came around. "You're smart, Sharon," the art teacher, Mari, kept saying. "It's never too late." Sharon had finally agreed. Why not? Her son was grown. She had no social life. The Pell Grant covered the tuition. Her job would pay more if she finished her degree. Naturally the car breaks down.

"Everything okay there, neighbor?" The call through the frosted window startled Sharon. Henry Smalls. His house was behind her apartment. His wife had died—heart attack at only fifty—four years back. He'd asked Mari about Sharon's romantic interests during breaks from dry-walling Mari's kitchen.

"I think he likes you," Mari teased.

"*Romantic interests?*" Sharon had snorted. "That's a good one."

Henry opened the door. "Car broke?"

"Just when I need to get to town for class," she confirmed.

Henry, pushing sixty but still muscled, no beer belly under his camo jacket, grinned down at her. "I'm on my way to the V.F.W.," he said. "I'll give you a ride." Pink circles bloomed on his cheeks.

Grabbing her books from the backseat, Sharon hid her smile. "Thanks."

Like warm rain after hibernation. His muscles like roots under mud. Viscosity, writhing, skin on skin. Smells— muck, ferns, wet fur. She'd moaned, kept her eyes squeezed shut. Air chilled her skin, hot against him, slick with him. Iced-over places steamed within. Thawing. Her body filled with light, heat, yearning. And her mind had emptied.

His teeth gleamed in the light-beam. "Hey!" Randy swung down from his Cherokee. Hiking boots, denim-clad thighs, slim hips. Sharon flushed, grateful for the poncho's shadow. Staring at his crotch like a schoolgirl. "What's the count?" he called.

"Not much." Sharon's rubbers squelched obscenely. She extended the clipboard. "Just frogs."

Randy pulled her in by the clipboard, tipped the brim of her cap with his face, and pressed his mouth to hers.

Sharon's body jellied. Their tongues bumped like tadpoles. He lifted her up from her muck-stuck wellies. His erection sprouted under layers of denim, wool and plastic, and her gut warmed. Damn.

Another vehicle geared down into the gully. The roadside squished. Sharon pushed Randy back. What if it was someone from the college? The high school? Someone she knew? Randy's feral grin, mocking. Stupid, she thought. Sex has made me stupid.

Henry Smalls rolled down his window and squinted. "You folks okay?"

On the first night of class, Sharon had penciled *"Randy"* into her notebook. Thirty-something, Sharon guessed.

Jeans, plaid shirt, fleece vest. Her teacher was maybe ten years older than her son.

Randy reviewed course requirements, texts, the service project. "Big Night," he said. "First warm spring rain. You'll help salamanders cross the road." A younger student laughed. Randy touched his fingers to his upper lip and smoothed his mustache into his goatee. "Voluntary," he said. "Not 'til April." Maybe he was nervous too.

Student introductions followed. Besides Sharon, four looked older than Randy—a waitress, a disabled factory worker, a husband and wife who took a class together every winter, "to keep busy." Three high school students earning transferable college credits; five twenty-somethings. Sharon remembered Candy, who had dropped out from Neweden High, pregnant with the baby in the photo on her notebook cover. "I'm here to show him how important learning is," Candy said to the class.

Next, Sharon swallowed and said her name. Randy looked from his roster into her eyes. "I'm here because—" His tongue slipped out to touch his moustache. "Because I want more—"

"Sharon," he repeated, interrupting. She'd meant to say *more pay*. He stared. Her neck prickled, not a hot flash.

Sharon filled three pages with on the local ecosystem that night. She'd never thought of Neweden—plants, animals, streams, people, roads—as enmeshed. Why, even the Taurus on the roadside, buried in the next snowstorm, a hiding place for mice and voles. Left there, metal would rust poisons and minerals into the earth. If she got it running again, it would flatten creatures too stupid or slow to move, change the air. A mosquito trapped in Neweden could carry encephalitis cross-country. "We're all connected," Randy said. "One big organism."

Sharon contemplated this huddled in her coat outside during the class break. What about the not-young, not-old woman with grown kid, no man, no one? What part was she in the organism?

The smokers' cigarettes looked like fireflies out of season. She guessed she was going to have to get a new car. Something reliable and solid. Practical.

"A little ecosystem of their own, huh?"

Sharon inhaled, startled. "Sorry?"

"Smokers." Randy nodded. "Like a little phylum, a social group." He leaned close, smelling of hemlock. "They even create an atmosphere." He grinned. "Smog."

Sharon swallowed. "I guess so." A satellite crossed the Milky Way into blackness. Worlds up there looked so close together. "Not for me," she said. "I quit when my son was a baby, long ago."

Randy shuffled. Why was he talking to her? A young woman looked over from the smokers and waved her cigarette.

"I think she likes you." Something she might say to her son, she thought.

"Hmm."

Sharon raised her eyebrows. "Not interested?"

"Not my type." His voice purred.

"And a student."

The silence stretched. The smokers stamped out their butts to return inside. An owl hooted.

"I heard you ask Candy about a lift home."

Sharon blinked. "My car died," she said. "But she, Candy—"

"Doesn't live in Neweden anymore," he finished, starlight reflecting in his pupils. "I do. I'll give you a ride." His finger pressed her forearm. "Okay?"

Sharon couldn't concentrate on the video in the second half of class. He was her teacher. She was old, past menopause. She was plain, dumpy. Surely he was just being nice. The salamanders on the screen pressed over and around one another, stirring muddied rainwater into oil, copulating.

She hadn't been surprised when his hand slid from the gear-shift onto her thigh, the Big Dipper low over the highway. Her body's zinging response had been the surprise. The motor rumbled. Her belly squirmed. She covered his hand with her own, tracing skin like fine leather between his fingers. Smooth. Like his penis later, inside.

"She's an old one." Randy approached the salamander hesitating at the asphalt. "Big."

Henry's eyebrows lifted. "Salamander savior, eh?"

Randy's fingers straddled the salamander's legs and belly, lifting her up. "You're something, old girl," he crooned.

Sharon watched his full lips, accentuated by his goatee. The salamander struggled, skin sheening in the light. Randy puckered. No, she thought. Randy kissed the creature lightly on the head.

"Uh." Henry grunted. "That just ain't right."

Sharon resisted the urge to spit.

Randy released the salamander into unfurling fiddleheads on their side of the road. She hurried lopsidedly downhill. "Thirteen inches," Randy said.

Sharon started. "Huh?"

"The chart." Randy looked at this watch. "10:25. Spotted Mole Salamander. Family *Ambystomatidae*. Female. Thirteen inches."

"Oh." Sharon fumbled for her pen. "Right." She scrawled the data.

Randy looked at Henry. "They can live twenty years."

Henry's smile-lines twitched. "Zat so?"

"Endangered," Randy continued. "The vernal pools where they mate—destroyed. Development. Pollution. Roads."

Henry nodded. "Cars get 'em."

"Yep." Randy stroked his goatee. "Unless someone helps them across."

"But odds . . . ." Henry cocked his head. "I mean, they been crossin' roads without help pretty much all along, right?" He spat. "Somp'in inside tells 'em which way to go, right? So maybe somp'in inside tells 'em *when* to cross the road too. Maybe the ones get squished just ain't meant to. Maybe meant to be dead. Lived out their usefulness."

Randy snorted. "Natural selection, you mean." He thought Henry was dumb, Sharon realized, just a woodchuck who shot deer and fished from an ice shanty. She shifted backward, boots sucking.

Henry scratched his chin. From her living room window, Sharon had watched him cross the street to the library every Saturday, and late on winter nights, illuminated by a lamp in his Laz-E-Boy, a book in his lap. Henry was no dolt. Something wise and warm underneath. Plain. Not dumb. "Yep," he said. "Natural selection. Got to evolve to survive, right?"

"They're slow to evolve." Sharon spoke suddenly. She'd read it for class. "Some animals take too many generations to evolve. Civilization's too fast. It overwhelms them. They die out before they adapt. That's why we have to help, right? *One salamander at a time.*" The Big Night project motto. Sharon flushed. "They don't know the road is dangerous. They can't *not* cross . . . ."

Both men stared, Randy as if she had performed a trick, Henry grinning, eyes creasing. Sharon closed her mouth.

"Been learnin' somethin' up there to the college then, ain'tcha?" Henry teased.

Sharon laughed. Mist rose from the thawing earth and asphalt, fuzzy forest split by road.

Randy handed her the clipboard. "I'd better check in with the next crossing guard."

Hadn't he known she was a good student? Sharon wondered. They hadn't talked about class, hadn't actually dated—"I can't compromise my position," he'd said—but he'd come to her apartment twice more. Once each month. Just sex. A condom in the wastebasket the next morning. "Protection," he'd said. Not from pregnancy. Hell, Sharon thought, at her age sex should have been even freer than the "free love" of her youth. Now it was safety. Separation from dangerous fluids. She watched Randy start his Cherokee. He'd kissed a damned salamander.

"You need company?" Henry put a hand on her shoulder. "Got an umbrella in the truck. Keep those critters out of the damp whilst they cross the road."

Sharon laughed.

Sex with Henry was like late summer sun. He watched her face, and she watched his.

Henry had stood on the centerline and flashed his light at the driver of a Volvo until it stopped, and the salamander wriggled across on her own. "What say we go see this salamander party?" Henry had said, yawning. "Then I gotta call it quits. Okay?"

He'd read her mind. "Yes," she said. "I've been wanting to follow them all night."

Henry folded his umbrella. "Thought so," he said.

Their boots sucking and squooshing mud, ten minutes downhill into the darkness, the salamander scurried into a crescent-shaped pool of snow-melt. In a month it would dry up, eggs hatched and the next generation launched into summer ferns and forest floor. Tonight, though, the water, darker than the sky, swirled with shining bodies. "Whoa," Henry said.

"It's magic," Sharon murmured. Dozens of salamanders writhed, bodies pulsing, rippling the surface. "Coming home. Getting on with life." Her breath fogged, twisting in mist. Trees overhead plopped droplets. Water swished, frogs peeping.

I'll buy a car, Sharon thought. She slid her cold hand inside Henry's coat, felt his heartbeat through flannel. A two-seater. Something fun.

LABYRINTH

Not a maze, but a labyrinth. Lawrence surveyed the patch of bare earth. He had no use for mazes with their dead-ends, forking paths, choices at every turn. Too easy to waste time, lost or circling. To tell the truth, he had no use for a labyrinth either, except as a project. He needed something to take his mind off Alice. Dead. Gone. Buried. And Rose gone too. Just wandered off, like always. A new garden for spring would be good for clearing out the cobwebs. And he needed to do something with the patch of dirt over the new septic system anyway.

Lawrence stood with his tools, surveying the flat stretch of bare earth, the leach field stretching downhill underground below him. He remembered standing hand in hand with Alice, newlyweds back in '55, at the labyrinth at Chartes, the last romantic moment of his life. She'd said it then: *Labyrinth would make a good pattern for a garden.* Lawrence thought it would be a good project to pass the time. What little of it he had left.

He hoed out the middle cross of the labyrinth, chop-drag, chop-drag, mounding dirt. He didn't miss romance. What a waste of time that was. Life demanded attention, a clear-eyed pragmatism. Chop-drag, earth divided into a map. You were born, you lived, you did what you could with the life you were stuck with, and you died. If you'd lived well, maybe you didn't leave the place worse than you'd found it. Maybe your kids appreciated you. Maybe you left a nice garden.

Lawrence consulted the printout of the design he'd gotten from the Internet during the long winter, alone for the first time in almost fifty years. A lot of hooey about the labyrinth on the Internet. Now there was a place for romantic notions. He dumped the bricks and muttered. *Journey to center of your life and back, my eye.* Nice pattern, that's all. Those folks all trying to make it all mean something. Lawrence had no use for any of that crap anymore. Waste of time.

He pushed the wheelbarrow to the pile of old bricks by the road. He planned to lay bricks into the design level with the black Vermont soil so he could mow over the whole thing in the fall. He picked up one, cold and solid in his bare hands—edges rounded almost smooth. It bore the date—1932—it was made, the year of his birth in this same house. He harvested two at a time, clanking them into the wheelbarrow. He stopped to pull away poison ivy from the heap, cars whooshing south on the highway beyond. The straightaway had cut off their road back in '67, after the third baby, a dead-end.

He didn't see the snake at first, draped under the vines and over the bricks. It didn't move, like a decoration. Lawrence felt his neck go cold. He started back, eyes widening before the thought—*Snake!*—registered. The wheelbarrow handles caught the backs of his knees. He toppled it. Bricks spilled into grass. His arms windmilled as he fell, and his head bit an edge. Blackness.

A machine steaming with black tar black tar black tar. Men pick-axed the bricks from the road and piled them on the edge of the property. Black tar to make the new road. He remembered his father's hands, as cool and rough as the bricks, as he twirled him around in the air, singing, *Swing low, sweet chariot, coming to carry me home*—. Pap died when he was seven—tree fell on him at the logging camp—but he still felt that brick-grip, smelled black tar for the new road. Dead-end now.

Light bloomed against his eyelids. Lawrence felt warmth on his arms. Not God, just sun. He opened his eyes to the patterns of maple leaves, bright greens against the blue sky, brown branches in whorls around the mottled tree trunk, upward. Toward heaven. Lawrence blinked. Pap might've seen this. Had his God helped him in his last bit of time? Nope, none of them.

Lawrence touched the side of his head where a lump bulged. Just a scratch. He couldn't have been out more than a minute. He rolled onto his side. The snake, still draped over the pile of bricks, hadn't moved. It was a milk snake, least that's the name Pap and Mother always used. A constrictor. A short thick snake, patterned in orange rectangular blotches edged with black. Good for keeping the mice out of the barn. Not poisonous. Not dangerous, except for clumsy old men. Lawrence re-sat his hat on his head. The snake seemed heavy with heat, the curves pressing over the heap of bricks. Lawrence rolled to his knees, then pushed himself to his feet. He rested a minute. The snake moved, almost imperceptibly, then stopped. When he'd caught his breath and all dizziness had passed, Lawrence reloaded the bricks. Maybe the snake would be gone when he got back. He hated to bother it. So calm, so still.

He trundled the loaded wheelbarrow across the yard. Here his mother had hung sheets, shirts, and trousers, laundry for working men that kept them fed after Pap died, on lines criss-crossing the yard. He used to run between the clotheslines, tree to wall to post, twisting starched rows to nowhere, fabrics billowing in the wind. Mother yelled. *Keep those filthy hands off.* Lawrence remembered his mother's red fingers dropping seeds into his own palm. *Idle hands are the devil's workshop,* she'd always said. She'd thought milk snakes drank from the udders of cows too. Mother took ten years to die of the TB. Not like Pap. More like Alice with the cancer, that maze of chemo and hair-loss and hospitals and home again. Men don't linger, don't hang on like that. Boy grows up quick tending the sick. Lawrence reckoned he'd drop over quick too, someday, likely soon, maybe next time he saw a snake.

After a sandwich and a dab of rubbing alcohol to the bump on his head, Lawrence edged the path of the labyrinth pattern in a double row of red brick, around then in, around then in, toward the center. Oriental poppies, echinacea, lupine, and columbine would divide the paths in garden areas between the bricks. He'd seed the paths with grass. He thought of walking barefoot on spring grass when he'd been a boy. No choice back then. No extra money to waste on shoes. Penny saved, penny earned. *Waste of money, like time, is a sin,* his mother'd said. Now Lawrence thought maybe he'd take off his shoes and walk barefoot in summer through the labyrinth, turning around and back on himself. He touched his head. Bump must've addled his brains.

What to put at the center? He liked fruit trees—practical, useful—but you couldn't plant a tree over a leach field; roots might eat into the pipes. A bench then. A birdbath. Maybe both. Alice would've liked that. A still place where she might hold his hand and watch the birds. He remembered her holding his hand over her heart at Chartres, her breath on his knuckles. Alice's whisper had seemed loud in the great cathedral. *You are my center.* That hand had felt as warm as the earth in the sun. He'd been aroused by it, even in church, before that God in whom he had since stopped believing. He'd felt ashamed, excited, dangerous. Sinful.

Lawrence dragged chunks of granite from the stone wall, watching for snakes. He wouldn't be surprised again. He turned first one, then the other, over and over, rolling it to the center of the labyrinth garden. He would need a plank to make the bench. Though he'd never been one to sit still for long. He might have stopped with Alice for an instant, but then he would have noticed a branch fallen in the flowers, or some dead-heading, or weeds that wanted pulling. She had been a sentimental woman. Holding hands like they were youngsters with nothing else to do. *Retired ain't dead,* he'd always said. Lawrence pushed at brick that wasn't level with the earth and flexed his fingers, the arthritis aching a little. *I should have stopped longer with her.* Alice's hands had pulled him down into the French comforter again and again in their room in Paris. The skin of her hand on his belly had been smooth. So bad and so good all at once. A new life for him. Then the babies had come, and died, that third one, Forrest, making it all the way to two before that sick took him. Before Rose.

Lawrence pushed the wheelbarrow back to the brick-pile. The milk snake had inched a little further along. He paused. It was shedding, the thin, translucent layer—a version of itself—had slipped away. The bricks snagged at the snake's belly, freeing him from the old skin. About half of the skin dangled from his tail. The snake seemed completely still. Lawrence loaded up without disturbing him, and headed back to his project.

He connected the dots to the ends of the pattern with the curving lines described in the diagram, one brick after another, until the circuit was whole. His shoulders ached with wheelbarrowing, his bones stiff. He held the hoe like the baby's tiny hand had circled his thumb. He couldn't remember which one. Maybe it didn't matter. A baby holds on for all time, whether he lives on or not, at least 'til they wander off. Black-flies swarmed when he turned the afternoon earth. Earthworms, those ugly pink brothers of serpents, worked back down into darkness again and again.

Back around the house to the barn, to the brick pile. Three-quarters of the snake was out of his old skin, new scales glistening in the spring sun.

Lawrence went into the barn, waiting for his eyes to adjust to the darkness, listening. He found a thick board, about five feet long, rough-hewn. In the light that slivered through the sides of the barn to pattern the stone floor, something moved. Maybe a mouse. Maybe a ghost, if you believed in such things. Alice had, part of her romantic side. *I'll wait for you on the other side,* she'd said. But he didn't believe in heaven any more than in sitting still. Lawrence went inside for a drink, and then carried the bench-seat back to the garden center where he balanced it on the granite blocks. Time slanted tree-shadows across the labyrinth.

Evening approached. Lawrence brought out seedlings in plastic trays from the cold-frame and went to the cellar for the bags of perennial corms Alice had watched him divide last fall. *Don't hate me for dying, Lawrence,* she'd said, her wheelchair perched at the edge of the slate patio. *Don't hate God.* He tucked in the little plants. Annual seeds—nasturtiums and marigolds—he poked directly into empty patches of crumbling dirt. No God to hate. He tossed an earthworm to the robin lurking on the edge of the labyrinth.

For Rose, that strange child who had finally stuck in Alice's womb, who had finally lived into a whole blond adolescence and adulthood, he mixed the seeds for bluets into the grass seed to be scattered along the path. She had liked bluets. Maybe Rose would come to see his labyrinth when the flowers bloomed. Lawrence remembered Rose's little hands wringing bouquets of shredded bluets, brought late to the dinner table. *Wash your hands, Rose,* he'd said. *Cleanliness is next to godliness.* Rose, whom he had never really expected to stay. Rose, who had stood on the pile of old bricks to watch the world rush past on the new highway—*Where does it go, Daddy? Why are they going, Daddy? Why?* Rose, who had rambled off to college, to California, to India, to an ashram, to Texas, to who knows where? Like a vine, a weed, a dandelion on the wind. Lawrence raked the seed into the soil of the paths between the bricks, sweeping the tines to fan the lines into arcs. Looking for something to believe. Some romance.

Lawrence didn't believe a hoot of that blather on the Internet about the labyrinth's spiritual purposes. Foolishness. New agers. Romantics. Like Alice, wanting to scatter the garden seed instead of planting in rows, in a neat pattern with a plan, a map, then surprised when the weeds choked out the vegetables or a carrot turned up in the pumpkins. Like Rose, who hadn't even enough sense to keep touch with her old folks. Surprised when an old, sick mother up and dies and she hasn't heard in time for the funeral. Sorry Rose. Too late for Alice.

Lawrence punched little holes in the dirt with his hoe and dropped in corms. The soil pushed under his nails as he buried them, painful and cold. He wound his way along the path, planting and mulching as he moved inward toward the center on his knees. He wore the pads she had given him for Father's Day. *I know you won't wear them,* she'd said.

In the middle of the garden, he sat on Alice's bench. It wobbled, needed another stone for balance. The center wanted for something else too, a birdbath, a special plant. He brushed dirt from his hands, rubbed the knots of his knuckles. The robin ran crossways over the pattern, stopped and yanked out an earthworm. A car whooshed past on the highway.

Lawrence stood. The labyrinth lay around him, brick-lined paths arced with raked seeds, dark bark mulch tucked close around little plants in the dividing strips of garden. The pattern pleased him. Not a maze. A path in and back out. A labyrinth over shit. Maybe he would plant a rose here at the center. Something with thorns. Something sweet and bright.

He loaded the wheelbarrow with his tools and trundled it to the barn to put it away. The snake was gone. He'd left his skin though. Lawrence picked it up. It felt like air, like lace. Skin as translucent as frost, faintly patterned. Like Alice's thin papery hand on the hospital bed, the ugly IV tube still puncturing it, the blue veins fading as the blood settled. Why had they left him all alone?

Little Rose would have kept the snakeskin to show him when he came in from work. She would have met the car and taken his hand and led him to the spot where the old snake had become a new snake. The world had seemed hers, and she had shown it to him, holding his hand.

Lawrence held the snakeskin, saw his own mottled brown hand shaking a little. How had he gotten so old? He carried it to the labyrinth and walked the path that turned back and forth, in and around, to the center, where he laid it on the bench next to him. If Alice were a ghost, this is where she would come. He listened to the breeze, watched the slant of long tree shadows. He was still, waiting.

Rose should come home. Lawrence sat still. She would not hesitate to walk the grass path of the labyrinth, bluets between her bare toes. He would go in and find the number of the ashram, wherever. He would call her now. I am sorry, I will say. I will say to her, *Come home.*

In the wind, the snake skin whispered something dry, a hiss, a snicker. Rose would laugh too, he knew. The romance of a labyrinth. Just like him to plant it over shit.

FISHER

David opened a can of tuna and called "Here kittykittykitty, here kittykittykitty." Then he heard himself, his high-pitched sing-song. He tried a manly "Hey, Killer, come on boy," but he knew it wouldn't work. Killer—a twenty-pound Maine coon cat with tufted ears and a tiger's yellow glare—might look like a tough guy, even a wild thing, but he was a marshmallow, a city cat, accustomed to a lambswool bed, designer food from tiny cans and petting on demand . . . at least he had been before the baby. David worried. Killer had only been venturing outside for a couple of months, since the snow melted in April, just after the baby came. He had never stayed out overnight before. Neither David nor Vicky had even thought about Killer until yesterday. They had been away three days.

When Vicky phoned from the hospital, checking to see that he'd made the drive home safely (two hours; no, he didn't speed) and to report the number of seizures the baby'd had since he left (only one, thank god), David didn't tell her about Killer. The cat will come home in the morning, he told himself, missing Killer's weight on his feet at the end of the bed. He didn't sleep well. Something rustled in the farmhouse wall behind his head, scratching and gnawing at midnight, and he banged with his fist until it settled down. He started awake again when the screeching from the pond began. *Peepers,* he remembered, the locals call them peepers. Then he dreamed that he was free-climbing the rock face behind the house. The granite split open between his hands with a wail, and he hung by one hand, proud of the muscles in his arm and shoulder but knowing, even in his sleep, that he was ridiculous, dangling in the air, the smell of warm stone sharp in his nostrils. A shadow slipped from the crack and faded into the darkness down the cliff, toward his house.

The can of tuna on the porch was untouched in the morning. "Killer!" David called. "Here, kittykittykitty!" Nothing.

Dawn streaked the eastern sky pink. He wished Vicky was here to watch it with him, the view so different now that the trees had leafed out. He remembered holding her just-swelling belly in his hands in October, standing behind her here on the porch in the morning, their first sunrise in the new house. "Our baby will grow up in the country," they had bragged to city friends. In private, they had wondered—being both city-raised children—what will her life be like? Barefoot. Naked sometimes. Close to nature, a little wild even. We'll get her a pony. We'll read together by the wood stove in the evenings. But by January, it had become so quiet when they ran out of talk, playing game after game of gin rummy, slapping the cards down, shuffling, that they had finally called the cable company. We'll just watch the good stations, they said to each other, educational TV. Maybe A&E or Discovery. No commercial stuff. But the woman at the cable company told them that they were three miles from the end of the cable.

Even the local radio station, on the far side of a hill, came in scratchy, as if from an earlier era. The nights stretched to sixteen hours, the winter into a frozen March, and Vicky's belly grew. David sometimes missed the rumble of the subway far underground, shaking their little apartment. He didn't tell Vicky about his own cravings, for oil-shiny hot dogs and for the simplicity of running down the stairs to buy one from the cart on the corner below their old apartment. Here, coffee at the local diner required layering skin in long-johns, flannels and goose-down, shoveling snow from the dirt road, warming the car, and driving four miles down the mountain to town. David longed for friends too. Even though he'd eaten breakfast at the diner nearly every morning for six months, the men still only nodded when he entered. Life here should be different. They had moved to Vermont for community, for closeness as well as simplicity and safety. But the winter had come and snowed them in, and then the baby had come too soon and all wrong. Parts put together wrong. The world gone wrong in the birth of that misshapen product of their love.

The phone rang. "Two seizures last night, one at nine and one at 11:45. I almost called you," Vicky said. "But nothing since midnight. I slept a little. I think maybe she's better."

David drew in his breath. Better. But she'd never be fine. Why had this happened to them? He pinched his tongue between his teeth. No. He exhaled carefully. "Good," he said. Should he come to the hospital?

"No," she said. "Work. Get some work done. There's nothing you can do here. It's too far. You should just take care of business. Get some sleep. I—" She faltered. David heard her draw in a breath, ragged at first, and then she exhaled, controlling the air. She made her voice strong again. "I'm fine. I'll go over to Care House later for a nap. A shower. I'm fine."

David hesitated, ashamed. He should insist. He should make the drive up to Dartmouth to the hospital. Two hours isn't so far. He should say, No, I'm coming. You'll need me. I'll be there. But he couldn't. He didn't want to go. He didn't want to watch the baby quiver, the blue lines jittering on the screen above her crib. He didn't want to sit in that little room watching television, waiting for the next specialist to breeze in and deliver his new edict contradicting the last specialist's edict, for some city friend to call and ask "How is she?" and listen with that antsy tone of obligation, making excuses to disconnect as soon as possible, while the pristine green hours of Vermont summer stretched on in the other world outside. "Are you sure?" he said. The gruff note in his voice masked relief. "I should get those asset management team reports done before the deadline." He heard his words hurrying. Don't change your mind, he thought. "We'll need the money from that project," he said.

He worked from home now, but it was still a job. And it was still new enough—this working from a distance—that he felt the pressure to prove himself, to prove that he could produce just as much, complete just as many projects and reports, process as much data, all that stuff that disappeared into the electronic void, off to the city, as if he were still just down the hall a few blocks from that ragged gap in the lower Manhattan skyline.

"Yes," Vicky said. But David knew money meant nothing to her. Nothing but the baby had meaning now. Keeping the health insurance and paying the bills was his business. Keeping the baby alive was hers. They'd never had that kind of relationship before, divided according to some biological tradition, but here it was.

"Killer," he said before he could stop himself. Damn.

"Is he okay?" Vicky asked. "I bet he was glad to see you." She laughed a little. David imagined her standing again beside him on the porch watching the sunrise, Killer winding around their legs. For one instant, he felt her escape the hospital. Then he remembered the way the baby looked in the crib, the blue lines on the screen.

"Uhm." David stopped. He couldn't tell her. "Yeah," he said. A silence widened between them. He hoped she was smiling, thinking of the cat. "Well," he said.

"Okay," she said. "I'll call later. Maybe after my nap." She sighed. "I need to sleep."

"Yes," he agreed. "The nurses will call you at Care House if . . . if they need you. Right?"

"Yeah," she said. "Yes. They will."

"Okay," he said. He scanned the reeds beside the pond and the line of boulders that marked the brook disappearing into the trees. No cat.

"Work hard," she said. "I love you."

David could hear the bleeping of the baby's heart monitor. "Me too," he said.

After eight hours at the computer, the evening still pristine with daylight in the approach to solstice, David drove the Cherokee to town for chicken-fried steak and mashed potatoes at the diner, four-berry pie with ice cream for dessert. He stopped first at the general store, the town hall, and the gas station to pin the flyers he'd made to the community bulletin boards:

Lost Cat.
Grey tabby. Very large.
Pink collar with bell.
Answers to Killer.
367-4236.

David regretted the pink collar. The bell was to keep Killer from the birds at the feeder, but it was really unnecessary. Killer preferred sleeping to hunting, and they hadn't remembered to fill the bird feeder since the baby had come in April. The pink, like Killer's name, had been a nod to the irony of the cat's size and fierce appearance. Only once had Killer shown any natural instinct, cornering a mouse in the kitchen one autumn night soon after they had moved in, while he was still restricted to the indoors. As he stuck a thumbtack into the board beside the door to the diner, David recalled the lazy batting of the giant paws, the *ee-ee-ee* screaming of the mouse. "Get it away from him!

Don't let him torture it anymore!" Vicky had cried. David had dropped the soup pot over it, slid a magazine under it, and flipped it out into the early crust of snow on the still-green grass. The mouse had dragged a leg, cowering under a leaf. It had probably died there from exposure, or had been eaten by some other predator, a real predator who killed quickly and efficiently, for food rather than sport.

"Cat gone missin', eh?" The man who held the door open for David was his neighbor down the hill just past the trees, Arnold Chamberlin, an octogenarian who still tapped his sugar maples with buckets instead of rubber tubing. David blushed, remembering Arnold's look when he'd explained to him in March, just before the baby, that no, the trees weren't tied together with string; those folks were just sugarin' the new-fangled way. They both took seats at the counter, leaving a stool empty between them, and looked up to read the Specials board.

"Evenin' fellas," said Ellie, the thin, grey-haired waitress. She opened a bottle of Bud and put it in front of Arnold, then stuck one hand into the back pocket of her jeans. "No stew tonight, Arnold," she said. "You want the meat-loaf instead?"

Arnold took a swig of beer and nodded. "I reckon," he said.

"How 'bout you, sir?" Ellie looked at David. "Chicken fried steak? Gravy on the side, right?"

David smiled. "Yep. You got it."

Ellie laughed. "What to drink tonight?"

David hesitated. He preferred microbrews, but he could feel Arnold listening. "A beer," he said. "Bud's fine."

"How's the wife?" Ellie lowered her tone and frowned. "That baby doin' okay now?"

David sighed and shook his head. He pulled the corners of his mouth down. "She's back in the hospital," he reported. "Seizures. Vicky's up at Dartmouth with her."

Ellie shook her head. "I'm sure sorry to hear that," she said. "You tell her I'm thinkin' about her." She turned and went to the kitchen to put in the orders, and probably to spread the news. Even though they were new to the little village, everybody seemed to know about them and their business. Not insiders yet. Not quite outsiders either.

David ate, following Arnold's lead, in silence, newspapers propped against the sugar holders on the counter in front of them. He tried to focus on a story about a discovery of new cave paintings in the French countryside, a farmer uncovering an old entry with his plow. He imagined the cool air rushing out of the darkness, ripe with images of something older than time, the secrets, perhaps, of a people who worshiped the creatures they killed, people who lived closer to the edges of death and life.

Ellie asked when he'd see Vicky again and David set the paper aside. "Oh, I'll go back to the hospital day after tomorrow," he said. "After I finish up a project for the boss-man in the city." He didn't want the locals to think he was a trust-funder. He wanted them to know he worked.

Arnold may or may not have been listening. Another man had stopped to ask if he could borrow a chainsaw. Arnold nodded. "Just go on in the back and get it out the mud room next time you're by," said Arnold.

"Door'll be open?" the other man asked.

"Shoot. Lost that key thirty years ago," Arnold laughed.

David tasted his pie, listening. No one around here locked their doors. How could you just trust the world like that? He thought of the old apartment in the city, the satisfying clunks of the deadbolts at the end of the day, being alone and safe with Vicky inside. Then the Towers fell. Then they had moved here.

David put cash down on top of his check and stood up to go.

"Fisher prob'ly got'im," Arnold said, still looking at his paper, open to the story about the French farmer.

"What?" David asked, not sure he'd heard right.

Arnold looked sideways, his bushy white eyebrows dipping in at the middle in a scowl. "Fisher," he repeated.

"Hate to say, but your cat's prob'ly dead. Fisher cat." He wiped one hand across his mouth. "Fishers kill off a lot of house cats 'round here, 'specially them that's new to the woods." He folded back the newspaper page. "I'll keep my eyes peeled," he said, "but like I say, prob'ly already been got."

At home, evening light stretched out in bright streaks against a deepening blue and David, shouldering long-handled branch-loppers, followed the path down from the house around the pond and into the trees, stopping to cut saplings sprung up almost overnight as he walked. He and Vicky cross-country skied right from the back door last winter, before she'd gotten too big, and now the New England forest seemed determined to reclaim even the little strip of a trail he'd cut last fall. It must have been hard for farmers to keep their fields clear before bush-hogs and tractors. He couldn't imagine the labor involved. After the interminable bareness of winter, spring had seemed to happen in an instant. The trees became lush with green, and weeds and ferns and vines shot up from the ground to obscure rusted hulks of old cars and tumbling foundations and stone walls as if humans had never touched the land. Maybe it just seemed to have grown up so quickly, David thought, because of the baby. He whacked a low pine branch with his pruners, cracking it off onto the ground. Maybe he just hadn't noticed. Because of the baby.

The land folded in on itself, hiding even the closest neighbors—the Chamberlin place down the hill, Hop and Gracie Peletier and all their kids and grandkids past the rise, the lesbians from Boston, Chris and Mari, across the road, and next to them, Wesley and Raven, the middle-aged hippies who trucked organic vegetables to yuppie restaurants around Amherst. David still felt a little scared alone like this in the woods, thick with hemlocks and maples and oaks, and the poison ivy he'd learned to see everywhere after a rash made his face swell in May.

Anything could happen. Like that logger who died when the tree fell on him, or the hunter who'd broken an ankle and hobbled out after two weeks. Cell phones couldn't get a signal; he wouldn't be able to reach even a neighbor for help. But he made himself walk the trail—a gentle loop into the woods, through a break in the stone wall, around and back out into the meadow again below the granite face of the little cliff—once a week with the pruners. "Keeping the wilderness back," he laughed to his old office-mates in those casual empty minutes before conference calls. He didn't bother to put on the plaid flannel shirt anymore, didn't see himself in his mind's eye, a Paul Bunyon, ax on shoulder. The green, long-handled loppers from the Walmart over in New Hampshire worked better than an ax, and their firewood was delivered by a guy with a dump truck and gas-powered splitter, a man unafraid of a chainsaw. David wasn't even sure where the ax was now. Maybe buried in the undergrowth.

"Killer!" he called as he trimmed the trail. "Here kitty-kitty!" The darkness between the trees, the thick mat of pine needles, the bird songs and blue sky patches between the leaves overhead sucked his voice into silence. Arnold saying, *Fisher prob'ly got'im.*

David had looked up *Fisher Cat* in the *Britannica* online: *Martes Pennanti.* Not actually a cat at all, though he'd been imagining something like a mountain lion, the fabled cat-amount that became extinct in the New England wilderness before the turn of the century, hunted to death by the settlers. The fisher was a member of the weasel family. The size of a medium-sized dog, he'd read, with short legs and dense dark fur. The name is a misnomer: it doesn't fish; it's not a cat. It kills rodents, squirrels, occasionally a small deer. An inveterate foe of the porcupine. And house cats. Especially the soft, domesticated kind.

The phone screamed him awake in the middle of another earthquake dream. 2:53 blinked to 2:54 on the digital clock beside the bed as he fumbled for the phone. "Hello? Vicky?" She had been with him in the dream, partly a memory of a day in their senior year at Oswego; they used to go climbing every weekend on the cliffs. They were engaged. He couldn't believe his luck in finding her. In the dream, they rested on a the rounded curve of an enormous boulder, the valley spreading out green and thick with trees below. In the dream, he reached for Vicky, intending to kiss her. Earthquake. A jostling at first, and then a crack. The smooth round granite opened between them, like a crusty roll broken by huge invisible hands. "Vicky?" He snapped on the light, sitting up.

"They say she's dying, David." Her voice shook. His wife. Vicky. She sobbed once, hiccupped a breath. "They say if you want to see your daughter before she dies, you should get here now."

David was already out of bed, stepping into the shorts he'd left on the floor. "I'm on my way," he said. "I'll be there soon." He hung up the phone and zipped his pants in one motion. He crammed his feet into his sneakers and dialed the number of the sheriff's office in town, tying the laces while it rang. When the sleepy voice answered, he said, "I'm David Wells, up Scott Hill Road. I'm leaving for Dartmouth-Hitchcock. My baby is dying and I've got to get there fast." He gave the woman his cell phone number and described his black Cherokee.

She would radio the State Police and get him an escort. "Go with God," she said.

The words stayed in his head. *Go with God*. David's chest seemed about to split. What kind of God would give a baby just to take it away, just to fuck with your life like this? *Go with God*. He grabbed his keys, opened the door, and stepped into the night.

The bushes rustled. A creature. Something large. It growled, a savage sound, guttural. The hairs on David's neck sprang up. A frightened little noise escaped from his throat—"Ah!"—and he stood inside the kitchen before he was conscious of moving his feet. He held his breath. The sound crawled against his skull, something that lurks, something from wilderness, darkness. A predator. David swallowed. Vicky. The baby. He flipped on the porch light. He pushed the screen open and forced his feet to move again across the threshold. A black hump, the size of stone too big for a man to carry, slunk away down the slate sidewalk. David gripped his keys, hesitating. It looked back. The eyes reflected the porch light and fangs gleamed. *Fisher.* His adrenalin pounded. His knees felt bare and cold, damp in the night air. The animal faded into the brush.

She breathed. She stopped breathing. The machine squealed. A nurse turned it off. Another machine clicked, clicked, clicked. Her bulging eyes moved under a thin blue veil of eyelids. She seized, twitching while they watched the lines on the monitor. Then she coughed and breathed. Vicky thumb-stroked the baby's arm above the little fist, clenched like an unfurled fern. She kissed the Neanderthal-broad but porcelain-white brow. The baby looked like a fairy tale creature, human but disproportionate, hunched and protruding in all the wrong places. David still couldn't believe this was his daughter. *My daughter. Angela.*

"You should hold her," Vicky said. "Can we hold her?" she asked the nurse.

The woman smiled. "Of course," she said. "Let me help."

David resisted the urge to step back, made his feet heavy and felt the hardness of metal like a tower thick in his spine and shoulders. *I can do it.* He thrust his chin out, a motion he suddenly remembered from his father, whom he barely remembered at all, a drunk who'd left him and his mom when he was seven, jaw bone stiff, shrugging his mom off as she grasped at his sleeve, walking away.

The nurse held the tubes and wires to the side while Vicky lifted the baby—*Angela, my daughter*—from the crib. The baby opened her mouth in a tiny dark O, like a normal baby, and her tongue poked out to taste the air. Vicky settled the odd little shape into his arms, which he held in the regulation way, cradled, shifting stiffly to the side to take her. The tubes and monitor wires draped over his arm like threads, connecting the baby to life, to the machines.

The doctors had inserted the tracheotomy tube last week after their rush back to the hospital. The baby had been born eight weeks too early, in April, because of the deformity, the problem they hadn't known about until the ultrasound at six months, because Vicky had been too afraid of the needle for the amniocentesis. "I wouldn't have aborted her anyway," Vicky had said. "She's my hope, my little angel."

The doctors said she would never be normal. "Babies with these problems don't usually live past three." They weren't even sure where some of the organs were inside her little round abdomen.

"I can't believe it," Vicky had said. "She seems so strong." The baby had come home in June for two weeks before this last crisis. And those two weeks home, watching the sun come up while the baby—so small, so oddly shaped, but theirs—had nursed at Vicky's breast, had seemed almost normal. Maybe she'll be okay, he'd thought then. Vicky loves her so much. And the day they had looked out to see a moose eating the lilacs they had even laughed at the sur-real scene, like a hallucination brought on by exhaustion, as if they were, like all new parents, just so tired.

And then the seizures, the ambulance ride north, sway-ing side to side around the curves. The doctor said that she wouldn't live without a trach tube. Let her go, David had thought, but he had said instead, "Whatever you want, Vic. You decide."

And now, watching the eyeballs roll under their lids, the little tongue probing the air from its cave, he wondered, will she die now? Will she finally die?

The weight of a baby—*this baby, my daughter, Angela*—is nothing, less than that of a cat. Killer. Fisher prob'ly got'im. The baby moved in his arms, a little stretch, then gaped her mouth into a yawn. Her eyes opened, and she blinked. David felt his jaw move. The pounding in his skull, the little hairs at his neck, his bare knees. Fisher. She looked into his face, searching. She had his father's eyes. They seemed to meet his. Her brow creased, a frown. Then she was blank again, smooth. His spine seemed to loosen.

Vicky slept on the bench beneath the wide window. Pink streaked the sky. Asleep, just like that. She must have sat down after she put the baby in his arms. He stood still, conscious of the rhythm of air pushing in and out of the baby through the tube, the steady beat of the heart monitor. The nurse was gone. Vicky's face was smooth, her hair tousled. She slept slouched, one hand over her heart, as if pledging or protecting. A hollow yawned in David's chest, pulled apart. His cheeks were wet. If he were alone in the woods, he would scream. He wished he could to go back to sleep too. He wished he could wake up with his wife beside him and the world sane. The baby moved, and he looked down at her again. A little reddish-blond hair had come in on her scalp, like the ragged goldenrod he couldn't seem to get rid of in the flower bed beside the porch. Gracie Peletier said that it secreted a poison through its roots that killed off other flowers. David had pulled it all out, but it was stubborn, it left roots, and he had seen— had it been just yesterday?—that it was coming back again. Hanging on. Tough.

When David drove up that evening, Killer sat on the porch, washing his whiskers in a trance of pink tongue-to-paw circular motions. He glanced up, blinked his yellow eyes once, and returned to washing. He was not dead. The fisher had not got'im.

"Hey there, boy." David leaned down to rub the cat's ears. Killer purred and stretched, lengthening himself into a yawn. There was a note stuck in the screen door. *Hope you don't mind we let ourselves in to put some food in your fridge. We're thinking of you. Hop and Gracie.* He hadn't locked up in his rush to leave—the snarl of the fisher—last night.

Killer looked at him, waiting to be let inside. Where had he been? How had he lived?

David remembered his father, that last time. A year or so after he had deserted them, David had come home from school to find the old fuck-up passed out on their stoop. Some big kids had been poking him with the toes of their shoes, laughing and jumping back when he snorted in his sleep, just another homeless guy. David remembered focusing his eyes on the cracks in the sidewalk, pretending not to know who the drunk was. He had skirted the lump of his father's body to climb the steps to the building. He remembered smell of stale beer, the hoots of the teenagers, the scrape of his book-bag against his knees. The reassuring clunks of each dead-bolt lock as it turned inside the apartment door. He had never told his mother. The door had been granite as he had leaned back, trying to catch his breath, the adrenalin thudding black against his skull. And his father had vanished into the tall buildings and alleys. Killer purred under his finger-tips and David focused on the mountains layered into the horizon. What had happened to him out there? He stroked, fur warm with sun under his hand.

The baby hadn't died. Angela hadn't died. They didn't understand how or why. She was just better, breathing on the machine, not throwing up the breast milk Vicky continued to pump for her, not seizing. David had looked at his daughter, sleeping, his wife, sleeping, and had watched the sun rise, blackening the face of the mountain into darkness. He thought, I will not fuck this up.

Now he opened the door for the cat. He would call his mother later, ask her come to stay for awhile to help, even though she said that the country was too quiet and the mountains scared her. He would call the visiting nurse, and the hospital supply company that delivered the oxygen tanks and the monitor. He would finish the asset management reports and email them to the city. Maybe he would push the lawn mower down the trail through the woods. He would call Hop and thank him for the food, maybe see Arnold down at the diner for a Bud. Try the meatloaf.

David switched on the lamp before the broad windows and dialed the hospital. He jingled his keyring, waiting to be put through to Vicky in the pediatric intensive care unit. The face of the pond below was a dark circle, but the green-shaded light beside him reflected, like the eyes of an animal before a car or in a porch-light, in ripples across the water. Vicky came on the line. Stars pricked the purpling sky.

"How is Angela?" David asked.

Killer jumped into his lap. David listened—*The doctors say maybe Angela can come home again next week . . .* He unbuckled the pink collar and tossed it into the wastebasket. Killer scratched the deep crease in the fur at his neck against the edge of the desk, his groan of pleasure erupting.

David worked the house key loose from his ring and dropped it into the deep lower desk drawer, which he closed. "Yes," he said. "Home soon."

SHORTEST NIGHT

We feed her and are hungry with her, and our fear and shame and joy in this hunger makes us more ravenous, gluttons.

She is on the move under a velvet sky, pricked with golden lights of the universe. This too is the universe. Her territory. Our territory. This is shortest night.

She knows that it is also the night of every week that we leave our offerings to her—to our own hunger—on the roadside. The cubs follow, eager for the game, waiting for her to topple the barrels so they might rake their tiny claws through the thin white plastic bags, the bounty of our gluttony spilling into their laps. Every seventh night, we two-legged animals line her route with barrels of chicken bones, melon rinds, salty potatoes, thick white grease fragrant with pork, sweet crumbly cakes. All for her and her cubs, and for the mice and the rats and the raccoons and the possums and the birds and the insects and the bats who fed upon the bugs and the owls who fed upon the mice and all the rest. All the universe. We two-leggeds are generous with the world on these seventh nights. And because this seventh night is the shortest night, we two-legged have gathered around a fire, light in the darkness, sparks leaping

into the sky, while she keeps her cubs to the bushes, waiting to tip the offering until the roadside grows dark again.

Mari feels a flutter in her abdomen—the first time in her
five-month pregnancy—as she stands before the bonfire.
It's a baby, like a salamander, she realizes, flipping over,
swimming inside her. She holds her breath, mouth open,
eyes following sparks into the midsummer night sky. The
night when everything begins again, the new cycle of life,
the universe turning. She and Chris always have a party
for Midsummer's Night. How right that the babies should
make themselves known just now.

"Congratulations," whispers Katherine Crossly. Mari
blinks and closes her mouth, turning to her. The girl is
lucky, having a wife instead of a husband, Katherine thinks.
Might be some help with the babies. "I heard the news,"
she says, holding out the paper bag she has brought. "A gift
for the twins," she says. "Not much. Just some little blankets
I crocheted."

Mari smiles, and the firelight winks in the wet in the
corners of her eyes. "Thank you so much, Mrs. Crossly."

"Katherine, please," Katherine says. "You make me feel
old." Though I suppose I am, she thinks. "Twins! My, my.
You'll be busy, I reckon." She catches a glimpse of her husband's back as he stoops over the coolers on the back deck,
digging for a beer in the ice. Jack was never one to miss
a party, even at the "lez-beans'" house, as he said, if there
was free alcohol to be had. And food. For a scrawny man,
he was never satisfied, never full. Katherine's own stomach
growls at the aroma of burgers. She too is hungrier these
days.

Mari puts her hand over her little belly. "I think I just
felt one move," she says. Her eyes are round, a little awed.

Katherine flashes back to her own first pregnancy, that
sudden feeling that something bigger and wider than her
own life had opened within. That there would need be

more and more. A need for more. A warm breeze lifts a curl at her forehead, and she looks up into the expanse of sky. All those worlds up there. All those places. "Yes," she says. "Your life is going to change."

Sharon lets Henry take her hand after she shuts the truck door, and lets him keep holding it as they walk through darkness up the dirt drive toward the bonfire. Something huffs off in the darkness, and she shifts closer to him. Henry squeezes her hand.

"Smells like bear," he says, voice low. "Best stay close." He tugs her arm under his, and his voice contains a note of laughter.

Sharon smiles, safe in the darkness, and licks her lips, tasting his kisses. She would like another. What will folks say? The first time they have gone out in public together. A couple. Couple of old fools, most likely. A branch cracks in the trees. Henry puts his arm over her shoulder, and she hooks a thumb into his back pocket. Why not? The world keeps turning around.

Brandi Pelletier watches Mr. Smalls and the secretary from the high school walk into the firelight with their arms around each other.

"Ew, gross," whispers Krystal. Brandi watches as the older girl puts her hand into her boyfriend Trevor's lap. "Old people shouldn't be allowed," she says.

Brandi isn't so sure that scrawny Trevor, who is always stoned, is all that much of a prize, but at least Krystal has a boyfriend, unlike herself. Even fat Krys could get a guy. Brandi knows how she does it. She looks around at the other kids. One of these guys might be the one she'll give up to. Maybe tonight. Soon anyway. Her father moves between her and the fire, his silhouette dark and scary. He shifts and she sees that his arm is over her little brother's shoulder, of course. Dad loves his sons. He doesn't even see her, and Brandi feels empty in her invisibility. Why doesn't he see her? Look for her? Why doesn't he love her? She scans the circle of teenagers sprawled on the log seats just far enough away from the fire that nobody will notice the beer bottles they've snuck out of the coolers. Maybe that kid just back from college—what was his name? He looks angry, sullen.

Jared scowls and takes a swig from his beer. Why isn't he getting drunk faster? God-damn his dad for showing up tonight. God-damn it. Why did he have to bring that guy here? Big fag. This might be the shortest night of the year, but it seems to Jared like it will never end.

She sways her big head back, forth, scenting the air, smelling us and our food, listening to us and our hunger. We have gathered in the light of the fire, out of our shelters, seeking something we desire, something to fill us on this shortest night. She listens. The roaring moving things are silent along the roadside. The bucket of offerings smells sweet. The cubs are restless. She is black with night. She is black with night. She is hungry, as are we.

Mari observes that Paul Dean's son is glaring at him and the guy he's brought to the party. Change is hard for kids, she thinks. Will her own kids—the twins growing within her now—hate her for being gay? Jared is sitting in the dim shadow of the studio with the other kids—some of them her own students at the high school—and she hopes against hope that they aren't drinking, or if they are that they won't try to drive home. She wonders if she should find someone to tell. Maybe Chris. Maybe one of their parents.

Then the mysterious fluttering again in her gut. Mari's mouth opens, but she can't speak. Oh. She thinks, oh. Change. Yes.

Ashley stands silently in the darkness just at the edge of the woods. Her brother, Wes, and the Pelletier boys have left her here, holding an empty paper bag. She is five. Mommy will come find her soon. If she stands still enough, though, to catch the snipe, which she thinks might be like a little fairy or maybe a mouse, the boys will give her an ice cream. Wesley said so. The hot dogs on sticks held in the fire smell yummy. She hopes there will be s'mores later. After Mommy comes and finds her. Another smell wafts from the trees behind her, something dark and huge and warm, but there is no moon, only the endless stars overhead, and she cannot see the animal that moves there. Maybe the snipe, she hopes. Then Wes and the big boys will see that I am big enough to play their games.

David can see the bonfire at his neighbor's house through the trees as he drives down the mountain. On his way to the hospital again. In the night again. This is shortest night, but he knows he is driving himself through a longest night. He wants so much for it to end. But it is never ending.

She rears up on her hind legs as if one with us, the two-legged. She places her forepaws upon the offering and pushes, spilling the bounty from barrel to road, where the cubs and she will feast in darkness that is so short, so timeless. We share it with her, guilty in our shared hunger, our need. It is the shortest night. With dawn will come the longest day.

FRESH AIR

"It was Tinker Bell, Daddy!" Ashley screamed from the back seat. "You hit Tinker Bell!"

Hal pulled the minivan to the side of the interstate, heart pounding, the darkness pushing in from all sides. He clicked on the emergency flashers.

"Whoa." Kareem's voice was deep for a twelve-year-old. "What was that?" he asked.

Ashley started crying. "Daddy. That looked like Tinker Bell!"

"God, what a baby," said Will, with typical big brother derision. "That's stupid, Ash," he said. "Tinker Bell isn't real."

"Will—" Julie's tone was warning. "Ashley, sweetie, it's okay." She unbuckled her seatbelt and twisted back toward their daughter, seated between Will and Kareem, the inner-city kid the family was hosting for four of the summer weeks.

Ashley sobbed. The van rocked as a semi whooshed past.

"What happened, Dad?" Will's face was blue in the light from his Gameboy.

Hal's heart still thumped. "I don't know," he said. He couldn't take his eyes off the smear where the thing—not

Tinker Bell, of course, but what?—had smacked the windshield. A luminous body, maybe five or six inches long. Wings? Out of nowhere from the freeway into his headlights. Not a bat. Too small for an owl. They'd all ducked, except Will, who'd been checked out into his own animated electronic world as usual. Hal had braked by reflex, but the thing—*she*—hit the windshield with a decidedly un-fairy-like *thunk* and tumbled over the roof of the mini-van—*th-thunk*—into the dark.

"Daddy," Ashley cried. "You've got to find her. You've got to find Tinker Bell. She's hurt!"

"Honey," he started. "We'll be late for the fireworks." They'd never get a good parking spot.

Julie squeezed his arm. "Just get out and look around," she hissed. She turned toward the backseat again. "Ashley sweetie, of course Daddy will look for Tinker Bell." Julie gave Hal *the look*, her eyes black in the light of a passing vehicle. "I'm sure she's fine, honey. Probably just flew off into the night. She's magic, you know." Julie reached back for Ashley's hand. "But Daddy will check, right Hal?" she said.

A week ago, Hal had washed dishes watching the chickens in the yard, Tinker Bell the last thing on his mind. The view of undulating Vermont mountains through the six-over-six panes of the kitchen window was stunning, lush and green in late June summer, the valley mist just clearing. One of the roosters—too many of them—jumped a hen, who squawked, flapping her wings, and ran off. They were going to have to do something about those damned roosters.

He soaped the coffee pot. He tried to forget the chicken problem, returning his thoughts to the email he'd just received. The dean was going to offer him the chairmanship of the English department. At last. He'd busted his ass for fifteen years. About time they recognized it. A fat raise, some respect, an *in* on all the really important business.

The authority to whip the department into shape, tighten the ship. Oh sure, he'd have to work with those old duffs who'd had tenure so long they were rotting into dust, but a little quid pro quo would take care of that. Control of the department budget would even things out. Shake things up a little anyway.

"Daddy!" Ashley jumped up and hooked onto his arm. The glass he'd been washing squirted into the air and smashed to the floor, shattering.

"Shit," he said. "Ashley! What the hell?!" He heard the harshness in his tone too late. She burst into tears. "Don't move, sweetie," he said, trying to get his voice under control. "It's okay, baby. Don't cry. It's just a glass. You just surprised me." He lifted her up into his arms, suds dripping down his elbows. She gripped his neck, sobbing, and he rubbed her back, surveying the mess. Fuck. One more thing to do. The tears subsided, and Hal set his daughter carefully onto a wooden chair before a fresh bowl of Cheerios with a kiss, then turned to sweep up the broken glass, shoving the laundry basket aside to get at the pieces beside the washing machine. A puddle of water. Shit, another leaking pipe. Nothing like an old house to keep your plumber in business. He dumped the broken glass into the garbage.

Will wandered in, still in his pajamas, opened the refrigerator and stood in the open door, scratching his head. "We never have anything good to eat," he complained.

Hal ignored him.

"Cheerios are good," Ashley said.

Will scowled at her, but he grabbed a bowl and spoon and the cereal box and slouched into a chair. "No bananas," he said. "Man."

Hal turned his back on them and put his hands into the soapy water again. Damn Julie. She had to go and get a job right now, didn't she? Not like they needed the money. Hell, he had projects to finish during the summer break. And now this promotion. Shit. What had he been thinking? Taking care of the kids and house all summer had seemed a breeze a month ago. She had caught him when he was dazed from the spring semester with commencement looming and a zillion faculty meetings and registration advising at full tilt. "Honey," Julie had said, rubbing his chest, "it's a great opportunity. Counseling at the Women's Crisis Center is just the kind of thing I've been wanting to do. Ash starts kindergarten in the fall; Will is old enough to watch her after school if I'm late on one of your class days. It's a perfect job for me. I'm ready. I've waited twelve years for this. I need to go back to work." And he'd been feeling generous. The three glorious months of summer had seemed to stretch out ahead of him then.

"Sure, honey," he'd said. "Of course you should take the job. I'll manage the kids. It'll be easy. No problem." Idiot, Hal thought now, sweeping. What the hell had he been thinking?

The phone rang. Julie. "Yeah?" he answered.

"What's the matter?" she asked.

"Fucking Tinker Bell," Hal muttered under his breath. He wanted a cigarette. No way to do that, not here, not with Julie and the kids sitting right there in the car on the side of I-91. He glanced back. Ashley had pressed her face to the dark window, leaning over Kareem. He could see the whites of the boy's eyes beside the little girl's face. Will's GameBoy purpled his son on the other side, highlighting the sharp cheekbones that seemed to have emerged suddenly this year, the softness of childhood melting away. Will looked a lot like his own father now, Hal thought. Crickets whirred in the tall grass on the Interstate's edge. Almost thirteen. A little man. Where had the years gone?

He walked away down the shoulder behind the car, swinging the flashlight back and forth as if looking for whatever they'd hit. Mostly he hoped that any oncoming traffic would see the beam of light—and his silhouette in the car's red emergency flashers—and not kill him. Something rustled in the trees. He pointed his torch. A yellow-eyed reflection. His neck hairs prickled. Predator of some kind. He hoped it was just an owl on a low branch.

Hal thought of his dad again, the long square chin and high hard wedges of bone above concave cheeks, the lines etched deep when he lay in the hospital dying. It struck Hal that his dad looked a lot like the pirate in that old Disney Peter Pan movie. Hook. Obsessed with a crocodile. With revenge. Getting his man. He'd never retired, never taken a day off except to play golf on Saturday and go to church on Sunday. And both of those were for business anyway. Contacts to be made, connections to be worked. All about getting ahead. Captain Hook. His dad had nearly had an embolism when Hal had told him he was going to get his doctorate in English lit all those years ago. *Knew you'd never amount to anything,* the old man had scoffed.

A semi truck growled up the incline and Hal waved his little light up and down. It seemed feeble. The trucker blasted his horn, but he moved over to the outside lane as he passed. Fucker.

Maybe Will was turning out to be a little like Hal's dad. Obsessed with that stupid computer game. *Gotcha, dude,* Will would say, gloating, when he scored a kill and the Gameboy made that sad *wah-wah-wah* sound. That and the skateboard. Always begging Hal or Julie to drive him someplace with concrete. Kid didn't appreciate what he had—room to roam, tight community, good school, gorgeous green mountains, safety. Still, Hal thought he understood. Kid wants to know what's out there, what the world is like. "Maybe we've kept them too protected here," he'd said to Julie. "Maybe it'd be good to try the city for awhile." Sure would be easier for me, Hal thought.

Something glinted on the roadside in Hal's light. He walked into the grass and bent down.

•

"Yeah, I'm okay," Hal had said to Julie on the phone, "but we're going to have to move." He stared out at the chickens in the morning sun. Stupid things. "The Dean's going to give me the chairmanship after Bob retires next year. I'll need to be in town, on campus, most of the time. Can't be commuting with that schedule."

"What?" Julie sounded taken aback. Hal felt another surge of anger. She'd known this might be coming. He'd told her. It was the next logical step in his career. Did she expect him to keep driving a hundred miles back and forth from Vermont to the University in Connecticut forever?

"Move?!" Will yelped. "Are you kidding? You mean get out of this hicksville at last? Yes!"

Ashley started to wail. "But I like this house! What about Raggedy?"

Will scoffed. "No roosters in the city, Ash. Guess we'll have to eat'im."

"Will!" Hal said as Ashley burst into tears again. Great.

"Hal," Julie said, her voice strained but quiet through the phone, trying not to disturb the calm of the Crisis Center, Hal guessed. "We'll talk about this later. I—" He heard her swallow. "It's great news, honey. Congratulations." Yeah, Hal thought, that sounds sooo sincere. "I just called to remind you that you have to meet the Fresh Air bus at 2," she said.

Shit, he *had* forgotten. "Right," he lied. "I know. In the Co-op parking lot." He rubbed Ashley's shoulder as she sobbed and hiccupped into her security blanket.

"And make sure Will clears out a couple of drawers in his dresser," Julie said. She paused again. "Really, honey. The promotion is great. We—I— it's just a lot to take in right now. I didn't really think— My job—" She sighed. "Well, we'll talk about it."

Hal felt his brow furrow. Talk about it. That wasn't the deal. The deal was that this is what they were going to do.

Move. Sell the house. Get on with his career. "Sure," he said. "Whatever." We'll see about that, he thought.

"I'll see you all later," Julie said. "I'll meet you at the Co-op so I don't have to bike home. Don't take the rack off the car. Love you!"

"Yeah," Hal said. "Bye." He punched the Off button on the phone.

It was a gun, a pistol, lying in the grass beside I-91. Hal stood over it, shining his flashlight on it. He'd never touched a gun in his life. His dad had hunted once in a while with clients, but Hal had refused the one or two invitations his dad had offered, preferring to stay home and read. Mostly he hadn't been able to stand watching his dad do the hearty buddy-buddy salesman thing. It was so transparent. But those fat-cats had seemed to suck it up.

"Look at that. Heat on the side of the road."

Hal started. He hadn't heard Kareem approach. "Uh, yeah," he replied. "I can't imagine how it got here."

Kareem snorted. "Someone tossed it," he said. "Prob'ly."

Hal felt his face warm and he was glad for the darkness. Of course. It had probably been used in a crime, maybe down in the city, dumped out the window of a car heading north. "Guess we should turn it in to someone," he said. "The cops."

Kareen laughed. "Cops," he repeated. Hal heard the silliness of the word. "Yeah," Kareem said. "Can't leave it here. Some kid might find it." Hal heard authority in the boy's voice, experience.

Hal bent and picked the gun up with two fingers through the trigger loop like they did on NCI. It was heavier than he expected. It slipped a little in his grip.

"Whoa there," Kareem said. "Point that thing the other way."

Hal heard the car door open and he glanced back. Will. Kareem reached over and thumbed down a little lever beside the trigger. The safety. Of course. Hal looked at

Kareem. "Don't tell Will," he said. "I don't want them to know." He wasn't sure why.

Kareem's eyes met his for a long second.

"Hey guys," called Will. "What'cha doing? Find Tinker Bell?" He laughed derisively.

Kareem nodded once, and Hal slipped the gun into his jacket pocket.

Kareem had come off the bus holding a black duffel and a skateboard, a good-looking African-American kid just about Will's height. "That's him," Julie had said, pointing. She had been waiting at the Co-op when Hal arrived with the kids. "I recognize him from the photo."

"He boards!" Will said. "Cool." He flipped down his own skateboard and held his mother's shoulder while he rolled back and forth.

The woman at the bottom of the steps—Mary something, Julie knew her—greeted Kareem and checked her clipboard. "Stevens!" she called out, looking over at them and beckoning.

Julie untangled herself from Will and stepped forward, followed by Hal carrying Ashley. Will tried a little jump off the curb and failed, his skateboard clattering to the sidewalk, wheels spinning. He picked it up and tucked it under his arm.

Kareem stuck out his hand toward Julie for a shake, but she ignored it and circled her arm over his shoulders in a hug. "We're so glad you're here, Kareem," she said. Her own skin seemed darker next to Kareem's, her Mayan nose flatter and wider. After fifteen years of marriage, Hal sometimes forgot his wife's Guatemalan heritage. She had been adopted as an infant by a slightly flaky single American woman, Rosie, his mother-in-law. Raised in liberal but white Vermont, where she'd been the only person of color in school, Julie—*Juliana* really—was the one who insisted that they host a Fresh Air Fund kid. They'd always meant to, but the time had never seemed just right. "Hal," she'd said.

"Will and Ashley need to see people with dark skin. They need to know that white is not the only color. They see me, but they don't. They have my blood in them. They are darker than their friends, and they need to know that that's not weird." There was no argument for that, Hal knew. He agreed with her anyway. And that was back in the winter, before Julie's job, long before his promotion.

He watched the boys eye each other. "Hey," said Kareem. He nodded toward Will's skateboard. "Nice board." His own was scuffed and a little splintered, the wheels black with tar.

"Thanks," Will answered. "Not much terrain around here though. Skate park at the Rec, but we live out in the sticks. Dirt road." He rolled his eyes. Shrugged. "Maybe Dad'll bring us to town sometime, to the Rec. That's cool."

Kareem scanned the mountains over town with a little smile. "Sure is green here," he said. He looked at Hal and stuck out his hand again. "Thank you for inviting me, Mr. Stevens."

Hal smiled, shifting Ashley, and shook hands. The kid had a firm grip. "Call me Hal," he said. "And we're glad to have you."

Kareem glanced at Ashley. "Hey little sister," he said. He held up his palm. "Give me five."

Ashley giggled and slapped his hand. "I have a rooster," she announced. "His name is Raggedy. He's magic."

Will laughed and shook his bangs out of his eyes. "And he looks de-licious!" he teased.

"Dad-dy!" Ashley wailed.

Hal met Julie's eye. "We won't eat Raggedy, sweetie," he said. "I promise."

"Will, don't be mean to your sister." Julie sounded tired.

Kareem shifted his bag.

"The car is over there," Hal said, leading the way, Ashley heavy in his arms.

"Well, Mom," Will said, "Dad said we had to do something about all those extra roosters."

Behind him, Hal heard Julie shush Will.

"Mo-om," Will said, "I know that means we've got to kill some of them."

"Will," Julie said, tough and low. "That's enough. You know we won't hurt Ashley's pet."

"So where's Tink?" Will asked, looking into the pool of light on the side of the expressway.

"Nothing yet," Hal said. The weight of the pistol pulled his windbreaker downward. He put a hand in the other pocket to even it up. He swept the grass and asphalt with his light. "I think we'll just get on to the show, what say, guys?" He turned toward the car.

"Whatcha gonna tell the kid?" Will asked. "The fairy's flat? The fairy's flown the coop?" He laughed harshly.

Hal sighed. Were all teenaged boys such shits? "Give it a break, Will," he said. "We'll tell Ashley that Tinker Bell must have flown away so she's fine."

They walked single-file back to the car, Hal bringing up the rear. As soon as he opened the back door, Will cawed. "How many points do you get for hitting a fairy, anyway, Ashley?"

"Chill man," said Kareem. "Don't be a jerk." He slid in next to Ashley and put his arm around her shoulders. "She wasn't there, little sis. Flown off we reckon."

Will snorted. "Grow up, Ashley. There's not any such thing as fairies. Jeez."

"Hey man," Kareem said. "No need for that." Hal got in on the driver's side. He drew the seatbelt across his lap and checked the mirror for headlamps as Kareem finished. "Let the kid be a kid for a little bit more." Kareem's eyes met Hal's in the mirror. The gun thumped against his thigh, solid and somehow mean. "Grown-up is way overrated."

Indeed, Hal thought. He reflected on the honors seminar he was prepping for the fall: Childhood in the Literary Imagination. It was all the rage on the list-serves in his specialty since 9-11—the "joy" of childhood, the so-called "innocence." Right, Hal thought. Take Hook, for example. He heard himself lecturing to his future students. Hand lost to a crocodile, the whole clock-in-the-croc metaphor, a skeevy dude trying to catch up with a bunch of "lost boys" who "never grew up." He'd definitely have to add *Peter Pan* to his list for the class. What could be more ripe for a little undergraduate analysis? Hell, it cried out for it. College students were all a bunch of kids refusing to grow up anyway.

"Honey?" Julie said.

"Sorry?" He'd missed something. "What?" A burst of fireworks showered blue and red off in the distance, some other small town's celebration. A semi-truck shook the car, passing. They'd have to hurry to get to the ball park before the Brattleboro fireworks started.

Julie's hand stroked his wrist, and Hal felt a surge of shame. The gun. The argument. "Aren't we going to go?" she asked.

The boys had adjourned to Will's attic bedroom to unpack Kareem's things that first night, right after the fried chicken, corn on the cob and fresh strawberry pie. "This is awesome food, Mrs.—uh, Julie," Kareem had said. "Thank you." The kid had excellent manners. Hal tried not to think *for some-body from Harlem*. He wasn't like that.

Hal could hear their low voices overhead as he sat on the toilet seat reading while Ashley splashed in the tub. Kareem had seemed sweet, a good kid from a tough place. Wasn't that the whole idea of Fresh Air? Get those kids out of the city for the summer. Let them live the good life out in the country. If only his own kid wasn't so hostile.

Hal had to admit that he resented the whole thing a little himself. Hell, he sure could've used a break from the suburbs when he was their age. A break from his father. All that money, but no way was the old man going to let him have any of it. Stay home and work, earn it, he'd always said. But Hal hadn't caddied at the club like the old man wanted him to. Nope. Nor even washed cars at the lot. Nope. He'd gotten himself a job at the library, shelving books. Air conditioned. Quiet. Not much to do. Lots of time to read, all those books for company. *What are you, boy, some kind of fairy?* his dad had asked. *Get a man's job. Get a tan. Get some muscles.* I guess I showed him, Hal thought. Chair of English. Maybe into the Dean's Office after that. Jerk.

"Daddy?" Ashley's voice brought him back to the bathroom. The bathwater sloshed. "What's going to happen to Raggedy?" Her little pixie face was bearded with bubbles.

Hal blinked. Shit. "Nothing, sweetie," he said, turning his book on its face. He forced a smile. "Raggedy is your pet. We won't let anything happen to him."

"Can he move with us to the city?" she asked, patting bubbles in the water, glancing sideways at him then back down. She was worried. She pushed down on another bubble.

"Well," Hal hesitated. "I don't know." He thought of the shabby black bird pooping all over the doorstep, crowing at the crack of dawn every morning. The city? No fucking way. "We might not be allowed to have a chicken in the city, sweetie."

Ashley bit her lip. "What will happen to him?"

A moth hit the screen, trying to get to the light. This one was grey with little black spots that mimicked eyes in the center of his wings. The screen was covered with stupid flying things every night, trying to get to the light. "Well, maybe we can find a home for Raggedy," Hal lied. Nobody wanted another rooster. That was the problem—one of many problems—with keeping chickens. One rooster was enough. What did you do with all those extras? The answer was obvious. Will had it right. Dinner.

"Ashley sweetie," Julie said, entering the bathroom, "time to get out." She lifted her daughter out of the tub and wrapped her in a green towel hooded with a frog face.

"Daddy says I can't take Raggedy to the city when we move," Ashley sniffed. She crouched low on the bathroom floor.

Julie frowned at Hal over Ashley's head. Uh oh, he thought. Here it comes. Julie knelt down to look Ashley in the eye, cupping her chin. "Sweetie," she said. "You don't need to worry about that. We might not even move. Nothing—" She glanced hard at Hal—"*nothing* has been decided." Another moth thumped against the screen. Laughter came from upstairs, deep and masculine. The boys sounded like men, Hal thought.

They made it to the ball-park and spread their blanket on the wet grass before the fireworks. Julie opened the backpack and doled out sweatshirts. She poured hot chocolate from a thermos and scootched closer to Hal. Her breast pressed his thigh as she handed a cup over to Ashley.

"Hey, there's my crew," Will said, pointing to a group of boys hanging over the chain-link fence that marked the back edge of the outfield.

Hal snorted. *My crew.* Where the hell did he pick that up? He leaned back on his elbows. The gun in the pocket of his windbreaker swung under his back and poked into his ribs. He sat up again, leaning away from Julie. The gun was on her side. She glanced at him and frown lines shadowed in her brow. Hal felt a twinge. Damn. He wanted to make it up. If only the gun—.

"Can I go over there with the guys, Dad?" Will asked.

Hal looked at Julie, who shrugged. "No firecrackers," he said. "And stay in sight."

"Can I go too, Daddy?" Ashley asked. Her upper lip was mustached with chocolate.

"No way." Will jumped to his feet and started walking. "Come on, Kareem," he called.

"Will—" At the sound of his mother's voice, the boy's shoulders slumped. He slowed, but he didn't look back.

"Will!" Julie said it louder, warning. The family at the next blanket stared.

"Hey, it's okay," Kareem said. He held out his hand to Ashley. "Come on, little sis." He flashed a smile at Julie. "I'll keep an eye on her," he said.

"Nice boy," Hal said, watching them walk away.

Jules looked at him, her eyes black. "Good thing somebody's being nice," she said.

Hal put his hand on her back, trying to keep the gun pocket behind him. "Sorry," he said. "I've got a lot on my mind."

A fizz lit up the hill as the first rocket shot off. The light disappeared into the black sky.

"Yeah." Julie sounded mad. "Listen, Hal. It's just not all about you, okay? We've got to think about the kids. About me. My career. I'm happy here. The kids are happy here. I know this is what you want, but it's not just about you, you know." The sky went silent for a long instant, then the blue and red sparks bloomed and the report boomed like a cannon. "Oh!" she said, her face tilted upward, alight. Another fizz and another.

Hal wrapped his arms around his knees. So that was how it was going to be. Fine. He leaned his mouth close to Julie's ear. "I am going to take the promotion," he hissed. "You can't stop me."

She looked at him. The fireworks glittered, reflected in her eyes.

Was she crying? Shit. That's it. Turn on the waterworks, Hal thought. The explosions came closer together now. Julie shook her head, blinking. She looked up again, the air lit white with smoke drifting in ghostly feathers. Hal glanced over at the kids by the fence, who were laughing, reaching up into the sky to try to catch the ashes floating down. Suddenly Julie's face was in front of his, her eyes closed. She grabbed the back of his head with one hand and kissed him hard, passionately. She forced his mouth open with her tongue, and then just as suddenly pushed his chest so that he fell back hard, the gun jabbing his shoulder blade. She reared up over him, her face a shadow. "You can do what you want, Hal," she said, her breath steamy and sweet with chocolate. "Nobody is going to stop you." Her words came louder in the gaps between explosions, muffled when the rockets cracked, like the scratchy soundtrack of an old movie. Her face was completely dark, haloed by the exploding greens and blues and yellows in the sky overhead. "But I don't think it's worth it—the city, the job, the lifestyle. We're free here. The kids are free here. It's a good place to be a kid. I don't want them to grow up too fast. And that's what will happen there. I know it. You know it. Look at Kareem." She kept her palm spread wide on his chest and dragged her other sleeve across her eyes, glancing up at the fireworks. Her long braid thumped against Hal's shoulder.

He watched a fizzler shower yellow sparks beyond her profile. The smell of gunpowder bit sharply in his nostrils. "I—" He stopped, not knowing what he wanted to say, his words lost in the boom-*boom*, delayed.

Hal made himself climb the ladder to Will's attic room to see how the boys were getting on in their first evening together while Julie read Ashley her story, the dumbed-down Disney version of *Peter Pan* that he hated and for which Ashley begged over and over.

"They're gonna off 'em tomorrow," he heard Will say. "A bunch of roosters. It'll be cool."

Kareem hurumphed. "You think so?" he asked. "You seen something killed before?"

Hal hesitated below the loft opening, gripping the ladder rungs, listening.

"Sure," Will said. "Like in the movies, right? Blam! Cool." He snorted. "Chickens like run around after you cut off their heads, right? My grandma said so. Blood spurting out. Crazy."

Silence. Hal squeezed a rung of the ladder. He and Julie had talked about it. It was a moral thing. You eat chicken; you should kill the chickens. She didn't think Will ought to see it, but Hal said the kid ought to face the reality. Time he knew what it meant to eat those birds magically plucked and clean and packaged in plastic at the Price Chopper meat counter. Now he wondered. Will seemed so charged up about it.

"I saw a guy die once," Kareem said. "Kid about 15. Wasn't looking and got hit by a car. *Ka-thunk* and he was down. Car wasn't even going that fast, but kid hit his head on the curb. Blood coming out his nose and ear, but he just looked asleep. Real still. That was it. Fast."

Julie came out of Ashley's room, switching off the light, and paused at the bottom of the ladder. She touched his foot, looking up. "Everything okay?" she asked.

He nodded, relieved. "'Night, guys," he called. "Lights out soon, okay?" He backed down the ladder. What could he have said? He hadn't learned guy talk very well. He hadn't even been there when his old man had died. Kareem's voice rumbled from above.

"'Night, dude," Will called. *Dude?* Hal thought. What had happened to *Dad?*

At home after the fireworks, Hal locked up while Julie got Ashley ready for bed. He wanted to put the gun into his desk, somewhere safe. The boys sat at the kitchen table with a bag of cookies and a gallon of ice cream. "Don't eat it all in one sitting," Hal said, passing through on his way through from the attached winter barn and chicken coop and into his office.

"Okay," Will said. "Hey Dad?"

Hal stopped in the doorway. "Yeah, Will?" The gun in his pocket thunked the wooden door.

Will frowned, glancing at his father's jacket.

"What, Will?" Hal repeated, stilling the gun with his elbow. "What do you want?"

Kareem kept shoveling ice cream into his mouth, but his eyes followed Hal, serious.

Will shook his head. "Will you take us to town tomorrow, Dad? I want to show Kareem the rec center. Maybe meet up with the guys and hang out."

Hal sighed. "I need to work tomorrow, Will." His paper, he thought. His plans for the department. Email his acceptance to the dean.

"Maybe Mom?" Will asked. "If we get up early, we can hook a ride down with her."

Hal shook his head. "I need you to keep an eye on Ashley, Will, so that I can work."

Will exploded out of his chair. "Jeez, Dad! Ashley? What am I? Your babysitter? Your slave?"

Hal cringed at the word, his eyes darting to Kareem. "Shut up, Will," he said. "You know better than that." He let his fingers touch the cool smooth metal inside his pocket. It made him feel tough, like he did when he smoked a cigarette outside in the cold after class. He breathed carefully. "Everybody helps out around here. That's the rule." The gun reassured him.

Kareem put his spoon down, clinking the inside of his bowl. "How 'bout if we take Ashley with us?" he asked.

Will spun on him. "Are you nuts?" he said. "That baby tagging along all day?"

Kareem shrugged. "We can take her to the library or something," he said. "Give the man here a little break. Maybe see if there's something doing for little kids around town." He cocked his head at Hal. "Maybe the man'll cut us a little slack later for pay-back."

Hal giggled suddenly. He closed his hand into a fist inside his pocket, resisting the urge to touch the gun again. "Okay, deal." He looked at Will. "You could learn something from this guy about bargaining," he said. "You guys take Ashley to town with your mom in the morning, and I'll bring the bikes down and pick her up for the afternoon." One finger slid the short length of the slick gun barrel. He touched the safety lever. Hal felt a little thrill at the back of his neck. "You can stay and ride back with Mom."

"Yes!" Will pumped his fist then held his palm out to Kareem. "You rock, man."

Kareem slid his palm lightly over Will's hand. "You're welcome."

Julie held a black rooster in her arms. "Do we really have to do this ourselves?" she asked. The bird cocked his head and blinked, his fat red comb and wattle flopping from side to side.

Hal looked down at the 12x12 block left over from building the porch and swallowed. He turned the heavy cleaver in his right fist. "I think we do, Jules," he said. "It's the right thing." He'd given in on making Will participate, but if they were going to keep chickens and eat chickens, they had to kill them too. "You're the one who wanted chickens," he said. "You're the one who wants to live on a farm." He remembered building the porch—cutting the 12x12 for the support post—with her when Will was still a toddler. They'd had to work during his naps. He remembered laughing, handing her the hammer, the nails. She was the better carpenter too.

Julie petted the rooster. "Sherman said he'd do it for us," she said. "I just don't want to be the one." She reached her hand out from the feathers to touch Hal's arm. "Please?" she said.

Hal sighed. The spot where her hand rested warmed another memory, her hand on that same arm the night he'd met her. "I can't do it if you won't hold him," he said. He snuck a look at her. Here was an out. The thought of chopping the head off the rooster made him queasy. Julie's deep brown eyes seemed huge in the shade of the willow. The kids' laughter floated out from the barn where they'd sent them to play. Kareem had never been in a hay loft before. Never touched a horse or gathered eggs still warm from the hen. Hal couldn't resist. "Guess you're not really cut out for it, huh?" he said, thinking about their fight after the kids had been asleep last night. Julie squeezed her eyes shut. "Maybe you're the one who needs to move to the city."

"Don't, Hal," she said. She knelt down and positioned the rooster so that his head was on the block. The bird looked around, blinking. "Don't screw it up," she said. "Do it quick."

Hal's pulse quickened. He grabbed the rooster's head in his left hand, just as their neighbor Sherman had instructed, and stretched the neck out across the block. The black feathers shone in the glittering light under the willow. Julie averted her face and closed her eyes. Hal held his breath. He raised the cleaver. He could feel the chicken's pulse through the leathery skin under his thumb. One of the kids—Ashley—shrieked with laughter out in the barn. The ax handle was slick and warm with sweat. He gripped it tighter and felt his bicep bunch. The blade fell, shooting from his shoulder, the metal green and bright with sun through leaves. Hal felt a grunt release from his chest. The cleaver sort of bounced on the rooster's neck. The feathers were hard. The yellow beak opened against his left hand. Hal quickly chopped down again, firmer this time, and the head fell to the ground from his hand, blood spurting from the body Julie held. He stepped back, gasping, his heart thudding. The cleaver slipped from his palm to the ground with a *thunk*. Fuck. He tasted bile.

A sob burst from Julie. She released the body of the rooster, which collapsed in a lump, and sat back into the grass, face buried in her arms, back heaving.

Hal stood for a moment, then knelt and folded his arms around her, turning her from the dead rooster and into his chest.

The morning of July 5, Hal knew something was wrong the instant he opened the sliding glass kitchen door. Silence.

Complete and total silence. "Morning, chickens!" he called as usual, stepping out into the stable. The cheeriness in his voice was forced, false. No response. No clucking. No rustling of feathers. No squawks as the roosters stretched their wings in the coop. Hal's heart rate increased and his ears started to ring. He flashed back to the fairy-thing hitting the windshield last night—*thunk*. Something bad was going to happen. Had happened.

"Daddy?" Ashley tugged his bathrobe and he jumped. He hadn't heard her get up. "What is it? Why are you standing there?"

Hal put his hand on the top of her head, the gossamer softness of her hair under his fingers. He swallowed. "I think something's wrong, honey," he said. He listened again. Still no sound from the coop. Definitely wrong. "Something bad has happened."

"Raggedy?" Ashley's voice rose an octave, the note prior to a wail, and she pushed against his leg trying to get through the door into the stable.

"Whoa there, little sis." Kareem held her shoulders and pulled her back.

Thank god, Hal thought. His eyes met Kareem's. "I think you should wait here, honey," he said. "I'll go see about Raggedy and the other chickens. Maybe they're just sleeping late today."

He patted her head and stepped out into the stable, conscious of the need to step confidently, her eyes on his back. But he didn't feel brave. Something bad out there. Something ugly. Maybe dangerous. The gun, still in the back of his desk drawer. That heavy cold weight in his hand. He glanced back. Ashley's eyes were round and wet, Kareem's arms surrounding her, hugging her. His brown gaze was serious, somber, knowing. Too late to go back for the gun.

Hal breathed in and took the steps down to the coop. The familiar stale chicken smell but something else too, something sharp, dark, feral. Something metallic. A small sound from the coop. The hairs on the back of Hal's neck prickled. He forced himself to keep walking.

Inside the chicken wire fence, feathers. Two white cockerels, lifeless on the floor. In the darker back corner, a heap of chicken bodies. Hal swallowed and held his breath. He saw an arc of blood spatter on the plywood wall. A chicken head, eyes closed. Hal swallowed. He forced himself to walk to the stable door, unlock it and swing it open. Ashley was watching. She should see him make all the normal moves, an ordinary morning. Cool damp air rushed into his lungs, sweet with hay and spruce. He walked the door open and fastened it with a shutter-dog. Hidden by the wall from the kids, he gasped and stood still, leaning with a palm on the wood.

God. What had happened? Predator, obviously. Fox. Weasel. Something crazy.

And he was going to have to deal with it. He was going to have to look, go in there, be a man. A sob rushed out of his chest and throat. God. No. He was supposed to just open the door and throw out some corn, maybe collect a couple of eggs, go back inside and sit at his desk writing about Peter Pan and Captain Hook and Tinker Bell and the island of lost boys, glancing out to watch the chickens wandering around the yard eating bugs off the tomato plants all day. He heard the sliding glass door of the kitchen opening.

"No!" he yelled, and stepped back into the stable. It was Will.

"Hey Dad," he called. "What's up?" He stepped out and made a face. "What's that smell?"

"Will," Hal said, "go back inside." The boy didn't need to see this. He was too young. He was still too young.

Will hesitated, then glanced back at Kareem, still holding Ashley inside the kitchen, watching. He straightened his shoulders and started down the steps toward Hal.

"No!" Hal yelled. "Will."

He enunciated each word for emphasis. "Go. Back. In-side." He stepped toward his son. "That's an order." Will stopped, his face registering surprise. Hal realized suddenly that he didn't usually speak to Will like that. When had he stopped telling his son what to do? Will was only twelve. Just a child. He didn't need to see this. "But Dad—"

"Now." Hal pointed toward the kitchen. "Back inside now." A sound in the chicken coop distracted him. A rustling of feathers. He looked into the darkness. He took a step toward the wire.

"Whoa." Will hopped down from the steps and leaned past Hal. "Oh man," he whispered.

Hal reached out and pulled his son close to his side. He placed his palm on Will's cheek, trying to turn his head into his side. "Don't look," he said.

Will refused to turn his head. "Dad," he whispered, his voice small, shocked. "What happened to the chickens?"

Hal shrugged, moving his hand to the back of Will's neck. The boy's collarbone felt bony through the t-shirt. "I don't know. Fox maybe. Predator." Will pressed into his side, warm. They were silent together, looking at the dead chickens, the blood, loose feathers floating in the little breeze. The aftermath of a pillow-fight gone terribly wrong.

Will looked into his father's face. "But it didn't eat them, Dad. It just killed them." Hal met his eyes, wide and sad. "Why did it kill everything, Dad?"

Hal felt helpless, stupid. Fathers were supposed to have all the answers, right? His dad always had. Hadn't he? He shrugged. "I don't know, Will." I'm not my father, he thought. He repeated the words, almost to himself. "I don't know."

Will swallowed in a hiccup. "But it's so mean," he said, and the boy's sob escaped despite his attempt to keep it in. "Dad?" His face was wet when Hal looked down, and this time Will let Hall pull him into his embrace, and they stood together for a long moment, Hall feeling the warmth of his son's tears through his t-shirt.

The rustling came from the darkness inside the coop again. Will sniffed and drew his sleeve across his eyes, and they both looked into the hen house. Something moved. Hal stepped forward and opened the latch, his arm dropping from around his son's shoulders. Will slid his hand into Hal's, squeezing a little. How long had it been since he'd held his son's hand? Hal stopped and met Will's eyes, so like Julie's. He saw trust there. Love. He remembered Will as a toddler, picking up the hammer, playing in the sawdust while they built the porch. He's not lost to me yet, Hal thought. He squeezed Will's hand.

The door to the coop swung open and Will followed Hal inside, stepping around the bodies of the white cockerels toward the darkness. The body of the big brown hen was headless. Yellow chicken feet stuck out of a heap of bodies. The row of nesting boxes had been tipped onto the floor. Hal didn't see the big rooster, Mr. Fancypants, anywhere. The straw underfoot was a mess of blood and feathers and chicken shit.

"Dad!" Will dropped his hand and stepped into the darkest corner. He knelt, gathered something, stood and turned. "It's Raggedy," he said, his face breaking into the light-stream from the stable door. "He's okay, Dad." The little rooster huddled, blinking stupidly, into Will's arms. Tears streaked Will's cheeks. "He's okay, Dad." He stroked the grey and black feathers gently. "You're okay, boy," he crooned.

PTSD, Hal thought. Raggedy looked dazed. What a scene he must have witnessed. "Let me take a look, Will," he said. He didn't want Ashley to see Raggedy injured. Hal combed the silky feathers to the white skin, row after row, while the little bird stared ahead, unblinking. Hal could see Raggedy's heartbeat in his neck, and, remembering the other rooster he'd killed, Hal stroked it gently. He remembered the heaving of Julie's back as she'd cried in his arms.

They wouldn't do that again. Raggedy seemed untouched, at least physically. He was very still. Not even trembling. Frozen. How had he managed it? "Lucky little fellow," Hal murmured.

Will carried Raggedy back out of the coop and toward the kitchen, Hal following. Ashley's face broke into a grin, and when Kareem let her go, she rushed to the door and slid it open. "Raggedy!" she cried.

Will glanced back at Hal, eyes somber. He smiled, streaks of dirt and tears wrinkling on his cheeks, and answered Ashley still looking at his father. "You're right, Ash," he said. "He's magic."

A week after the slaughter, Hal sat back at the top of the crescent-shaped plywood ramp, a half-pipe they'd built behind the barn, to watch Will take the first run. It was full-on dark, but they'd been working all day and the moon was full. The meadow was bright, and he could see all the way to the hills in the darkness. Skateboard wheels rumbled down then up, down, up, a kind of low-pitched song. Will tried to twist in the air and fell. Kareem laughed and jumped into the structure to help him up. "Come on, man," he said. "Give it another try." Will picked up his board and started to climb up toward Hal. "This is awesome, Dad," he grinned. "Thanks."

Hal smiled. "You're welcome, son." He reached a hand down to pull Will up, squeezing the smaller palm in his for an extra minute. Will grinned and stepped onto his skateboard again.

Something about the chickens, the predator, the grim work of burying all those wasted bodies, had stopped him. Hal couldn't stop feeling that feathered neck in his hand, Raggedy's shallow heartbeat. He had spent the last week ignoring the Dean's emails. Let him think the Internet was down. Everyone in Connecticut thought Vermont was wilderness anyway. Out in the sticks. Off the grid. Cute but crazy.

Instead of working on his paper, Hal had built a tree-house with the kids. He'd gone bike riding with them. He'd taken them to the river to swim, even climbed up and swung out on the rope swing to show the boys how it was done, letting go and flying out and down into the freezing water. Hal smiled, remembering the moment his hands had released the rope, the pure motionless moment in blue sky, green hemlock height, before the plummeting breathlessness toward water.

When it got really hot yesterday, the kids had begged him to go to the matinee down in town, and the idea of the darkness and the air conditioning had been too delicious to pass up, so they packed into the car and stood in line with a hundred other kids and their parents. The feature had been *Peter Pan,* the old Disney version rather than Spielberg's *Hook.* Hal guessed he ought to see that version before the fall semester.

His paper lay idle on his desk with a pile of books he'd ordered from the library. It seemed so stupid—the theory, the writing, the office politics—all of it. He'd studied children's lit because it was quick. He liked the picking apart more than the reading or the writing. He liked making it mean something. He'd been a good grad student. Hell, that was what had brought him here in the first place. Researching Kipling up at the old house above Brattleboro—the place where the great man had written *The Jungle Book*—the place where Hal had met Jules at a cocktail party. She had reached out and put her hand on his forearm. He could still feel it there, warm, natural, human.

Hal looked up at the stars, the moon huge and white over the house. He could see Julie in the lighted bathroom upstairs, toweling Ashley off after her tub. The paper could wait.

"Hey Dad!" Will and Kareem clamored up to the top of the ramp, both grinning. Will thrust his skateboard out toward Hal. "Your turn, Dad."

Hal laughed. "No way. I'll break something."

Kareem slid off his elbow and knee pads. "No excuse, old man. Time to take a risk. Live on the wild side." His teeth gleamed in the moonlight.

Kareem and Will had helped clean out the chicken coop that morning. They had appeared in the stable, pulling on pink latex dishwashing gloves, wearing rubber wellies. They'd set their jaws and grabbed up chicken bodies and tossed them into the wheelbarrow alongside Hal.

"Mean, just mean," Will murmured.

"Poor old stupid birds," Kareem replied. "Defenseless. That fox or whatever just killed everything that moved. Nothing they could do."

Hal thought of Raggedy. "Except hide," he said, dragging the body of a cockerel from under the tipped nesting boxes. "Be still."

Will understood. "No, Dad," he said. "It was just a miracle. Magic. Just magic."

They'd raked it all out, scrubbed the walls, hauled the nesting boxes outside and fixed the hole they found in the chicken wire. The predator had dug right under. They went to the feed store and bought more fencing, installed a second layer of wire. Hal screwed three more bolts onto the coop door even though none of them could imagine getting more chickens for awhile. The work had taken all day, and Will hadn't complained once about his lost skateboarding time.

Hal showered twice during the day, and then, when he couldn't sleep that night, had run a hot bath. He lowered himself into the water and lay back, closing his eyes, feeling sweat bead on his upper lip. He could still smell the hen house. Blood. Fear. Predator. He put his face into the water and snorted in and out, trying to clear the gunk from his nostrils. He would never forget this. Those stupid defenseless chickens locked in, asleep, dreaming chicken-dreams. Free-range, sure. But you had to deal with those extra roosters somehow. They'd called Sherman to take them after that first one. The only one they'd been able to kill. And now this. Some killer in a frenzy. Crazy. Crazy like him keeping that damned gun. Hal breathed the steam, tried to force his muscles to relax, let go. He thought of it in his desk drawer downstairs, the cold weight of it like a drug, a fantasy. Bubbles ticked up from his hair. It was past midnight.

When he opened his eyes, Julie stood at the window, her long thick braid like a pendulum down her back, the white of her nightgown a screen. She was beautiful.

"Hey," he said. "Sorry I woke you."

"Hal," she said. "Look." She stepped to the side and pointed toward the dark window. A huge moth, green luminous wings spread wide, a long white body, bigger than his hand, hung from the screen. "Luna moth," she said.

Hal sat up, water streaming down his spine. He felt his mouth open. Tinker Bell. Of course. A moth. "It's beautiful," he said. He reached out and placed his palm on Julie's calf.

She sat on the rim of the clawfoot tub and laced her fingers into his. "Bad day," she said. "Evil things." She kissed his knuckles and whispered into them. "Don't be afraid, Hal."

Hal felt his throat tighten. "I've got a gun in my desk drawer downstairs," he said. She stroked both their hands with her thumb. "It was on the highway that night. I should have told you," he said. "I—" He breathed in, felt tears on his cheeks. "I'm sorry," he said.

Ashley carried Raggedy around all the time, petting him, whispering to him, hand-feeding him bright yellow kernels of corn. She wouldn't leave him alone in the coop overnight, so they'd built a little hutch in her room on the promise that she'd keep it clean. That the chicken would stay in the cage to sleep, not in her bed. Raggedy still looked dazed. At first he had stood still for hours wherever placed, but now he followed Ashley around when she set him down. The attention seemed to be working. His feathers, still askew, gleamed.

Ash had even pulled him up into the tree-house they were building via the basket-on-a-pulley they'd rigged. Hal had lifted him out of the basket and set him on the wood floor. The rooster stepped to the edge and fluffed his feathers, cocking his head. "I don't think he likes it up here, Daddy," Ashley said.

"Looks like he wants down," Kareem said. He laughed. "Go on, be a bird, Raggedy! Show us what those wings are for."

Ashley shook her head seriously. "No Kareem. Chickens don't fly. They have wings but they don't go very far."

Raggedy blinked his little black eye and clicked his beak.

"It's all downhill from here," Will commented, leaning back against the tree trunk, his hand looped firmly into the back of Ashley's shorts. They hadn't finished the sides of the tree house yet. The view was astonishing, Hal thought. All that green in the undulating folds of the mountains. All that blue sky. Fresh air. The three children's faces were smooth, varying shades of brown. Kareem sucked on a straw between his teeth, and Ashley bit her bottom lip, reaching for Raggedy

The little grey rooster opened his wings and jumped. "No!" Ashley cried, held from falling over the edge by Will.

Hal sat up on his knees. The kids all leaned forward. Raggedy floated down like a weightless grey mophead. He plopped into the long green grass, ruffled his feathers, and strutted a few steps. It was as if he'd been flying all his life. Hal and the three kids all looked at each other, mouths and eyes open wide before the air burst out of them into laughter. Raggedy cocked his head to look sideways up at them, hopped up on the fence post, and crowed.

Kareem slid the knee pads up over Hal's jeans and Will snapped the strap of his helmet under Hal's chin and helped him to his feet. Kareem positioned the skateboard.

"You guys are crazy." Hal looked down at the sloping plywood valley. "I'm way too old."

"Oh, grow up," Will said, patting his back. "Relax and let gravity do its magic."

"Keep those knees bent," Kareem advised.

Hal put one foot on the board. This was nuts. "I'm gonna break something," he muttered.

He looked up at the moon again. Julie and Ashley were silhouetted in the bathroom window, pointing at something on the screen. Luna moth. He could see the wings open, close, open.

The Dean needed an answer. The gun was gone, turned in to the police, and Hal was glad. Sherman had a couple of hens he was willing to sell. Mary, the Fresh Air coordinator, had extra cockerels she couldn't bear to kill herself. Kareem had to go back to the City in three days, but he wanted to come back next year. Julie had been offered a promotion at the Crisis Center. Hal felt Will's hand on the back of his calf, urging him into the U of the skateboard ramp. He remembered again the *thunk* of the moth against his windshield on the 4th.

The moth detached from the bathroom window above. She looped back, then up, into the full round white light of the moon. Jules turned off the light in the bathroom, and Hal drew in his breath at the stab of absence in his chest. He blinked.

"Look boys," he said, pointing to the moth, illuminated by the moon. "Tinker Bell." And then Hal put his foot onto the back of the rolling board and rumbled downhill, his heart pounding, his cheeks damp with night air. Because maybe, he thought, maybe for a minute, we fly.

INDIAN LOVE CALL

Swimming upstream, his strength just equal to the river's current, Jared's concentration—stroke, breathe, stroke, breathe—broke when a small brown face bobbed up from the water two feet away. He gasped. Water rushed into his mouth and the river pushed him under. Long strands of his bangs feathered before his eyes like seaweed. He forced his body to relax and twisted onto his back to float downstream. His face surfaced in hemlock-sweet air. What was it?

Sky, clouds, and green leaves whirled overhead, dizzying—Mom and Dad's divorce, Dad's "announcement," making first-string soccer in fall, picking a major, Maddy, Hojo— No. Don't think. Jared closed his eyes on the deepening blue of the sky and saw the brown face again in his mind. Otter? He'd never seen one himself, despite having grown up on the river.

Jared rolled and dived toward the bank. His shoulders heaved at the water—left, right, left, right—hands scooping the current. He swam every afternoon after working mornings as an assistant at his old-high-school coach's summer soccer camp for little kids. Coach had yelled at him this morning, and Jared's ears burned at the memory. "They're just eight," he'd said, "just kids; don't be so hard on them." Shit, Jared thought. Soccer was a competition, a battle. "Let 'em play," Coach had said. What did Coach know anyway? He'd be stuck teaching math and coaching part-time in the sticks of southern Vermont the rest of his life. Soccer took hard work. Excellence, a will to win. It was a fight, not just a game.

In a calm pool near the bank, Jared's toes grabbed a small boulder. His thighs and calves—iron hard from soccer—stabilized his stance so he could push out of the water and scan back upstream looking for the animal face again. He squinted. Something splashed near the curve of the river, and a brown tail, fatter than a dog's, flipped up like an arrow toward the setting sun and slipped underwater. It had to be an otter.

The river's riffles pinked under the streaked sunset sky, the deeper water steely blue to black under the sheen of reflected surface light. The constant background clatter of smooth rocks shifting, the rush and splatter of water, and Jared felt himself alone, his body warm in the cold river. The hair on his shoulders prickled. There, six feet away, looking back at him, the small brown face, a little larger than his fist, silvery drops of water shimmering from long whiskers. The black eyes seemed to suck at Jared's gaze, like the dark swirls where the big brown trout grew under river rocks, pulling him. With a soft blip, the sound of water surface tension barely disrupted, the otter vanished.

"Your dad called again," Mom said. The kitchen door slammed behind Jared, and he settled onto the wooden bench to take off his running shoes, still damp from his scramble along the bank from his swimming hole to the house. She turned from the stove, stirring spaghetti sauce with one hand, the other on her hip. "You need to call him." She frowned, her green eyes crinkling at the edges. "He's still your father, Jared. You can't just ignore him."

Jared shrugged and tucked his sneakers under the

bench. "Yeah, sure," he muttered. When hell freezes over, he thought. He stared at the wooden seat. His finger traced the familiar path where the grain bent around a circle that had once been a branch. His dad had found this slab of maple along the riverbank below the house after the flood, the year Jared was born. The bench was part of their family lore. The story of the flood and his mom going into labor. The volunteer firefighters showing up and pounding on the door to get out before the rise of water, his mom with her bag all packed for the hospital anyway and his dad staring at the puddle on the floor when her water broke. "Guess that dam didn't hold," Dad had said.

Dad—Paul Dean, Esquire, a great guy, fantastic local lawyer, suit and tie, good looking, tall, athletic, family man for twenty years—*faggot*. Jared thought the word and clenched his jaw. My dad's a faggot. Telling everyone everywhere, all over town. Coming out. Thank God Jared had been about to leave for college when his dad had that "epiphany." At least Jared had been spared that year of embarrassment. He'd stayed with Mom at Christmas break, ignoring his dad completely, and he'd gone to Florida for Spring Break. All his friends here knew though. Hell, everybody knew now. Mom and Dad had decided to have an "un-wedding." They'd even sent out invitations. Jared hadn't said a word to anybody at college, of course, not even Maddy, but now she was on her way up to Vermont to visit, Mom's doing. Why had he given her the home phone number? Just his luck that Mom had picked up and had a "nice long chat with her. Seems like a nice girl," Mom'd said. "So I just told her that she should come up and stay over for a few days, get away from the city. I asked her to stay for the unbinding ceremony." Maddy would arrive tomorrow, Thursday. The unbinding party would be Saturday.

Jared pushed his hands against his eyes and temples and raked his hair back from his face. He groaned softly to himself. It was too much.

"Call him, Jared," Mom said. "You're not a child. Punishing your dad for who he is is not rational. He was brave to face the truth and come out. Don't you be a jerk."

Jared sighed. "Yeah, sure, Mom." Later, he thought. Maybe. Maybe when hell freezes over. "Just not right now," he said. "I need a shower."

His mother shook her head, stirring the spaghetti, eyes out the kitchen window, watching the river. She was wearing the lime green t-shirt and black nylon shorts of her softball team uniform. Katie Dean had been playing during the summer in what she called "the old-ladies, slow-not-dead-pitch league" since Jared was little, on the same team with most of the same players. They'd not won a single game in their first four years together, but, miraculously, when Jared was twelve, they'd been the town C-league champions. He'd been the bat-boy that year.

"You going to the ball-park after dinner?" Jared asked. His best friend from high school, HoJo, so named for his love of the restaurant's chicken-fried steak dinner after soccer games, and where he now worked as a line cook, might be off tonight. HoJo had moved to town—Brattleboro—after graduation, and in with his girlfriend, Krissy, who had been pregnant. Maybe HoJo could hang out.

"Yep." Hi mom grinned at him. "The slow-not-dead-pitch league," she said. "You should come along. The ladies would love to see you." She put the noodles into the boiling water on the back burner. "Get a move on, though. I've got to be there by seven."

Jared thought his mom looked pretty good for her age. She worked out, kept her hair long and blond, swept back now in a pony-tail for the game. She was cool, for a mom, a little older than his friends' moms maybe, but more relaxed, chill. She was smart, a physical therapist at the hospital.

What the hell was Dad thinking? They'd been such a tight little unit, the three of them. And now Dad had wrecked it.

"Sure," Jared said. "I'll hit the showers and be right back."

Jared and his mom drove south following the river downstream from Neweden to Brattleboro. "So what do you think we should break?" Mom asked.

"What?" Jared looked up from his cell phone. The service signal still hadn't beeped, though the valley was starting to widen out. His phone would work when they got nearer the interstate highway.

"The ceremony." Mom kept her eyes on the road, hands in the ten-two-o'clock position. Jared smiled. Always safe, always in control. Mom was pulling for him to declare pre-med his major. Safe.

"What ceremony?" Jared blinked. The un-wedding. "Oh." Shit. "What do you mean 'break'?"

She frowned, giving a bicyclist in the shoulder lane a wide berth as she passed. "Something symbolic, of course," she said. "Something to symbolize the ending of the marriage."

"Uh." Jared sighed. "That's dumb," he said. God, it was as if they wanted to embarrass him forever. "Why do you guys have to do this anyway?" He looked down at his cell phone again.

He heard his mom *tsk*. "It's important, Jared," she said. "For us. This is the end of a part of our lives. We need to acknowledge that ending. No pain, no regrets. Just a break-up, an ending. We made something wonderful together—" She let go of the steering wheel to squeeze his shoulder, but Jared didn't move. He kept his body stiff and his eyes on the phone. Mom sighed. "It's really okay, hon. Your dad and I are fine with this. We've got our own individual lives to live and there's no reason to make anybody suffer just because we've changed."

Jared's jaw tightened. What about him? Wasn't he suffering? Be a man, he reminded himself. "I just don't see why you have to have this stupid party," he said. That was the worst part. The party. The un-marriage party. Everyone invited. And they weren't going to let him get out of coming to it either. The phone beeped. Signal. Thank God. Jared flipped it open.

"Hon—" his mom started.

Jared punched in HoJo's number, ignoring her.

"Jared, we need to let everyone we love know that this isn't one of those awkward divorces where our friends have to choose sides. This is a celebration of a new part of our lives. It's a good thing—"

"Hey," Jared said when he heard his old buddy's voice. "Whatcha doin' tonight, man?" He felt his mother slump in the driver's seat, but he kept his eyes on the river opening up into the wide shallow lake called Retreat Meadows ahead. The road curved away up the hill to the first stop sign at the edge of town.

A baby was crying in the background. "Hey man," HoJo said. "Hang on." His voice softened, went into a singsong. "It's okay, baby. It's okay. Daddy's gotcha." The wailing eased. It was weird, HoJo with a kid and all. "What's up?" his voice normal again.

"On my way to the ball-park with Mom," Jared said. The car swung into town, old Victorians painted pink and purple up and down the hills. "Meet me there."

HoJo sighed. Jared heard the baby gurgling a rhythm in the silence. HoJo was probably bouncing it. "I don't know, man. I got to babysit," HoJo said. "Krissy's at work with the car."

Jared snorted. "You kidding me? You can't walk six blocks to the park?"

HoJo sighed again. "I'm pretty tired," he said. A bell dinged. "I'll see. I gotta eat first. Maybe." The baby made a sound. "Oh shit," HoJo said. "Gross. I gotta go, Jared. He just spit up." The phone gurgled like water down the drain as the connection ended. Jared shook his head, staring at the screen. People sure fucked up their lives in weird ways.

•

At the high school the next morning, Mom reached out and grabbed Jared's arm as he opened the car door get out. "Call your dad." He looked down at her hand. It had two big brown spots on it that hadn't been there before he went off to school. Like Grandma's, he thought. He wished he'd run the five miles to soccer camp this morning.

The softball game had gone late last night—Mom hit an awesome double in the last inning to win—and the ladies had insisted on his mom and him joining them at the bar for a beer. One of the dykes on the team, Scooter, had sneaked him one near the restrooms when his mom wasn't looking, which had been cool. Scooter still looked like a teenaged boy though she had to be about forty. No boobs, short hair, freckles. She'd always been willing to play catch with Jared when he was the little kid on the side-lines at practices. She hadn't babied him but threw hard pitches that popped like gunfire in his glove and left his hand stinging later.

"How's New Joisy treating you, kiddo?" she had asked last night. "Got yourself a girl? Good grades?"

Jared felt his face warm. He shrugged. "I guess," he said, taking the cold long-neck Scooter offered. "Yeah."

"Ah—" She reached up and patted his burning cheek with a cool palm. "So you do have a girl," she said, grinning. "Cute? Blond? I like blonds," she teased. "What's her name?" She glanced around the dim room. The Rainbow was technically a gay bar, but in such a small town, whatever was open on a Wednesday night was fine for most everybody. Jared saw a girl he'd dated in high school dancing with a football player a couple of years older than them who had lost his college scholarship and dropped out. The dance floor was small and the DJ terrible at mixing songs, skipping from something new back to something from the sixties to a line dance without any transition, the beats never matching. But the music was loud and nobody much cared. It was summer, the sky still light at nearly ten, and the air warm and the beers cold.

"Maddy," Jared answered. "Not blond," he said, "so back off." He grinned. Scooter, like the rest of his mom's team, was like a big sister or aunt to him. He'd grown up going with his mom to practices and games at least once a week from April through August, year after year. "Thanks for the beer." The first time Scooter had sneaked him a beer had been last summer, from a plastic cooler at the playoffs, right before he'd headed off for freshman orientation at Rutgers. It seemed like another lifetime. One year. Jared stood up taller. Nothing much had changed around here. Scooter had broken up with another girlfriend, bought herself a new pickup truck. HoJo—who hadn't shown up at the ball-park but called instead to make a plan to meet up after soccer camp on Thursday—had knocked up Krissy and got married. And his mom was getting a divorce from his dad, the queer. Jared guessed maybe things did change around here.

Jared saw Mom laughing with two of the other women on the team and the husband of one who acted as the team's manager. She looked young with her hair still in a pony-tail like that, her t-shirt sleeves rolled up to show her biceps. A scar of red dirt on her calf from a slide into second. Divorced. Man. What if she got hooked up with one of these dykes? Like Dad with the fags. Jared closed his eyes and shook his head. No. She wasn't like that.

Scooter clinked Jared's bottle with her own, startling him. "Oh, I know you got a fake ID in your wallet," she said. "I know a thing or two about college-life." She clinked her bottle against his. "So what about this Maddy?" she asked. "She good enough for our little bat-boy?" She tilted her bottle and drank deeply.

Jared glanced over at his mom again. She wouldn't get with a woman, would she?

Scooter tapped his elbow and beer sloshed up and out of his bottle. "Wake up, boy," she said. "What's going on inside that head of yours?" She turned to look in the direction Jared had been staring. "Ah. Mama." Scooter met Jared's eyes. "What's up, kiddo?" she asked.

Jared blinked and looked at his bottle. Shit. He took a quick swallow and shook his head. "Nothing." He turned a little and lifted his Red Sox cap, shrugging his forehead against his sleeve so Scooter couldn't see him wipe his eyes. Fuck, man. He tilted his head back, tilted the cap low over his eyes, and swallowed the beer in big gulps.

"Hey." Scooter pushed his bicep down. "Slow down, bat-boy." She squeezed his arm. "Your mom told us she and your dad were splitting. No biggy."

Jared groaned inwardly. Of course. She'd told everybody.

"Look kid," Scooter said, "so what? Your dad's gay. You got a problem with gay?" She grabbed his beer hand before he could take another swig. She was short, maybe 5'1 or 5'2, so Jared found himself looking down at her hand on his beer, her eyes like blue steel just beyond. "You do not have a problem with gay," she said, as if daring him.

Jared had shook his head once, blinking back tears. "Nope." Of course he didn't. He'd grown up with dykes, even one or two gay dudes around, like Al who ran the café in the village. He'd shook his head, meeting Scooter's eyes. "No problem with gay," he'd mumbled.

And Scooter's face had softened so he could see the girl part of the teen-aged-boy face, and her hand had loosened on his wrist. She patted his cheek. "No kid," she'd said. "You remember that. This thing with your folks—" She'd nodded toward his mom at the bar. "It might be weird and suck and all that, but you remember, you got no problem with gay."

Standing in the open door of the car on Thursday morning, Jared looked at his mom's hand on his arm, the age spots that hadn't been there before. He felt something tighten in his chest. "Really, Mom?" he asked. "You really want me to call him?" he asked. "After all this shit?" He looked at her. The little lines in her forehead were like waves, squiggles. Her mouth half-opened. "I've got nothing to say to him, Mom. He's not my dad any more." He dragged his arm from her hand and slammed the car-door behind him. "Who needs him?"

Then he made the little red-headed soccer kid cry.

Chris. Eight years old, skinny, floppy orange hair, really fast, but full of himself. Not much of a team player. He'd been stomping around the field, kicking clods of mud, obviously cussing out the boy on the other scrimmage team who'd accidentally tripped him. His little face was blotchy and scowling. Mad. He spit onto the grass. He kind of reminded Jared of himself when he was little. But a real player had to learn to fight back, play harder, act like a man and not just get mad. Hell, thought Jared, he'd had to learn that himself on this field.

Jared blew his whistle and ran over to him.

"Unsportsmanlike conduct!" he yelled. "Red card. Go sit it out, Chris."

Chris scowled at him, crossed his arms and planted his feet. "I didn't do anything wrong!"

"Get off the field, Chris," Jared said. He gave the kid a little shove, the silky shirt slipping over the bony shoulder.

"No." The other kids started wandering toward them. "Leave me alone," Chris said.

"He didn't do nothing," said the kid who had tripped Chris. "It was a accident. He fell down. He didn't do nothing."

Jared glanced around the circle of sweaty little boys. "He was being a jerk," he said. "You can't act like that. You can't say stuff, you can't stomp around and spit. It's unsportsmanlike. In a game, you get red-carded." He looked around. The kids were watching Chris. Jared raised his voice. They should be paying attention to him. "You guys can't act like babies just 'cuz you get knocked over. You gotta get tough." One of the kids snorted. Another rolled his eyes. Jared's jaw tightened. "Hey. That's just the way it is. No reaction. Just get up and get back in it. Be a man about it."

Chris' face collapsed into mush. "I'm not a baby," he wailed. His shoulders went limp, his whole thin body sagging. The baggy green soccer shirt and long shorts made him look even smaller, and he cried in heaving sobs. "I'm not a baby," he wailed. He opened his eyes, saw the other kids standing around him, and turned and ran for the woods between the high school fields and the brook.

The other boys looked at Jared with fear, anger, disgust. Damn it. Jared thumped his head with his fist. Idiot. What was wrong with him? He wanted to scream. He glanced toward the other practice field. Coach, shaking his head, was trudging toward them. Fuck, Jared thought. He dropped his whistle. Chris's green jersey blurred into the foliage as Jared trotted after him. Shit shit shit.

The kid sat on a downed tree beside the brook that curved around the lower athletic fields on its way to the river below. On hot days, they brought the kids here to cool off, encouraging them to wade in and splash water over their heads. Chris' thin back jerked. Jared paused. He was no good at this crap. He didn't have siblings; he'd avoided babysitting his whole life; he just didn't know what to do with little kids. Hell, he wasn't even sure he'd been a little kid. Mom and Dad had treated him like one of them, talking to him like a grown-up, no subject off limits. They'd taken him everywhere with them. If he wasn't invited, they'd either not gone or just ignored the no-kids policy, and he'd followed the rules, sat quiet and listened. Chris' body heaved a deep breath. It looked like he was talking to himself, shaking his head every now and then, tilting his chin for emphasis. The brook rattled loudly, so Jared couldn't hear. He tried to walk quietly, his cleats, nevertheless, clattering on the small river rocks. Chris turned and scowled. His cheeks were streaked with dirt and sweat and tears, and his hair sprouted in strange damp tufts.

"What do you want?" he said, and, "I'm not a baby." He crossed his arms over his chest and turned defiantly away.

Jared sighed. "Nothing, man." He passed the kid and knelt at the edge of the water. "Just needed to cool off." He scooped up a double handful of water and splashed it over his face. "Ahhh." He exaggerated, but, damn, it did feel good. So cold. He closed his eyes and bent over to dunk the top of his head, then tossed his thick hair backwards so that the water arced into the air and splashed down his back. "That's awesome," he said, still squatting over the water, not looking back. Jared crossed his arms over his knees and watched the stream squirting between two boulders. He should never have taken the summer soccer camp job, he thought. He wasn't cut out for it. He should have just trained for the fall. No distractions. No baby-sitting kids.

He heard a small clack of rocks. Something landed hard on his lower back, near his ass, and propelled him forward, just enough that he tipped, arms flying up and out to the sides, into the frigid stream. Chris shrieked laughter. Spluttering and bruised, Jared sat up, his cleats scrabbling for purchase on the slippery rocks. "You little—" He was going to kill him. He clawed at the limb of a hemlock and hoisted himself up.

Coach stood with his hands on his hips, the sun glinting off his shaved pate, grinning, right where Jared had been kneeling. Chris, behind Coach, sniggered. Coach reached out a hand. "Like I said, Jared," the older man said, "kids got to play." Jared felt like an idiot, water streaming from his shorts, socks and cleats squishing. He stared at Coach and pulled himself out along the branch, refusing his hand. The brook laughed quietly behind him.

As soon as the kids' parents showed up, Jared stalked to the parking lot where HoJo and Krissy waited in their old Volvo. No work-out today. He had ignored Coach and Chris for the rest of the morning. Assholes, Jared thought. The Coach had had them all down at the brook in the water for a good half-hour, then had let them make up their own rules, for Christ's sake, for the final scrimmage of the day. And the stupid kids, of course, had played for "fun," no teams, everybody shooting goals anywhere anytime. How would that get them ready for competition? How was that training?

Krissy sat in the driver's seat, HoJo riding shotgun. Jared squawked opened the back door, and slid onto the cracking leather seat. The baby was strapped into a car-seat in the middle. It looked at Jared with round eyes, a little yellow spit rolling out of its mouth. It smelled sour. Jared punched HoJo on the shoulder over the front seat. "Hey man." He glanced at Krissy, who had gained more than a little weight with the baby. "Thanks for picking me up," he said to her brown eyes in the rear view mirror.

She squinted. "Sure," she said. "No prob. It's a good way to spend a hot day." They pulled out with a puff of blue smoke.

"Cheap too," HoJo added, yelling over the muffler. "Hell of a lot better than flipping burgers."

"Take me by the house on the way?" Jared called. "I want my swim trunks instead of these shorts." He planned to really relax this afternoon, act like he was back in high school again, forget the morning, forget everything with a bunch of those beers he knew HoJo had in the cooler. But when they pulled into his mom's driveway, Jared saw his Dad's Jeep parked between the picket fence and the road, and Maddy's Honda in the drive. The kitchen door opened and Maddy and his mom came out. "Oh fuck," he muttered. She was early. Maddy waved, smiling and gorgeous, and his mom said something to her, grinning, and touched her bare arm and they both laughed. Jared closed his eyes. He wanted to slide down into the floor of the car. "Damn."

They finally got to Indian Love Call just after 2. The hottest part of the day. They were all sweating and grouchy and Jared almost wished he had just stayed in the gym and lifted until he'd passed out. Without Coach there, of course. Without anybody there.

Maddy, reaching across the back of the seat from the other side of the baby, kept running her fingers through his hair. It itched, made tingles run down his spine. Not that it hadn't been wild when she'd followed him upstairs and walked into his bedroom where he had just put on his swim trunks and plastered her hot body up against his sweaty skin and kissed him full on with her tongue practically down his throat. Man. He'd had to push her away and throw lots and lots of cold water down his back in the bathroom before he'd been able to come back downstairs. Even so, he'd found the biggest t-shirt he had, hanging down nearly to his knees, just in case anything needed covering up. It was going to be torture having her sleeping in the same house. Maybe they could get away by themselves down at the river, he thought, and felt his shorts tightening again. He could see the stretch of her long brown legs beyond the car-seat.

At least his dad had left quick. He'd come over to hug him, but Jared made his body hard and still. "Missed you, kiddo," Dad had murmured over his shoulder. "Sorry about all this."

It creeped Jared out; his dad probably hugged other guys and said stuff in that same low voice for totally different reasons. Maybe guys like as young as Jared even. Shit. Gross. He threw his arms wide, breaking the hug and stepping back. "Yeah. Whatever."

Maddy stepped up and slid her arm around his waist, snuggling into his arm-pit. "Me too," she said. She leaned her face to his chest and Jared felt his heart pounding against her cheek. He squeezed, letting his hand brush her breast, staring his father in the eye. He bent and kissed Maddy on the mouth, intending to make it a good one, tongue and all, but Maddy pushed away, blushing. "Stop it," she'd laughed.

Dad had looked at the ground. Yeah, that figured. Didn't want to know about straight sex any more, did he? He'd been working out, Jared thought, and he'd grown a goatee and mustache. Grey hairs peeked out from his t-shirt, tight over a muscled chest and arms. He looked younger.

Mom stepped up and patted Dad's back, glaring at Jared. "Your dad's here to go over the unbinding ceremony with me," she said. She pointed at the plank bench from the mud room, now standing in the middle of the yard. "We've decided on what to break," she said. They all looked at the bench. Jared felt something twist in his stomach. Why the bench?

"Don't forget. Sunday afternoon," Mom said. "Two o'clock." She grabbed Jared's arm as he started for the house. "You'll be there," she said. It was a statement.

"Yes," Maddy chimed in. "We will."

Mom frowned, then took Maddy's arm. "Good," she said. "Come on, Maddy, I'll show you the river." Jared watched them walk down the grassy hill toward the Siberian irises, day lilies and hollyhocks that bordered the long, wide deck hanging out over the riverbank. Maddy looked back over her shoulder, eyes sparkling like light on river-ripples. Who was she to tell him what to do? Jared thought.

Dad sighed. "Come on, kiddo." He touched Jared's forearm. "Give us a break." His face was sad, his blue eyes creased at the corners.

Jared flinched. "I gotta go change," he'd said. "We're going with Hojo and Krissy to Indian Love Call." He pulled away and turned to the house.

Then Maddy had appeared in his bedroom and kissed him into almost forgetting that she had acted like she owned him. Dad had been gone when they'd come back downstairs.

Watching HoJo with the baby and Krissy was depressing. Sure, HoJo scrambled with Jared up the cliff on the far side of the deep, crystal-green pool of the swimming hole to take his turn on the long rope swing, but it was clear that his heart wasn't in it. He could hardly stop looking at the baby and girl below. A little flab hung out over his swim trunks. He seemed happy, Jared guessed, dope-happy. Stupid and slack, huffing for breath by the time they reached the top of the ledge.

The swimming hole was crowded, as usual on a steaming August afternoon. The shoulders of the highway were lined with parked cars tagged Connecticut, Massachusetts, and New York, and they'd lugged the cooler and towels down the trail with the baby crying the whole way. "Heat rash," HoJo had said, squashing the baby's hat on in the little harness pack. "Course, you don't care about how hot Daddy's belly is under there, do you buddy?" His voice had gone soft and goofy.

Jared watched his old friend catch his breath on the ledge. Man. What the hell had happened?

Krissy and Maddie sat in the shallows below, Krissy holding the baby so that its toes touched the water. It screeched and lifted its fat knees and the girls laughed, and the baby let his feet touch the water again, repeating the game. HoJo chuckled. Jared closed his eyes. Had everybody lost their minds?

"I know you don't get it," HoJo said.

Jared looked at him.

Hojo was still staring down, the river wide and smooth and deep, a bunch of little kids in swim suits jumping in off the lower boulders, three groups of adults with picnic baskets and coolers under the trees along the shore. The baby shrieked and HoJo grinned. He looked at Jared. "Nobody can tell you what it's like," he said. "Having a kid." He blinked. "A family."

Jared shook his head. It was hard not to think this was just another one of HoJo's crazy phases. He'd not stayed with a girl for more than a month in high school. He'd always been the one to talk Jared into cutting class and going swimming on the first warm day of May, or the one to throw a keg party in the woods in the middle of January. HoJo was nuts, wild, nothing but fun. "Yeah, right," Jared said. The warmth of granite seeped into his thighs and calves, relaxing the muscles. He felt drowsy from the beer.

Maddy called up. "Be careful!" The sun gleamed on the smooth dark hair framing her oval face, thick dark eyebrows like moons opposite her lips. "Is that safe?" Jared laughed and shrugged, turning his palms up. The ledge where they always jumped off holding the rope was about twenty feet from the emerald water, but Jared and HoJo had done this a million times. They would swing out and drop, right at the apex, into the deepest part of the water. No big deal.

"It's like I didn't know what it meant to be a man," HoJo said, his voice quiet. "Like I wasn't even real before them." He tossed a little stone into the water, plunk. It settled slowly to the bottom, rings widening across the surface. The water was so clear. "I really am now," HoJo said. "A man."

"Sure," Jared said. "Right." HoJo a grown-up? Please. Jared had the straight A's; he'd been the soccer captain when they took States. Hell, he'd had to drag HoJo out of bed with a hangover to get him to the game on time that day. Now HoJo had a job, a kid, a wife. Christ. But still on the rope swing at Indian Love Call. Same old same old.

"Yeah," HoJo said. "Sure. More a man than you, college boy."

Jared gripped the rough bristles of the rope and slid his hands snug against the knots. "Like hell," he said, sliding his butt forward. "Changing diapers makes you real? You are crazy, dude." He stood up, holding the rope.

HoJo laughed and then, just as Jared pushed off from the ledge, reached up and yanked his trunks to his knees. "There's real!" HoJo yelled.

Damn. Jared knew he had to let go when he reached the apex of the arc out over the water, even though his swim-suit was dangling from his foot and all his junk hanging out. If he didn't, he'd smash back against the rocks of the ledge. Even as he thought it, swinging to the apex and twirling around, his hands relaxed, and he saw the rope jerk back toward the cliff. HoJo reached to catch it, hand open, leaning just a little off-balance outward.

In Jared's instant of hanging, his ass cool and uncovered, he felt weightless, like he was a kid with nothing but the present before him, a big round pool of green. Time hung still. He spun slowly, free. He saw Maddy's mouth in a delighted O, her hand rising to point. Green leaves blurred against blue sky. He felt a grin bloom across his face. Just as gravity began to reclaim his body, pulling him down, he saw little rocks and dust squirt out from HoJo's foot on the ledge. Was he okay? Jared corkscrewed, plummeting. He closed his mouth and grabbed his nose, anticipating the splash. Ice cold water shrieked from his toes up his torso. He opened his eyes under water as he began to rise, and something brown shoot toward him, then down and past. The sleek tail brushed his knee. Jared surfaced, gasping. Otter!

A girl screamed. Jared twisted, and the pool erupted in his face. HoJo! Jared glimpsed legs cartwheeling, one foot smacking the rocks before disappearing into green water. A pink coil of blood bloomed into the current.

On Friday, Maddy's fingers twined Jared's, and he closed his eyes into the sun, the warm rubber tube massaging his neck, his ass numb in the river. They spun lazily downstream, water splashing in rapids, the big turns of the river winding away from the highway, under bridges, past the high school and the brook that emptied in past the soccer fields, and on toward the swimming holes—Jared's private work-out spot, then the other one just upstream from Indian Love Call. Jared planned to get them out of the water at his private swimming hole and walk back up the tributary to the house before that other one.

Jared's mom had dropped them off at the dam and they'd stood atop it to sun-screen each other. The lake behind the dam was closed to swimming this summer, the floodgates open and the water level low, down to river level. "The silt builds up over the years," he explained to Maddy, pointing to the bucket loader and bulldozer on the lake-bed below. "They scoop it out onto that hill. We used to sled there when I was a kid." He rubbed the sunscreen between her shoulder blades and then tickled the back of her neck with a fingernail. "They found a body down there when the water got low enough in May," he whispered, and she shivered.

"Really?" Maddy turned to look into his face.

Jared shrugged. "Yeah. Idiot kayaker. Spring run-off. Old guy, like fifty or something. You'd think he'd of known better."

Maddy squinted. "Why?"

"They all come up here from Boston and New York in Spring to kayak. Don't have the slightest idea what they're doing. What the river can do. Try all these fancy tricks when they've never seen a spring run-off river." Jared remembered the roar, the metallic scent of mud-colored water, the river three or four times its summer size. "Hard to imagine when it looks like this," he said, nodding at the clear, sparkling ripples. "But it's dangerous." He blinked and hefted the Styrofoam cooler onto his shoulder. Maddie started rolling the black inner tubes behind him down the trail. "When I was little, Mom and Dad wouldn't even let me go outside alone in the spring or if there were storms coming." His cheek burned again, and he scrambled ahead to the river.

At the river, he tied the floating cooler to one tube, and they splashed in for the three-hour float down to his house. Jared thought he'd never felt so tired, but he couldn't relax. He hadn't slept much either, not after the scene at Love Call, not after the scene with Mom and Dad. The un-binding ceremony was tomorrow. He'd only agreed to the tubing trip to get out of the house, where Mom and Dad were busy with setting up tables and cutting flowers. The last straw had been Dad trying to give him advice about majoring in sports management.

"Shit, Dad," he'd said. "That's what the jocks do, the lazy ones. The ones who just want to spend their whole lives playing. The ones who can't get on with a real life, serious work."

Dad had shrugged. "Nothing wrong with enjoying what you do, son. It's the lucky ones that get to do what they like to do in life."

Jared had scowled. "Yeah," he'd muttered. "No matter what it does to anybody else."

Mom's hand had bit his cheek, stinging, though there was no force behind it. Jared had thought of the otter's slick fur against his leg. Mom gasped and froze, her own cheeks suddenly wet, her face red. "Oh," she'd said. "Baby, I'm sorry." She'd never hit him before. Ever.

Jared listened to water rattling stones. His face still stung.

Maddy squeezed his hand. "Thinking about yesterday?" she asked.

HoJo's foot had been gashed, but not broken, which was "goddamn lucky," as Krissy had said. They'd stopped the bleeding and bound it with a ripped t-shirt, then helped him hobble back along the trail to the car, all the fun gone out of the afternoon. "What were you thinking?" Krissy fumed. "Acting like a damn fool. What would we do without you working? We got no insurance. We can't afford no hospital, no time off. You can't cook if you can't stand up. Who's going to buy diapers? Food? Gas? Who's going to take care of us?"

Jared rolled his head toward Maddy's inner tube. She sprawled across it, long limbs draped over the black rubber circle, her breasts barely contained in her bikini. She's so hot, Jared thought. How'd I get a girl like her? "Yeah," he said. "It was scary there for a minute."

Maddy squinted. "You didn't seem scared," she said. "You were in total control, like, 'okay, where's my shorts, let me cover up my dick, rip my t-shirt into a bandage, keep the injured guy calm, pack up the stuff, half-carry him back to the car, pack the baby into his seat, drive us all home, situation normal.'" She smiled. "Like you were the dad."

Jared blushed. "Boy Scouts," he muttered. "Sports. Coaching. You know." He rested his head on the warm tube. Swallows skimmed the water.

"You're good at being in charge," she said. "Too good at it maybe."

Jared scowled. "What's that supposed to mean?"

Maddy laughed, then pulled him closer by the hand, lifted herself up and smacked him on the lips. She hovered for a second, her face shadowed by the bright sky. Jared's felt his inner tube pushed down under her palms. "Just lighten up a little," she said. "Summer's short. Enjoy it." Maddy popped out of her inner tube into the river, where she swam a few strokes then rolled, ducking her head to slick her hair tight over her skull and down her back like a thick black fish. She floated, letting the current rock her body.

Enjoy it. Jared yawned, sighting the big power-line towers slashed between the green trees and across the river. They were half way from the dam to Brattleboro, coming up on Jared's private swimming hole, which was where he planned to get out and walk back up the tributary to home. He had to avoid that other swimming hole, that wild place upstream from Indian Love Call.

"Can we get out of the water for awhile?" Maddy clung to the tube she had recaptured, twirling in the current.

The river cut between granite stones worn smooth by hundreds of years of water. The trail home along the tributary of the main river emerged from the willow brush on the left bank ahead. Maddy was already climbing out onto a boulder. "Come on," she called. "The rocks are warm."

Jared sighed. He really didn't want to hang around
here. He paddled reluctantly toward her. They were
about an hour upstream from where the river path met
the highway, the same place they'd parked yesterday
to hike to Indian Love Call. On a long ago July afternoon when he was twelve, Jared had discovered that the
river upstream from Indian Love Call toward the power
lines—a minute or so downstream from the tributary,
from right here—hid several other swimming holes. At
one secluded sandy beach, a skinny bearded guy had
been making out with a skinny girl, both of them as
naked as jaybirds. He remembered the way his body had
reacted that day, the way he couldn't turn away, couldn't
stop watching, even when he knew he should go home.
Today he was hoping they'd just be asleep—whoever
might be there—sun-bathing, which, he'd discovered on
all his return spying adventures, was what they mostly
did. But it was the wild place just ahead—the other
skinny-dipping swimming hole, the one just downstream from his own home tributary—that Jared dreaded.
Stopping here was fine, so long as they didn't go past the
little river they could follow back up to the house.

Jared held onto a rock to anchor, resisting the current.
Maddie grabbed the rope and dragged the cooler up onto a
flat stone island about six feet long. Jared pulled toward the
rock, and his tube flipped, spilling him into the water. He
popped up, spluttering with cold, and Maddie laughed and
hauled his tube onto the rock before she slid into the water
and against his body, holding him at the neck, her mouth
hot on his, their tongues thick and fish-like together. Jared
closed his eyes and let the current carry them, half-floating.
Their legs swept lazily in an arc, swirling into an eddy, and
Jared felt gravel scrape against his back. Maddie's hipbones
pressed him down, and her legs straddled him. The water
laughed in little waves against his ears. He slid his hand
inside the top of her bikini, his finger on the hard pebble
of her nipple. He felt her groan and saw her teeth bite her

lower lip through the lattice of his eyelashes and her hair. She was like a mermaid or water nymph, he thought.

It wasn't their first time—he and Maddie had been doing it all spring semester whenever they could get his roommate or her roommate to give them some privacy— but this wasn't just sex either. It was wet and hot and cold and warm in all the right places. They were part of the whole big world, completely alone, completely together with the river and the green and the sky and the mountains. A veery started up in the dark woods, the metallic echo of bird-song and the taste of the river on Maddie's skin harmonizing. Jared's mind whirled, like the sky and clouds and leaves overhead when he floated. Maddie's hands shoved again and again into his chest. "Let go, Jared," she whispered. "Let go." And he did, and she with him, and they came back to themselves still lying in the shallow water, animal selves receding back under their surfaces.

Animal self. Jared had seen his mom's animal self when she had slapped him. Something wild and old and fierce, like a bear maybe, buried inside her. Something he'd been hurting, something scared, something mad. He closed his eyes. Don't think. Don't about Mom.

They lay naked on the big flat warm granite stone, almost asleep. The hairs on Jared's back moved in the lightest breezes. He watched Maddie's face, completely smooth, her nostrils moving in and out. She wasn't like the other girls he'd known. Tough. Not afraid to tell him to shut up. And the way he did, the way he just backed down. Why did he do that?

A smack of water drew his eye. Fifty feet downstream something moved on the riverbank. Jared's eyes shifted when a head bobbed up. The otter blinked, staring straight into him, before the nostrils closed and the head disappeared with a blip underwater. Willow rushes on the river-bank blurred the mud slope beyond, but Jared spotted another narrow brown and white body in the rocks. He touched Maddie's hand. "Look," he whispered.

Maddie opened her eyes. She smiled.

Jared's belly prickled against the slick granite. "Don't move," he whispered. "Just look." He tilted his chin toward the riverbank. Maddie rolled her head. Jared whispered into her hair. "Otter."

He heard her breathe in and smelled the river in her hair. The otter in the water scrambled uphill, his sleek body dripping. When he reached the perch of the other, he stood and sniffed. Suddenly, with a movement as natural and effortless as a kid with a sled on snow, the otter slapped his body down in the mud, pushing off. Maddie gasped and Jared felt the cool air he himself sucked in. He felt his mouth open. A slide! The second otter followed close on the first, nose to tail, twisting downhill. Both splashed into the water and were gone. Jared felt his chest move and air escape through his nose in a sound he didn't recognize at first. Maddy's face turned to his, her eyes round. She grinned, her teeth bright. She laughed aloud, and Jared laughed again, this time full and from his chest.

Jared pushed himself up on his hands. The otters—both heads in the river—stared, that same black look he'd met a few days ago, swimming against the current. He took a breath, swallowed.

"There's a swimming hole just around that bend," he said. "Gay guys hang out there," he said. "Naked." He knew he was blushing. He couldn't meet Maddie's eyes. "They hook up." He watched the motionless otters. "Most of those cars at the highway from New York and Massachusetts are gay guys, here for the swimming hole." Maddy's shadow fell over him, and the otters disappeared into the water with another quiet blip.

Jared looked at Maddie. The sun had dipped toward the mountains behind her, silhouetted against a sky the color of blue chicory. Maddy didn't speak. Jared couldn't see her face, but he could feel her watching him. He looked out across the river again. No otters. His heart thumped against his knee. "What?"

"Your dad's a pretty cool guy, Jared," Maddy said.

Jared felt his throat tighten.

"You know gay guys at school," she said. "That forward on your team is gay. I don't get why you're so weirded out by this." Maddy squatted beside him, but Jared kept watching the water. "Give him a break, Jared. Life's too short to be so uptight."

The otter's face popped up again, water rippling out in circles as if spotlighting the creature. Jared swallowed. "It's my dad, Maddy," he said, but he heard the whine in his voice. He licked his lips. He really wanted to explain it. "It's different." Jared knew he was being an ass. "I—" He thought about the kid he'd made cry. Chris. The way his face had got all red and mad and then crumbled into tears. He was acting like a baby too. His throat tightened. But where would he go home to next break? Dad's apartment? Mom wouldn't keep the house alone, would she? The otters slipped out of the water near the mudslide, glancing back at them like little kids. Jared stood up, keeping his gaze down, away from Maddy. "What if he's over there," he said, nodding toward the river-bend, "screwing some dude?" He sighed. "Why can't it just be the same?"

There were men at the next curve in the river, just below the tributary that led home, just as Jared had known there would be. Maddy had dozed off on the rocks, the otters disappearing, and he'd stood, finally, and slipped into his swim trunks and put on his sneakers and walked carefully along the rocks of the river, scrambling over boulders, stopping to pick up a stone or examine a piece of old glass smoothed by years of rushing water, just as he had done when he was a kid. He'd sat for awhile on a log and watched a trout in a dark green pool below his feet, barely moving. Finally, as he had done when he was a boy, he climbed the little path over the rock ledge to look down on the gay swimming hole. Two men were sunning themselves on slabs of granite flung there by floods or even glaciers. Another was in the water, the sun bronze on his muscled shoulders. None were Jared's father. Someone laughed, and two men came from the trees, holding hands. Dozens—perhaps scores—of rock cairns stood in the river and along the banks, stacks of stone, phallic and magical. They toppled at every flood, at every high water, Jared knew, and the men returned and rebuilt them. He'd done it himself at his own backyard river after spying on the men when he was twelve, building this solid, fragile thing for no good reason. A kind of play.

None of the men was his father. Of course not. His father was with his mother, preparing for their unbinding. But he had probably come here, just down the hill from their house, Jared thought, some time. Some time. How long had his dad watched these guys play in the rocks, in the river? Jared wondered.

On Saturday, Jared traced the familiar whorl of wood grain with his fingertip. After the flood waters had receded and they'd all come home from the hospital nineteen years ago, Dad had found this slab washed up onto the grass. Jared remembered it first balanced over a log curing for firewood, an instant seesaw, his dad pumping his hairy muscled thighs on one end of the board to make Jared on the other end rise into the air and *plonk* back down against the ground, the two of them rising and falling in exact opposition. He remembered his mother taking a turn, her laughing face. Jared remembered trying to balance himself in the middle when he was a little older, seesawing his weight on one side of the plank, then down on the other side, riding the board like a ship at sea, experimenting with the laws of gravity, moving one way or the other to understand fulcrum and lever. Imagining himself setting sail, grown and out to sea. Then the board had served as a shelf in the kitchen until they'd been able to remodel with real cabinets, after which Dad had attached two-by-four exes at each end, legs, to form the bench that fit perfectly in the mudroom.

The bench on which Jared had sat to take off his first soccer cleats after games in elementary school, his snow boots clumped with snow from treks with Mom and Dad under a full moon calling for owls, his wet sandals at the end of a summer day following the river to spy on naked swimmers upstream, the shiny black dress shoes handed down from Dad and worn on his first date, the size eleven running shoes in which he'd escaped the house after his father had come out to him last fall. "I'm gay," he'd said, "but nothing between us will change." What a lie, Jared thought. Dad had taken the legs off the bench yesterday. It was just a slab of wood again, sanded smooth here, grooved with a bit of bark there.

Jared looked up. The little river below and beyond the deck chuckled and whooshed softly, background to the clumps of people on the platform with him and his parents. Maddie was smiling. Hojo held his kid and Krissy's hand. Coach. Scooter and the softball team. Dad's law partners. Everyone.

His mom took one end of the old plank and his dad took the other end. Jared was the fulcrum, he thought. He pictured them slamming it down on his head, breaking it over him. He could feel both of them tugging just a little, willing him to let go. Instead, he gripped tighter, holding on. It hurts, he thought. It does hurt.

The prick of the splinter didn't surprise him at all. He flipped his palm and watched the blob of blood well up. Jared blinked. He had expected it. He'd wanted it. He put the heel of his hand to his mouth and bit the wood and tugged it from under his skin, his blood metallic, like the flavor of the cold current filling his mouth. He flashed back to the little otter face bobbing up out of the dark river upstream. He remembered the way his body had hesitated and then relaxed into a float, swept downstream again by mineral-sharp water.

Dad's stupid little goatee had white hairs. Mom's hand on the board was spotted brown.

Jared pulled harder on the board. "No," he said quietly to his parents. "We're not going to break it." He met his mom's glance, and then his dad's. "Just let it go," Jared said, and they did. He hoisted the chunk of tree over his head and tossed it over the deck railing into the green water. From here, just below his home, it would float on the tributary into the main river, down past Indian Love Call and his hometown and eventually, maybe, out to sea.

JUST SO

Between trying to please two brides, working two jobs, worrying about two sons, and fighting with two insurance companies, the last thing Debra needed was a goddamn mouse at Naulakha. Mice always got inside during the fall, of course. In her own home—burned half down in April—Tigger would have taken care of the little bastard in a night or two. But Naulakha, Rudyard Kipling's historic home above Brattleboro, Vermont—Deb's part-time every-Saturday housekeeping job—was too special for the likes of a good mouser with sharp claws. A cat might pee on one of the antique rugs or shed on the velvet chaise or scratch the desk where Rudy wrote *The Jungle Book*.

Nope, I'm on my own against little Mickey, she thought. And right before the Westerly-Ryan wedding too. That rich bitch would freak out if she saw a mouse. Deb swept the little black mouse turds from under the stove. One week to kill the bastard.

The phone rang into the silence, and Deb answered it. "Hello?" She leaned against the stove, phone cradled on her shoulder, reaching to straighten the glasses into precise rows in the glass-fronted cabinet.

"Hey babe."

Debra smiled. She had married Bob twenty-five years ago, high school sweethearts, but his voice, like the purring of a cat, still made her feel tender and calm. "Hi hon," she said. "What's up? How's the hip today?"

She could almost hear his shrug through the phone lines. "Not bad," he said. "Only took one pill so far." Bob had been bumped by a rookie pallet-jack driver at the warehouse a week ago. Bruised his lower back pretty good. Lucky it wasn't worse—a broken leg or hip—though the medical insurance people would be faster to cover if it was, Deb thought. "So the adjuster called," Bob continued.

"'Bout time," Debra said. Five months after the fire, they were still waiting for the house insurance people to pay up so they could move out of the Tagalong camper parked in her folks' driveway in town.

"Yeah," Bob said. "But it's not good news."

Debra felt her sinuses thicken with tears. She closed her eyes and swallowed to keep any tremble from her voice. "What now?" They'd been in that house twenty-five years. Raised three kids in it. Since the fire, the house had been empty. Even the copper pipes under the kitchen sink had been stolen. Hell, the sink too. If she and Bob could just get the money, they'd start on repairs. Just knock down and rebuild the burned part, a garage they had converted to a family room with what used to be the kids' rooms overhead. Deb placed her cool palm on her cheek and waited for Bob to speak.

"He wants to declare it a total loss, babe," he said softly. "Wants to have it condemned."

Debra drew in her breath. She looked at the lavender sky descending on the New Hampshire hills east across the valley. "Oh Bobby." She sat heavily on a straight-backed chair.

Krystal came in from the dining room, the cloth in her hand wafting the air with lemon oil. "What's wrong, Mom?" she asked, frowning.

"Nothing, hon," Debra said. "I'll tell you in a minute." She gestured to the phone. "It's Daddy."

"Maybe it's better, Deb," Bob said. "Just take the money and start over with a new place. It's not enough to build, but I bet we can find something we like. Something small. Just us now anyway with the kids mostly grown." He laughed, trying to joke her out of the mood. "If they move out and stay gone, that is."

Deb wiped her eyes roughly with the back of her hand. "It is what it is, I guess," she said.

Krystal opened the fridge to get a can of Coca Cola, snapped the pull-tab, and grabbed the half-bag of Oreos left by the departed guests. Debra watched her daughter eat five in rapid succession, swishing them down with gulps from the soda. She hoped Krys would fit into the wedding dress, but she knew better than to say anything. She probably weighed over two hundred pounds by now, a real shame. Such a pretty face. While Bob talked numbers, the range of settlements the adjuster had suggested would be forthcoming as soon as he got some comparables, Deb frowned at Krystal and pointed to the black cookie crumbs on the floor. "I'm guessing it'll come in at about one-eighty," Bob said. "One-ninety if we're lucky. A hundred and a half to pay off the first mortgage and that home-improvement loan."

"Aw, hon," Debra said. "That sucks." They'd worked all their lives on that house. Paneling. Paint. Bushes and trees and flowers. Converting the garage. It was the house they'd bought with Bob's Army discharge money when the two older kids were just toddlers. They'd added on and fixed it themselves as much as they could over the years. Always paid the mortgage on time. Always paid the insurance and taxes. The apple tree had been loaded with fruit—hard, wormy little MacIntoshes—for the first time last year. Less than forty thousand for all those years of hard work. With inflation, they were nearly as broke now as they had been twenty-five years ago.

"It's enough, Deb," Bob said. "Has to be. We'll start looking. Might be fun to start over. Cash'll stay with your folks anyway. We don't need much now."

Debra bit her lip. Her baby, Cash, had graduated high school in June and got a job at the Parks and Rec in town. "Sure, babe," Debra said, thinking about his injury, wondering when he'd be back to full pay again. She tried to sound optimistic. "Yeah, we should be able make a down payment with what's left over after the bank's share. Maybe some new furniture, clothes, stuff to get started again." Maybe it would be okay. "Any word from Robby?" she asked. Their eldest, Robert Jr., would be home from Infantry School in Fort Benning by Thursday, just in time to serve as one of the groomsmen in Krystal's wedding, a week from tomorrow. Debra tried not to think beyond that. Definitely not about Iraq.

Bob laughed. "Nah. He's not gonna call us till he gets to the airport and finds a flight." He coughed. "Hey Deb, do you think Tigger's okay? He seems kind of scrawny." The receiver crackled. "You think he's losing weight?"

Deb thought she could hear the old cat purring on Bob's end. He was technically Krys's childhood pet, but Tigger had become her household companion after her daughter had moved in with Trevor, her fiancé. "Not especially," she said, "but I've been pretty busy with the weddings and all."

"He's been sleeping here on my belly while I watch TV," Bob said. "And he just don't seem quite himself. I can feel his ribs."

Deb sighed. "Well, he is pretty old," she said. "You think he needs the vet?" Another fifty bucks, she thought, despite her love for the old bugger. "We'll talk about it when I get home," she said.

The wooden chair on the other side of the table creaked as Krystal slid into it. She'd almost finished off the Oreos.

"How much longer?" Bob asked.

Deb closed her eyes and reviewed her Saturday work.

Eight beds changed. Three bathrooms scrubbed. Kitchen mostly done. She'd vacuumed all three floors, including stairs, swept the porches and basement. Polishing and mopping could wait until Monday after her shift at the candy factory. The garbage had been taken out, and she had loaded the recycling and dirty sheets into her minivan. She'd drop those off on Monday too. Krystal had just finished the dusting, though she'd do it again herself before the wedding party arrived from New York. "We just have to fold the clean towels," she said. "No more than an hour."

After she hung up, Debra held out the broom and dustpan to her daughter. "Not a crumb," she said. "There's a goddamn mouse in here, and I'm not leaving him any goodies, except in a trap. Sweep it up while I go down and get the towels."

Krystal shrugged and took the broom. "Okay, Mom," she said. "I don't know why you care though." She pushed herself up from the table. "A mouse is a good omen. Fertility goddess. Connected to Demeter, right? And some say mice are dead people's souls."

Deb rolled her eyes. "That rich lady from New York won't care if it's a goddess mouse or Mickey Mouse, now will she? She sees it before her wedding, she'll flip out and call *me* to take care of it." Deb started down the back stairs, calling over her shoulder. "Probably in the middle of *your* wedding!"

Krystal's footsteps thumped and the broom brushed overhead while Deb pulled the warm towels and washcloths out of the dryer. Krystal had planned herself a pagan wedding of all things. Called it a "hand-fasting." Thought she was a witch for Christ-sake. At least she was getting married. Deb sighed. She didn't hold out much hope for the groom-to-be, a greasy video-game addict named Trevor. No job, but he did take orders from Krystal pretty well. At least she seemed happy. Deb hoisted the laundry basket and carried it up the stairs to the scrubbed kitchen table overlooking the valley.

Krystal had stirred up a cup of instant coffee for her, and Deb took a sip before sitting down. "Thanks hon." The two of them started folding, looking out at the yellowing birches, the white trunks vivid in the rays of setting sun. Deb told Krystal the news from the insurance company. "But don't you worry about the wedding, baby," she said. "Me and Daddy's got that money all put away."

Krystal snapped a towel free of wrinkles. "Oh, that reminds me," she said. "The high priestess is coming up from Northampton to see the circle tomorrow." Krystal folded the towel precisely, twice lengthwise, once across, as prescribed by the nonprofit that owned the Kipling house. "You can meet her."

Debra rolled her eyes: *high priestess*. But she bit her tongue and managed to keep the sarcasm out of her voice. "Hmm," she said. "That'll be nice." She folded a fresh dishcloth and placed it on the marble counter beside the new sponge still in its package. "Oh, wait." She mentally reviewed her schedule. Sunday. No doctors, day off from the candy factory, something else . . . What? "What time?" she asked.

"Around noon," Krystal said. "Why?"

It clicked. "Melody Westerly. The gal from New York," Debra said. "The one getting married. I'm supposed to meet her here at one." She sighed. "Again."

"Oh, that bitch," Krystal said. "What's she want this time?"

"Caterer," Debra replied. "She's coming all the way from the city to meet him while he looks at the kitchen." She looked around. "What's to see? It's a kitchen. And he don't need her to look."

"Bitch," Krystal repeated. "So you'll be good for noon, meet Mistress Galena, then back here by one."

"Mistress Galena," Debra repeated. "Krystal, hon, are you sure about this? Father Frank would be glad to step in, I could call him tonight. Something more traditional, you know . . ."

"Mom," Krystal said, "no. That whole Jesus thing is *so* not me. I'm a witch, remember?" She frowned, the look reminding Deb of the toddler she'd once been.

Debra sucked in a breath but remembered to hold it rather than sigh. *Kids.* "Right," she said. "Just asking." At least she's happy, she reminded herself. Shut up and let her make her own mistakes. Deb had learned to keep her opinions to herself. Mostly.

When they finished the towels, Krystal balanced them in her arms to take them upstairs to the linen closet. "Don't forget to lock it," Debra called. "And go up to the attic storeroom and get me a mousetrap too, will you?" She looked around. The dishwasher clunked, finished with its cycle. She would unload it tomorrow. The house was supposed to sit empty until Melody Westerly's fiancé and their guests began to arrive midweek for the wedding next Saturday. She thought again about the woman's voice on the phone, her bossy tone. It'd be just like Melody Westerly to expect to stay even though they'd made a clear plan for an empty house so they could finish the extra cleaning and wedding preparations in the next four days. And the boss, Edwards, would say to make it happen too because the Westerlys were donors to the Trust that owned the house. Debra sighed. She'd better empty the dishwasher tonight.

When Krystal returned, Debra had her set the mousetrap and baited it with the last chunk of Oreo while she finished putting the dishes away. They checked that all the lights were off and stepped out the front door into the porch under the overhang where the Kiplings' coach drivers had once pulled through so the rich folk wouldn't get wet. Deb put her key into the heavy door and stuck her head back inside to call, "Bone appeteet, you little bastard," before pulling it shut and locking it.

Krystal snorted a laugh from the darkness near the cars. "You crack me up, Mom," she said. "A place for everything and everything in its place, but no place for one little ole mouse." Her sneakers crunched in the gravel. "Don't you think that little guy's got a purpose too?" The hinges of her car door squawked.

Deb looked through the gloom across the dull roof of Krystal's car. "Nope," she said, opening her van. "Not except to piss me off."

Krystal shrugged and lowered herself into her seat, the car listing. "Little things, Mom," she called. "Little things count too." The hinge squawked again. "See you at the picnic shelter at noon."

Deb glanced back at the long dark shape of the house to check that they hadn't missed any of the lights. A ship, Kipling had called it, and it looked like that now, long and tall on the edge of the hillside, roof slanting toward the open prow of the porches. The night smelled of frost and sweet rotten apples, and stars had begun to prickle the deep blue-black of the sky. Little things, Deb thought. Yep, they count. They count up to the million and one little things I have to do every day, every night, every week. All the little things to make the house perfect for rich guests, the little things to make Krys's wedding perfect, the little things to keep us on our feet, all together, all in one piece.

A star, a bit of space-dust, dislodged from the sparkle and streaked east, and Deb gasped despite herself. One little thing.

The trap was sprung, the Oreo gone, and the mouse still alive somewhere in the big house at one the next afternoon. "Shit." Deb put down her bag and knelt to retrieve the trap. Couldn't have it in sight when Melody Westerly arrived. "Bastard," she said, glancing around the kitchen. She could put it behind the garbage can under the sink, but somebody might move that to take the trash out. The huge cast iron stove—converted from wood to electric—stood up off the floor on legs, but she was worried that an industrious caterer might sweep under it or drop a spoon and get down to look underneath. The antique butcher block beside the stove stood solid to the floor, swaybacked and lined with cuts from a hundred years of chopping, freshly oiled and seasoned by her own hand yesterday, exactly according to the recipe and instructions in the housekeeping book Edwards had given her when he'd hired her. The trap would just fit in between the block and the wall, Deb thought, and the stove would hide it on the side.

Westerly was late, of course, so Debra fetched the heavy floor polisher from the third-floor storage room, carried it down the back stairs, rolled back all the old oriental rugs and set to buffing the hand-waxed floors in the first floor parlor, dining room, living room, and loggia. Only the entry hall and kitchen were polyurethaned and could be mopped with water. All the others had to be hand-waxed. During summer and fall when the house stayed fully booked, she got down on her hands and knees with a can of paste wax and coated, then machine-buffed one room every week. In the winter, when the house sat empty for long stretches, she'd spend whole days alone in the house, doing all the floors thoroughly, beating and airing rugs, flipping mattresses, polishing silver, whatever was needed. Sometimes she talked to the ghost that was supposed to haunt the house, though she'd never seen it and didn't quite believe in spooks. Anyway, Melody Westerly had reserved the house for the whole week before her wedding on Saturday so that Debra could spiff it up, do all the floors, Windex and clean, and so that lawns could be mowed and the tents and chairs for the wedding could be set up. Couple thousand bucks so that Deb could put everything just so. The things rich folks spend money on.

Deb sweated as she swung the loud, heavy buffer back and forth, reviewing her morning up at the picnic shelter above the ballpark. "I won't pay for it if it's not legal," she'd said to Krystal. The goddamned "High Priestess," it turned out, wasn't licensed to perform weddings in Vermont.

"But this is what I want, Mom," Krystal had whined, standing in the middle of the wooded clearing. "It's spiritual. I don't care about the legal mumbo-jumbo. It's a rite of the goddess, not the government. What's a license got to do with it?"

The buffer bumped the wall and bounced back, one round pad wobbling loose. "Fuck." Deb switched the machine off and rested, swiping her brow, before tipping the machine on its side to readjust the buffer pad. "I just won't pay for the wedding, the reception, none of it. Not if it's not legal," she said aloud. "Put my foot down." And now there was the cat to deal with too. Bob was right; Tigger wasn't looking good.

"Hello?" someone called from the front door.

Damn. "Hello!" Deb called out. "Coming!" She combed her fingers through her hair as she swung the dining room door open into the hall.

A young man in a pink polo shirt smiled and extended his hand. "You must be Ms. Westerly," he said. "Jeff Marsh."

Deb laughed. "Not hardly," she said. "I'm the house-keeper. Debra Leclare. Call me Deb." She shook his hand. "You're the caterer, right?"

Jeff nodded. "Yep. Marsh Lane Catering. Steve Lane is my partner." He looked around as he spoke, checking the place out. Though almost everyone in town knew about the Kipling house—there was a historic marker on the dirt road at the bottom of the drive—only the rich folks who rented it out by the week—and the cleaners—ever really got inside.

"You want to see the house?" Deb offered. "Ms. Westerly is late."

Jeff Marsh nodded. "Sure. I always wondered what it looked like."

Deb took him through the loggia, its tall windows looking out over the valley, spectacular with autumn foliage, and nodded a glance into the dining room. "I'll show you the kitchen through that door last," she said. They passed through the little study and into the living room, lined with bookshelves, and out onto the main porch overlooking the lawn. "I think she's going to have the ceremony out there—" She pointed to the south hill above the tennis court. "So she can come through that path between the rhododendrons. Deb leaned out and pointed back across the lawns below the house to the north. "And they'll set up the tents for the reception out there."

Jeff leaned out to look. "Kitchen's on that end?" he asked.

"Yep," Deb said. Back in the main living room, sweet with the leather conditioner she'd just rubbed into the couch, she gave him the spiel about this being the room where Kipling wrote *The Jungle Book*. Back through the hall and up the wide main stairs, Deb told Jeff about the Kipling family's tragic years in Brattleboro, the death of their daughter, the fights with the relatives. She showed him through the four bedrooms and three bathrooms, smoothing the wrinkles in one bedspread as they passed. "The ghost," she explained. "Two children drowned in the pool after the Kiplings sold the place. She's always messing things up like that."

He laughed uncertainly. "Really?" he asked.

Deb shrugged. "I don't know," she said. "But there's always something just a little out of place after I've left it perfect. Maybe a mouse. Maybe a ghost. Who cares?"

On the third floor, Deb showed him the pool table and the desk that Kipling had actually used. "They keep it up here so it doesn't get messed up," she said. "It's worth something, I s'pose."

Jeff ran his fingers over the curved wood. "Cool," he said. "I always liked that story. Orphan boy raised by wild animals and all that."

Deb shrugged. "Yeah," she said. "Good movie anyway." She'd married Bob right out of high school, had Robby ten months later, Krys a year after that, and little Cash two years after that. Not much time for reading.

As they walked downstairs, something clicked in Deb's memory. Of course. "You say your partner is Steve Lane?" she asked. "Stevie Lane who graduated about five years ago?"

Jeff's smile creased into dimples. "That's my man," he said. He waved his left hand so that the gold wedding band glinted in the sunlight. "Until death do us part," he said.

Deb laughed. Of course. "I always thought he was light in the loafers," she said. "He used to come over to my house every day after school when he was a little feller. Back when his mama was alive and working afternoons. I used to babysit some, but I used to tell his mama that I oughta pay *her* for all the help he was to me." They reached the ground floor and Deb led Jeff through to the kitchen. "I can still see him standing up on the steppy stool chopping carrots at my counter. That boy was a whiz in the kitchen."

Jeff laughed. "Still is!" He stood at the sink and looked around. "He runs the kitchen and I run the business," he said. "This is small for us," he said. "But it'll work." He walked to the stove. "Electric?" he asked. Deb nodded. Jeff shook his head. "Good for nothing but boiling water," he said. "But the food'll mostly be done before we get here anyway."

"Now I think about it," Deb said. "I think my Krystal went to your wedding-thingy. Her and Stevie were in the same class all the way through."

"Civil union," Jeff corrected. He frowned, thinking. "Krystal," he said. Then his face widened. "Big girl, funny as all get-out?"

Deb laughed. "That's the one. She's getting married too, next weekend, day after this Westerly gal." *If* she finds a way to make it legal, Deb thought.

Car tires crunched in the drive, and Jeff looked through the window. "I think the *grande dame* has arrived," he said.

In silence, they watched the young woman, her hair in a scarf like an old movie star, try to park her blue convertible sports car with the top down under the coachman's porch. A little brown wiener dog wearing a yellow sweater wriggled on the white leather passenger seat, barking. Discovering that the pull-through was too narrow to open the car door, Melody Westerly huffed, turned the engine on again, and backed into the middle of the drive to park. She scooped up the dog, whipped off her scarf and flung it onto the seat before stepping out. About twenty-five or so, she wore tight designer jeans with a yellow turtleneck and supple leather jacket, and her blond hair, free of the scarf, bounced in curls down her back. She left a smudge of red lipstick on the dog's head when she kissed it, her lacquered nails hooked under his chest.

"Just as Steven described her," Jeff murmured under his breath.

"Rich bitch," Deb confirmed.

They exchanged a grin and went to meet the client.

By Monday morning, Debra was glad to be going to work, her regular job. Eight hours of watching chocolate-covered cherries pass along the conveyor belt, snatching out any that weren't just right, her hair neatly netted and her whites still white, seemed nice and peaceful compared to the chaos of the rest of her life. First Krystal with her ranting and howling and carrying on about the priestess and the government and her mother trying to ruin her life, and by the way, Trevor really thought they should buy more than just two kegs for the reception party. And then her baby, Cash, roared into the driveway on the motorcycle her dad had given him, which got her riled up all over again, and then her dad had come out and said (again) why the heck couldn't a young man ride a motorcycle? He'd had that same bike when he was just eighteen, damn it, and it was just collecting dust in the garage. Then Bob yelled from inside the Tagalong that they should all just calm down: Hell, Cash was eighteen and graduated high school, not like they had any real say in the matter, and didn't she remember how him and her had ridden this bike to the prom? And Krystal was just going to have to find a priestess who was goddamned government-approved—it was freaking Vermont, after all; the State must've licensed some witches to marry folks for Chrissake; probably some wizards and trolls too! And would somebody please bring him the goddamn chooser so he could watch something besides f-ing golf on TV. Then Robby's call had made them all quiet. His unit would be shipping out for the Middle East before Christmas. Finally they'd each drifted off to bed—Krys to the apartment where she was living with Trevor, Cash in the spare room in Mom and Dad's house, and Deb with Bobby into the Tagalong in the driveway.

Deb took some TYLENOL PM but lay awake a long time, making a list of things to do the next day—first shift at the candy factory; call Father Frank; deal with the beer question; finish up the floors at Naulakha; check the weather; reschedule the mowers if it rained; take Bob to the doctor; go over the grocery list for the reception with her mother; check the email to see if Robby knew his flight in from Georgia yet . . . Tigger lay like a bag of bones, purring, on the pillow behind her head. She'd have to squeeze in a trip to the vet for this sweet old guy too. She had just dozed off when the phone rang.

Melody Westerly—who had, as Deb had predicted, planned to stay on at the big house through to the wedding to "make certain all the preparations were just right"—screamed into Deb's ear: "Vermin!" Deb looked at the clock. 12:30. "Jo-Jo is completely damaged!" Melody Westerly shouted. Deb blinked. The wiener dog was named Jo-Jo. "He's in pain!" the woman shouted. "He is a pure-bred champion-line miniature dachshund worth thousands! His poor little nose!" She stopped to comfort the dog. "Poor wittle thing . . . " Kissing sounds. Deb wondered if Melody was still wearing the red lipstick.

"I'm sorry," Deb said. "I'm not sure I understand, Ms. Westerly."

"Like hell, you don't," Westerly snarled.

Deb held in a deep breath, her eyes closed. Don't speak, she thought. Don't say it. She bit her tongue.

"There was a *mousetrap* in the kitchen," the woman hissed through the phone line. She sounded so offended that Deb almost laughed. Imagine that! A mousetrap in an old house.

Bob clicked on his bedside light and raised his eyebrows. Deb shook her head and mouthed *Naulakha*. He rolled his eyes and lay back in his pillows.

"Yes, ma'am," Debra said, using the same tone she used with a crying child. "Is there a mouse in the trap?"

"So you admit that the house has mice!" Westerly crowed. "Vermin! I can't believe you people let out a house infested with vermin!"

Deb opened her mouth to respond, but the woman kept shouting.

"For what my father is paying for this place, we could have had the wedding at the Ritz Carlton. And now this! Vermin!"

"Excuse me, Ms. Westerly," Debra said. "Is there a mouse in the trap?"

"My poor little Jo-Jo," she said. More kissing sounds. "No." Her tone hardened. "There is no mouse in the trap," she said. "Jo-Jo found the trap for me—didn't you good boy?—and it snapped on his sweet little nose." Her tone sharpened. "And let me tell you, if it swells up, I will sue." Her voice went sweet and distant again. "Sweet-ums has to look pretty for the wedding doesn't he?"

Westerly had introduced the dog to Deb and Jeff on Sunday afternoon, explaining that Jo-Jo was to be the ring bearer in her wedding. Deb hadn't bothered to tell her that no pets were allowed in the historic home. Mr. Edwards had made it clear: Melody Westerly was to have whatever she wanted.

"I'm sorry, ma'am," Debra said. "Is your dog okay?" And what was it doing behind the butcher block anyway, she thought.

"I have a call in to his veterinarian in the city," Melody said. "Dachshunds have very delicate noses, you know."

"Um-hum," Deb responded. She could care less about the stupid little mutt. "Is there anything I can do tonight?" she asked, thinking *bitch*.

Westerly huffed into the phone. "I am concerned about the very idea of vermin!" she said. "What if one of my guests is attacked! What if the food is contaminated?"

Deb inhaled and exhaled slowly, willing herself to speak carefully. "I don't think you need to worry about that, Ms. Westerly," she said. "That trap must have been left there a long time ago," she lied. "Probably a mistake. I haven't seen no mice in there for ages." Not quite a lie. She really hadn't seen any.

"Well, I certainly hope not," Westerly said. "I will see you here tomorrow and you will see to it. One sharp. I do not want anything to mess up this event."

Deb opened her mouth to reply, but thankfully the connection clicked off. "Oh!" she groaned. "That bitch!" Bob put a pillow over his eyes. "They do not pay me enough for this," Deb said. She reached across Bob and snapped off his light, then rested her head on his chest. His heart thumped against her ear. "Oh hon," she said, "if it's not one thing, it's another, huh?"

Bob hummed, "Yeah," his breathing evening toward sleep. One thump after another in her ear. Now they were nearly fifty, Deb listened for anything different, any sounds out of place, out of rhythm. Men died young sometimes, even healthy strong fellows like Bob. If only he could quit smoking. He'd done good the last time he'd tried to quit, until the fire and then the accident. Shit. And Robby joining up hadn't helped any. At least he'd be home soon. Thank God. Deb listened to Bob's good strong heart thumping along. One little thing at a time, she thought. One little thing at a time. Work at five. Don't think about nothing. Nothing but that.

•

Deb found the mousetrap in the corner of the kitchen on Monday afternoon, probably where Jo-Jo had flung it from his nose. She picked it up, put it into the pocket of her sweatshirt, and looked around. Three wine glasses that she had collected from the porch, a coffee mug that had left a ring on the wooden desk in the small sitting room, and a pizza box and empty plastic salad container sat on the counter by the sink. Two cabinets hung open, and coffee grounds had spilled from an open bag onto the floor. Coffee had baked into a brown crust in the bottom of the glass carafe. She clicked the coffee maker off. Parts of *The New York Times* had slid onto the floor from the kitchen table. Deb folded it so the headline with "Iraq" was inside and tossed it into the recycling bucket with seven empty Diet Pepsi cans. She put the dirty dishes into the dishwasher, wiped the counters and swept the floor. Melody Westerly was out, thank God, so Deb decided to finish off the living room floors.

Upstairs, she stuck her head into the bedrooms, one by one, just to see how they looked. Westerly had assigned the three rooms along the hall to her parents and to the sisters and friend who would serve as her bridesmaids and maid of honor. The groom would be staying at the inn in town with his family. Melody had taken the master bedroom for herself, of course; Deb could tell by the mess—clothes on the floor and strewn across the unmade bed and chairs. Hung from the hook on the front of a mirrored armoire, zipped tidily in a clear plastic bag, the frothy white wedding gown seemed spot-lit by the afternoon sun. The mirror behind it reflected golden foliage outside, surrounding the dress like a halo. Deb heard nothing outside but the rustling of leaves. The dress seemed enchanted. She stood before it without quite knowing how she'd crossed the room. The white pearl buttons down the plunging bodice little droplets of purity. Her hand itched to unzip the plastic bag. It was the kind of wedding dress a girl dreams of.

Her breath fogged the mirror in little bursts. Deb blinked, eyes damp. If only she could have given Krystal something like this. If only she herself could have been married in this dress. It was perfect.

The light shifted and flashed, drawing her gaze to the mirror. She heard a crunch of tires on gravel outside. A shadow, reflected in the mirror, crossed the threshold of the door, something small. Debra turned. Nothing there. The mouse, she thought, though no mouse would be stupid enough to come out in daylight. Would it? And if not a mouse, what?

The door opened downstairs. Debra shook herself and crossed silently to the stair again. "Hello?" she called down.

The little brown dog started yapping, and Melody Westerly looked up. "Oh, it's you," she said. Jo-Jo's nails clawed the floor as he hurled himself around the corner and started up the stairs, his front half dragging his back half up each step like a thick slinky toy. "I've been to see Dr. Woolfe, the vet," she said. "That yokel with the horse barn wouldn't know a champion dachshund from an ant-eater. He says Jo-Jo is just fine, but I'll have to have him checked out by a real doctor when I get back to the city." She started up the stairs. "You're here to clean, I suppose?"

Debra smiled as sweetly as she could. "I thought I'd finish the floors downstairs," she said. "If that's okay with you." She had called Krystal from the factory break-room this morning and asked her to take Tigger to the vet. She wondered if the two brides had passed each other in Dr. Woolfe's waiting room.

The girl shrugged. "Oh, I've got a terrible headache," she said. "Do it some other time. I really need to lie down." She flung a shopping bag on the bed. "Maybe tomorrow."

Jo-Jo made it to the top step and skidded into Deb's shoe, stood up and started clawing her jeans leg, panting and yipping. "Oh look," said Melody. "He likes you. He likes everyone, you know. Dogs are just so democratic, aren't they?"

Debra bent over and patted Jo-Jo's head, which felt silky smooth, almost oily. His long nose butted against her hand. His body felt warm and muscled. "I don't know if I'll be able to finish everything tomorrow," she said, thinking of the floors and windows to be done after her shift at the factory. "I can't get started until after one."

Melody shrugged. "Whatever," she said. "I'm sure you can shift things around a little so you can get here earlier. I'll be out all day," she said. "I'm going up to the spa for the day with my girls. My sisters and my maid of honor. I called and told them that they just had to get away and come up early so we could hang out. It's just too beautiful to be all alone," she said. She scooped up Jo-Jo and headed into the bedroom. "And a little spooky too," she said.

Deb opened her mouth to protest. "But, I work—"

"Yeah, sure," Melody said, "you can work all day tomorrow. We'll be gone by nine." And she shut the door.

Deb frowned. What would she do about her shift at the candy factory? The floors at the bottom of the stairs gleamed dully as she trudged down. Maybe she could skip the floors, at least not roll back the rugs, just buff around the edges. The windows of the loggia seemed smudgy. She couldn't skimp on the glass. Edwards himself was invited to the wedding; he'd notice if the windows weren't cleaned. Maybe she could get Krystal to help tomorrow.

In the kitchen to pick up her bag, Deb put her hand into her pocket for the keys and touched the mousetrap. She smiled. This time she'd put it all the way under the stove where the dog couldn't get it. Wouldn't want no vermin to spoil the goddamn wedding, she thought.

Tuesday, Deb arrived at the chocolate factory early for her shift at five, fresh from a good night's sleep. No midnight calls from Melody Westerly. No new worries from the kids or Bob or her folks or the insurance company. Except Dr. Woolfe had kept Tigger for some tests. No telling how much that would cost. Father Frank, of all people, had helped Krys find a new high priestess to perform her wedding ceremony—one who was licensed by the State of Vermont, "Mistress Isis" *sheesh!*—and Robby would be on leave starting tonight. Bob's doctor had said he'd be good to go back to work end of next week, "maybe," and Deb's mother had told her to go to bed at nine, offering to finish hemming Krystal's wedding dress. Things were looking up. All the little stuff seemed like it was taking care of itself. Maybe. She opened the van door into the cool darkness of the factory parking lot. She sure hoped so.

Deb saw Marcus through the window in his little office, so she waved and stuck her head in his door. "Hey boss-man," she said.

"Morning Deb." He sat back in his chair and waved toward the coffee pot. "Help yourself," he said. "What's on your mind?"

Marcus was the chocolate factory owner's son, fresh out of business school last May and comfortable in his new position as plant supervisor. He'd graduated in Krystal's high school class too. Deb liked him, but she knew he was all about numbers, not people. Not even people who were the mothers of the kids he'd gone to school with. If layoffs were needed, he'd do what needed to be done. Bottom line. Deb poured herself a cup of coffee and leaned over to top off Marcus's cup as well. "Nothing much," she said, then laughed. "Well, that's a damned lie. Krys' wedding, the house insurance, the Kipling house, sick husband, sick cat, you name it."

Marcus laughed. "That's right. This is Krystal's big weekend, isn't it?" He frowned and glanced at his computer screen, then back at Deb. "You've got it off, don't you?"

Deb nodded. "Oh yeah, no problem there. I just—"

"Good good." Marcus looked behind her to the door, then to the coffee pot, then back to his computer. "I don't think I'm going to be able to make it to the wedding," he said. "Maybe, but maybe not. I—" He glanced at her then away. "Why don't you take a big box of the seconds for the reception," he said. "The good stuff," he said. "We had that pouring glitch yesterday," he said. "Take the cherries. Take all of 'em."

Deb smiled. "Thank you, Marcus," she said. "That'll be really special for Krys. I'll tell her you sent them." She sipped from her Styrofoam cup. "I was actually going to ask if I might be able to take off a little early today. If everything gets done, you know. Not much orders coming up for fall season, right? A little slow these days?"

Marcus grinned, relieved that she wasn't asking for more. "Oh sure," he said. "We've got that wedding order to get ready for Saturday—West-Reilly or something—but all that's left there is the wrapping, right?"

Deb cringed. That woman was everywhere. "Right," she said. "It's all in the cooler now. Ready for trays."

"Sure," Marcus said. "You make sure that gets done right, and get the girls started on the regular batches, and you can take off." He stood up behind his desk, ready to be rid of her. "Guess it's pretty busy being mother of the bride and all, huh? Lots of details . . . ."

Deb stood and took her coffee with her toward the production floor. "Yep," she said. "A million little things."

Tigger was dying. Deb had stopped at the vet's on her way from the plant where she'd carefully placed a thousand perfect chocolate-covered cherries, their little stems each pointing the same way to form spirals, onto trays covered in gold foil and laced with sheer pink ribbons. Her hands were stiff from the hours of work in the cooler, but the twenty trays were safely boxed and tied and ready for transport to Melody Westerly's big day. The three boxes of seconds—cherries without stems, cherries that gleamed through gaps in the chocolate, cherries whose chocolate had discolored or just missed covering them—sat in the backseat of her van next to Tigger in his little plastic cat-carrier. It was already noon. The vet had wanted to talk for a long time about Tigger's condition—his kidneys were failing, old age, they didn't know what exactly—and their "options."

"I don't have many options," Deb had admitted. "I love this old bugger," she said, tears spilling onto Tigger's thin coat, "but he's sixteen years old. What good's it gonna do to throw money into exploratory surgery?" Tigger purred, cradled on her forearms, and she kissed him on the head. "He's like one of my kids," she said. "'Cept he stayed on with me. Put himself to good use, didn't ya feller?"

Dr. Woolfe nodded. "It's probably not much longer," he said. "He's pretty weak even after the saline." He reached over and stroked Tigger's head. "I think you're right to take him home for awhile," he said, "where he's happy. He might just decide to let go on his own, like animals do sometimes." He paused and tapped his stethoscope against his palm. "But if he hangs on and he seems to be in pain, you call me." He looked into Deb's eyes. "I'll come out to your house to put him down if you want."

Debra bit her lip. They'd had to do that with a dog once. Dr. Woolfe at the house with his bag, his needle. She hugged Tigger close, gently, then helped him into his carrier.

"You can have a nice little rest while I clean," Deb said to the cat as she pulled up the long curving drive to Naulaukha at 10 A.M. The blue convertible was gone, thank God. Deb considered leaving Tigger in the van, but she didn't want him to be alone. She hoped folks would do the same for her when her time came. Stay close.

She let herself into the house and called out "Hello?" but no one answered. Another relief. She put Tigger's crate on the first step and looked in at him, the yellow eyes huge and round, his pink nose twitching. He looked livelier. "Meow?" He tilted his head and reached his paw through the bars of the cage door.

"Hey boy," she said. He curled his claws around her finger. She sighed. Even thin, he seemed smushed inside the carrier. Deb looked around the empty hallway. Why not? She pinched the metal clasp and opened the cage door. Tigger stretched out his white paws, the tiger-striped grey body following, humped his back and sat down on the step to wash his white bib, eyes darting and ears tipping to catch any sounds. "Make yourself at home, old man," Deb said, stroking his sleek head and scratching his ears. "And if you see any little grey fellers, you take care of 'em for me, okay?" He stood and followed her into the kitchen where she set down a dish of water, from which he drank deeply. Kidney failure makes 'em thirsty, the vet had said. She picked Tigger up and carried him back to the loggia, where she sat him on a chair in a pool of sunlight. "I'm gonna miss you, old boy," she said. "But right now, I've got work to do. You take a nice nap, and I'll round you up in time to get gone before that witch gets back. You just take it easy."

But eight hours later, when the evening dark had set in and the floors were gleaming and the windows shining black rectangles and the dust all wiped away, Tigger was gone. Deb knew he was dead as soon as she touched him, body slack and already cooling, his fur soft and slick, bony underneath, still curled on the chair. "Oh Tigger," she said. "What a way to go." She felt tears welling. "In a rich man's house." She wiped her face on her shoulder and scooped her hand under the body to carry Tigger to the van, the cage in her other hand. It wouldn't be right to put him back in it. He was free now. She laid him on the back seat, and just as she shut the door, the headlights of the con- vertible turned in at the gate below. Deb got into the van and turned the key before the women reached the top of the drive. She lifted her hand from the wheel to wave but didn't stop, didn't roll down the window. She let herself cry all the way home, alone in the privacy of her vehicle under the shining stars.

On Wednesday, it rained, and Krystal freaked out. "What if it rains on Sunday?" she wailed. "I don't want to be married in the picnic shelter!"

Debra looked at her mother behind Kry's backside, shimmering with the white satin of the dress they were trying to fit her into. Mama just winked.

"Now honey," Mama said, "you keep going on about nature and all that larky. What makes you think nature-wet's any worse than nature-dry?" She sat back on her heels and looked at the mirror before the bride. "You'll be beautiful in any weather," she said. "All brides are beautiful." Deb followed her gaze to the mirror. She was right. Krystal was beautiful. The dress was tight, a little puckered here and there in the seams, but Kry's bosoms bunched up into a deep cleavage and her waist was cinched in as much it could be. Deb stood and lifted Krystal's hair into a twist on top. "Oh hon," she said. An image of Krys standing up in her crib, chubby and smiling, those brown eyes intense even then, flashed into her memory. She felt her throat close. "Oh baby. You're all grown up. You look so pretty."

Krys hugged Deb. "Mom," she said. "You know I've always been grown up. An old soul, you used to call me." They smiled together at their reflection.

Deb saw the cardboard box over her shoulder. "Krys," she said, "we need to get poor old Tigger into the ground before he starts to smell." Krys had insisted, when Deb had called her with the news last night, that she wanted to bury Tigger herself. "He's my cat, Mom," she'd said. But when she'd arrived for the fitting this morning, the rain had been pounding, and they'd agreed to wait. Deb glanced toward the window. "Looks like it's clearing a little," she said. Leaves pasted the ground, pulled down by the rain, and in the steam rising up under a direct sun, the world looked golden.

•

Deb's mother had already unzipped the dress, and Krys stepped out of it. "I'll finish the alterations," Deb's mother said. "You two go on."

"I want to bury Tigger in the circle," Krys said, pulling on her jeans and t-shirt. "Will you come up to the park with me Mom? I want Tigger to be there for the hand-fasting too."

Deb sighed. "But hon, I've got to get to the grocery store today, and pick up the linens for Naulakha, and call the mowers, and reschedule the tent and chair set-ups, and—" Krys' shoulders sagged. Debra relented. "Sure," she said. "It's my only daughter's wedding. I'll help you bury the danged cat in the circle."

Bob insisted on coming along when he heard what they were up to, so it was the three of them who drove past the ball fields and up the long hill that was the public ski slope in the winter to the picnic shelter at the top, parked, and made their way along the path into the woods, Deb steadying Bob, who leaned on a silver cane, Krys carrying the box in one hand and the shovel in the other. The trees dripped, though the storm had cleared off fast, leaving blue sky and a crisp autumn breeze. "Nice day," Bob said.

"The kind of day Tigger used to love," Krystal said. "Remember him chasing leaves when he was a kitten?" She paused as they entered the clearing. Sunlight streamed between the trees, lighting the semi-circle of wooden benches, mossy and damp, and the lectern at the front. "It really does seem like a magical place, doesn't it?" Kry said.

They stood and listened to the drips, a few leaves fluttering down into the light.

"You think we ought to bring up some towels if it rains on Sunday so people don't mess up their good clothes?" Deb touched the slime of a green bench.

"It'll be perfect, just like it is," Krys replied. She walked over to a spot past the lectern and laid the shoebox on the ground, then sliced the shovel into the earth. "Grandma's right. Nature-wet, nature-dry. All good."

Bob lowered himself to the nearest split-log bench, holding Deb's arm. "It'll be fine, hon," he said. "It's Krystal's place. Her day."

She shrugged, eying the puddles, the dirt, the sagging benches. "I guess," she muttered. She added towels to her list of things to remember.

Krystal dug until Bob judged the hole deep enough to discourage any scavengers, then laid the box inside. She knelt and removed the lid for a last look. "Godspeed little brother," she said. "Off to the happy hunting ground."

Little brother. Deb thought of Robby, of Cash, and felt her throat tighten. Even Tigger was gone now.

The earth thumped on the box as Krys kicked it over the grave. She put a patch of moss over the raw dirt and pulled a little candle from her pocket.

"Oh lord," Deb murmured. "Here it comes." Bob elbowed her ribcage.

Krystal ignored them. She lit the candle and held it to drip a spot of wax on the corners of a rough square, then four more between those. She set the candle on the hank of moss, closed her eyes, and said nothing.

It was so quiet that Deb could hear a truck gearing down the long hill out on the expressway far away, and the voices of children on the playground in the lower part of the park. Chickadees flitted between the branches, and the pine-sweet forest dripped. She stared at a silvery droplet on the end of a red maple leaf, swelling and trembling, glinting with sun. It fell. She heard a soft *bip* as it hit the pine-needled earth, and then the *bips* of a million more shaken off in a breeze. The forest whispered. Bob's fingers laced Deb's, surprising her, and she let her head tip onto his shoulder.

By the end of Thursday, Debra had almost forgotten the mouse. She spent most of the day at Naulakha. Sam

Fellows arrived at ten sharp with a kid helper, and they unloaded the mowers and set to work. Melody Westerly came out on the porch holding a coffee cup to complain about the noise and the hour, but Deb explained as nicely as she could that the tents and chairs couldn't be set up until the mowing was done. The big Rent-a-Tent truck pulled into the driveway just as she said it, neatly ending the bride's arguments. Three white canvas tents popped up on the freshly mowed lawn: one with tables and chairs and an area for the caterers, one for the wedding itself with a semi-circle of two hundred chairs, and a third covering a wooden dance floor. Deb showed him where to leave the china, silverware and glasses in the kitchen, and he used the hoist to lower port-a-potties into place on the edge of the driveway while the Westerly family drank martinis and watched from the back porch. The florist would arrive first thing on Saturday, along with the caterers, the musicians, and the DJ. Deb had just come up from the laundry room where she'd left the fresh tablecloths and linens from the cleaners when the little dachshund skittered into the kitchen. He ran to the stove and stuck his long nose under it, scraping the floor with his nails—painted red today, Deb observed—trying to push himself into the space. After the mousetrap again, she realized.

"Get!" she said, kneeling and pushing his wriggling body aside. She bent, her cheek almost touching the floor, and looked under the stove. The trap was still set. Jo-Jo got his shoulders into the narrow space. "You ain't too smart, are you?" she commented to the dog. Footsteps. She straightened up, her face burning.

"No," said Stevie Lane, the caterer, coming in the back door. "That is the dumbest dachshund I've ever met."

"Stevie!" Deb grabbed the stove door handle and pulled herself to her feet. "How's my little cook doing these days!" She put an arm around the small young man with the red hair and hugged him, then stepped back to look at him, his lime green polo shirt with Marsh-Lane Catering printed in pink, black clogs and jeans. "My God, seems like just yesterday I was changing your diapers."

Stevie blushed. "Not quite yesterday," he said. "And I hear Krys is all grown up and about to be a married woman too."

Debra laughed. "I hope you'll come," she said. She went to her purse and pulled out one of the Xeroxed invitations they'd made. "And your feller, Jeff, too, of course." She stuck it in his back pocket since he was holding a stack of platters. "Sunday at two," she said. "You can put those in the laundry room." She pointed at the stairs. "That's the 'staging area.'" She made quotes with her fingers in the air and rolled her eyes.

Jeff laughed. The dog, half under the stove, whined, now pushing back with his little feet. "I think that guy is stuck," he said, pointing his chin. "What's under there anyway?"

"Mousetrap," Deb whispered. "Don't tell." She grabbed Jo-Jo's back half and tugged until he slid out. She put him into the front hallway and shut the kitchen door. "You'll come to Kry's wedding, right?" she asked.

On Deb's way to her van—after securing a promise from Stevie—she stopped by the back porch to say that she'd be there by ten on Saturday to help with the set-ups and to keep the guests out of the house during the ceremony.

"And we'll need you to tidy up tomorrow evening," Melody Westerly called as Deb turned. "Come by around five. The rehearsal dinner is in town, so we'll all be out." She looked at her mother, who nodded. "Just to do up the kitchen," she said. "Maybe run the vacuum. Make it nice for Saturday."

Deb hesitated. Robby was arriving tonight, late. They'd planned a cook-out tomorrow evening to celebrate. "I don't know," she said. "I have plans."

Melody frowned. "But really," she said. "The house will be a wreck by then." She turned to her father. "Daddy—"

The big silver-haired man stepped toward Deb, his hand in his pocket. He set his martini on the railing and pulled out a wad of bills. "How about a little incentive," he said, peeling off a hundred-dollar note. He held it out to her. "Just a little something extra for your trouble. Shouldn't take more than an hour or so."

Deb sighed. He was right. She could whiz through it all in no time and still get home in time for a burger and beer. The hundred could be her gift to Krystal and Trevor. Something to help them get started. Something more useful than the lace tablecloth she'd pulled out of her old hope chest. "Okay," she said, taking the bill and putting it in the breast pocket of Bob's old flannel shirt. She'd never used that tablecloth herself; she doubted that Krystal would either. Too precious. Too fragile. All those little threads and holes, old and easily broken. "I'll be here at five," she said.

"Good worker, that gal," she heard Mr. Westerly say as she walked away. "Could use a few more like her around."

"Oh," Mrs. Westerly responded, "they all get lazy after awhile. You'd think they'd want to get ahead, but they don't." Deb slammed the van door and sat for a minute before turning the key. She could smell the newness of the hundred-dollar bill in her pocket. It crackled as she breathed deeply, trying to calm herself. Sometimes she hated rich people.

Deb woke on Friday to Robby's voice outside the Tag-along and smiled. Her first-borne was home safe. He'd looked so fine in his uniform coming through the security gate at the airport, more like Bob at that age than she'd remembered. A man. Grown up and on his own, but he'd dropped his green duffel and lifted her feet off the ground in a hug anyway. "Mom," he'd said, and "Dad," to Bob, clapping him on the shoulder. "Man, it's good to see you all." Robby had grinned at Krys and at Cash, who rubbed the top of Robby's skinned scalp with his knuckles.

If only they could be together at their own home, Deb thought, sitting up, stretching. She had cried at the airport, the stress of the fire and the weddings and Bob's accident and the money and even poor old Tigger dying suddenly wrapped up in Robby's homecoming. And Iraq. Nobody'd yet said that word. Nobody had to. Deb had gasped and cried some more and wiped her eyes. They were all together again. That was enough. Surely that was enough.

"It's a bomb," she heard Cash say outside, "but it's wheels. Guy's gotta have wheels." They must be talking about the bike, Deb thought.

"Bet Mom's pissed," Robby laughed. Their voices were so deep, so grown up. "How'd you keep her from killing you? Man."

"She still could!" Deb called through the camper's little screened window.

"Shit!" Cash said. "Mom! You scared me!"

Robby laughed. "Are you just waking up?" He stood from his crouch beside the motorcycle and peered in at Deb. "Roughing it must not be all that bad if you get to sleep in 'til nine." He smiled. "Reveille, Mom!" He tooted out the wake-up call between his fingers. "Rise and shine, soldier!"

"Pancakes, boys!" Deb's mother called from the house. "Come and get it!"

Deb pulled on her bathrobe, stepped into her slippers and descended from the camper to the covered carport. The old red motorbike stood between her and the kitchen door. Deb resisted the urge to push it over. Stupid thing. As if there weren't enough ways for a kid to get himself killed. She'd made Bob get rid of his after he'd laid it down—with her on it—one night down in Georgia. They'd been newlyweds, only eighteen or nineteen. She crossed her arms, pulling her robe together over her breasts. God, they'd been just kids. She might've even been pregnant already, just a month past the wedding, her graduation from high school, living in that little concrete-block house on the base, screwing like bunnies. She smiled, remembering. The bike's headlight had shined like the moon on the mirages ahead on the road that night. A warm night, smelling of ocean and the leather of Bob's jacket against her cheek, her arms tight around his waist. A little animal had scurried across the two-lane blacktop, a small dark shape, and Bob had swerved. Debra still felt the swinging out of their hips together, remembered the way the moon behind rows of pines had blip-blip-blipped like the line on the TV late at night as they turned, back end first, toward the woods. It had felt almost like a dance move, in perfect sync, until the asphalt scraped their right legs, the bike dragging them and squashing them, and they had slid together across the gravel shoulder and into the grass at the roadside. They could've died. Deb blinked, focusing on her own reflection in the curved mirror of Cash's Honda. Idiot thing. She'd discovered she was pregnant right after that, her leg and hip still bruised and scratched, and she'd put her foot down. "It's time to grow up," she'd said. "Be responsible. We gotta sell the bike and get a real car." And good Bob had done as she'd said. They'd both known it wasn't really about the baby.

The smell of pancakes and maple syrup, and the sounds of her family's voices brought Deb back. She opened the door to Robby and Cash singing "Goin' to the chapel, and they're gonna get married . . . ." Krystal and Trevor must have walked to Mama's from their apartment. Deb noted that they held hands under the table, and Bob leaned against the counter, grinning.

"Promise me you won't do that at the wedding," Krystal said. Deb could tell that she didn't mean it, secretly pleased to be the center of attention. Well, as she should. She was the bride, after all. Deb watched as Kry's brown eyes turned serious, gazing into her brother's face. She poked Robby's hand with the tines of her fork. "Promise me you won't do nothing stupid over there, big brother."

Robby glanced at Krys, then saw Debra in the doorway. He was so young, so handsome. "Not to worry," he said. "They'll probably just put me in the mess anyway."

Deb felt her throat tighten. It wasn't true. Robby'd put in for infantry training school. He'd made marksman in basic. They would put him in the action. Oh God. Right in the middle of the action. She closed her fist tighter, holding the neck of her robe together, broke Robby's stare and turned to the bathroom. She had to get a grip on herself. She had two weddings in the next two days. That was her job. No sense in thinking about things she couldn't change. She splashed her face with cold water. The woman in the mirror looked tired, but maybe not all that old. Mama'd just bleached her roots for her, and she'd kept herself out of the sun mostly, so there were only a few little lines around her mouth. Hell, she was only forty-seven. Not old at all. She stared at eyes in the mirror. Weddings. Cleaning. Everybody here. She couldn't let herself think about Robby going to Iraq. Not that.

The little pink foot in the trap and the splatters of blood on the floor and over the wall behind the butcher-block made Debra sick. The mouse had been caught, apparently, but he'd chewed off his foot or it'd been snapped off by the metal bar of the trap. She sat back hard on the kitchen floor, dizzy. She rested her forehead on her knees, forced herself to breathe. The sight of blood always did that to her. At least the idiot wiener-dog hadn't got to it first. Fuck. The goddamn mouse would probably die in the walls somewhere and stink up the whole place. Shit.

Debra forced herself to reach behind the butcher block and grab the trap by the edges with her thumb and forefinger to pull it out. The severed mouse foot looked like a baby's hand. She closed her eyes and saw floating colored spots. She remembered Robby's little fingers closing around her thumb. Hospital white and bright. Bob crying and grinning, both of them exhausted from the labor. They had been just kids, but they were a family in that instant. Those little pink fingers around her thumb. Oh God. Debra choked. Robby was going to a war. Her baby was going to a war. A sob welled up. She felt the mousetrap jiggle. Kids lost their hands in war. They got killed. She opened her eyes and saw the splatter of red on the wall again.

Debra cleaned it up, of course, because who else would? It's my job, she told herself. Just a job. She had calmed herself down and caught her breath, hauled herself to her feet, grasped the trap between thumb and forefinger—her hand trembling a little—then taken it to the garbage and dumped the whole thing—trap and mouse-foot and all—in. She'd gotten out the bleach and a rag. She had scrubbed the blood from the plaster. Bleach, rag, scrub. The wall pinked, then whitened. Think only about the house, she told herself. Think only about the work. Put the kitchen in order: dishes, counters, floor. She moved to the bathrooms, encasing her hands in yellow gloves, almost enjoying the burn of the chlorine in her nostrils, scrubbing and rinsing, wiping away little hairs from the shower, yellow pee-spots on the toilet seat, toothpaste spit in the sinks. She knew how to clean. This she could do. Make it all perfect again, clean. The Westerlys were out at the rehearsal dinner. The big empty house echoed and thumped with her movements up and down the stairs and hallways, in and out of rooms. She and Bob had looked at real estate on the Internet after breakfast that morning. She had found fault with every one of them: too big, too expensive, too small, busy road, too far out of town. She vacuumed the footprints from the Kipling rugs and made the beds, picked up dirty laundry, plumped the sofa cushions. Bob had called the realtor anyway, made an appointment for them to look at houses in their price range. As if she had time for that too. Debra stomped up the back stairs to the storage room for fresh linens, laid out a bath towel, hand towel and washcloth on each smooth bedspread. She returned to the first floor and shined the dining room table with wide circles that wafted lemon oil into the air. Her own face in the mahogany stared up at her, brow and mouth and eyes hard, the lines in her face like the grain of the wood. Debra stopped. Who was that woman? Why was she so angry? So tired? So old?

Something moved in the loggia, behind the planter, and she looked up. The leaves of the geraniums moved as if in a breeze, though the windows were shut tight, or as if they had been brushed by someone, but no one was there. A book lay in the wicker chair where Tigger had died. Debra stuffed the bottle of lemon oil and rag into her apron pockets and walked into the loggia. The floor-to-ceiling windows gleamed black with the darkness outside. She picked up the book. How had she missed it? She slid it into the empty spot in the shelf overhead, reading the title as she lined it evenly with the others: *Just So Stories.* She felt the corners of her mouth curve up in a tight smile. She ran her finger down the rough spine of the book. That's me, she thought. Making everything just so.

She heard a car-door slam in the driveway, and then the voices of the Westerlys, the key in the front door. Debra put on her jacket over her apron, the lemon oil and rag still in the pockets, and met them as they entered, smelling of whiskey and perfume and wool, laughing, cheeks pink. They didn't seem to see her as she slipped past, brushing the silks and taffeta dresses and stiff black of the men's evening wear, into the night. She stood in the driveway looking up at the lopsided moon, not quite full, shining.

Back at her parents' house, Krystal's engagement party was rocking. Deb's dad in his Kiss the Cook apron rocked back and forth on his heels, waving a spatula with one hand and a beer can inside a foam sleeve with the other. "Hey there, little girl!" he called. The smoke from the gas grill blew the aroma of steak into Debra's face, and she walked into her father's hug. "You ought not be working so late," he murmured. "Let your hair down. Enjoy life a little now."

Deb pulled back and looked at him, her hand around his waist. "Oh Daddy," she said, "you aren't just a little drunk are you?" She smiled and he grinned back. The music from the speakers perched in the house windows switched to the Rolling Stones.

"You know it, darlin'," he said. "But that don't make it not so." He waved his beer toward the bonfire where silhouettes of people moved about. "You let yourself have a little fun now and then. You ain't got to take care of nothin' tonight."

Deb laughed, thinking of the Westerly wedding tomorrow and Krys's wedding on Sunday, not to mention the house-hunting, the phone calls to the insurance people, Cash on the motorcycle, Robby . . . . "Sure, Daddy," she said. "Nothin' to worry about."

He put his flipper and beer down on the picnic table, leaned over and opened the big cooler at his feet, then plunged his hand into the ice and pulled out a Budweiser. "I mean it, daughter," he said, pulling the tab. "You stop thinkin' tonight, you hear?" He held the can out to her.

Deb looked at the beer. What the heck? She took it and raised it in a toast. "To letting go," she said, and gulped.

The beep-beep-beep-beep of the alarm at 9:00 seemed to split her forehead. Deb punched the off-button and sat up carefully, trying not to move her head too fast. Her tongue felt cottony and sour. Bob, lying on his side, mumbled something and tugged the blanket up under his chin. Deb put her palm on his bicep and nestled her face into the soft black hairs between his shoulder blades, warm and a little sour, smelling of grain and earth, from last night's alcohol and sex. She'd ridden him in the dark, adjusting and moving and whispering directions to him, her eyes closed, trying so hard to come, until he'd simply gripped her waist and rolled them both over, still joined, and put his hands on her shoulders and grinned down at her. "Let it go, babe," he'd growled. And slow, slow, agonizingly slow, he'd fucked her until she came, straining up against his calloused palms and narrow hips, fighting to lose control. Debra blushed, remembering that she'd tried to bite his shoulder, and the way she'd given in, finally, to the weakness and fullness, as if everything in her whole life, the whole world, had expanded into her body and mind, and just let go. Everything exploding. Vanishing. God, that had been good. She'd slept like a baby, no dreams, conscious only of the softness of her skin and thick emptiness of her body, like a cat sleeping in the sun. She petted Bob's bicep now, breathing against his back, thinking of Tigger. She missed his purr, the way he slept nestled above her head on the pillow. Bob smacked his lips in his sleep, and Deb smiled and pressed her lips to the hollow of his back, then slid out of bed, pulling the blanket up and tucking it in around him. Wedding day number one.

As she crept through her parents' kitchen, brewing coffee, showering and dressing, Deb flipped back and forth between blurry fragmented party scenes and her list of responsibilities for Melody Westerly's wedding. Dancing, singing at the top of her lungs to "I Will Survive!" in the basement, where the boys had hung a disco ball, turned out the lights and cranked the stereo. The jumble of bodies muffled the echoes from the cinderblocks, but she had heard nothing but the music, felt it pounding in her chest. Then a hand on her forearm, and she had opened her eyes, still singing, bouncing with the song. Robby, her son, had gripped both of her biceps, forcing her to stop moving, stared into her eyes and mouthed the words: "I will survive." God. Even through the fog of the Captain Morgan's, Deb had registered his blue eyes. The prickly blond scalp. The sharp angles of his jaws framing his smile. Her baby. She'd tried to wrench her muscles from his grip but staggered, tired from work, her body floppy from the booze. Deb remembered Robby's arm around her waist, helping her to the sofa, where she guessed she'd passed out until Bob had waked her with his sweet kisses. Deb tossed back four aspirin and a tall glass of o.j. in her mother's kitchen, blushing. Hot flash. She hoped she hadn't been too big an asshole last night. She splashed cold water on her face again. At least there wouldn't be much for her to do today. Only the wedding party—Westerly and her parents and sisters and maid of honor—and the caterers were to be allowed into Naulakha, so her job was to keep everyone else out. The guests would start arriving around one, and the wedding party would depart the house and march through the rhododendrons to the tent just before two. Deb had agreed to be there by ten.

In the end, there really wasn't much for Deb to do at Naulakha, and she felt lost with nothing in her hands, no work to attend to. She stood at the window in the loggia and watched the procession. The wiener dog at the end of a white leash held by a small boy, a white box dangling from the dog's collar, trotted down the red carpet path that had been rolled out between the shining dark green leaves of the rhodies. The bride in voluminous froth of white lace followed, on the arm of her father in black tailcoat, a long train slithering behind them. Worth more than her house, Deb thought. Probably getting filthy, despite the carpet, spilling over into the twigs, snagging and tearing. Deb snorted. Rich folks. It was pretty, though, a dream wedding. Like something out of a storybook. The wedding party disappeared under the white canvas, and Deb turned back to the interior of the house.

There was nothing for her to do.

Oh, she could go down to the kitchen, but Jeff and Steve had assured her that they had everything covered, and, to be honest, they seemed so busy—chefs and waiters shouting and moving from tray to stove to sink, up and down the stairs to the reception tent—that Deb had felt in the way. They hadn't even had time for gossip.

The big house felt hollow around her, still and quiet, but something subtle moving the air and dust from room to room. She often felt this in the winter when she spent days alone here hand-waxing the floors, cleaning under the old rugs, flipping mattresses. It was as if the house itself felt lonesome without permanent inhabitants, a family, sighing quietly like an old woman. Krys said it was spirits, of course, nothing mean, she assured her mother, just a few little ghosties wandering around, one of them a prankster who messed up the bedspreads and closed doors.

Deb stood for moment with her arms crossed. She heard a man's voice, raised, in the kitchen, then the sound of footsteps going down the stairs and the lower screen door slamming. The violins in the tent went silent. Through the back porch door, she saw birches gleaming yellow against the deep blue of the sky, a perfect late-September day. A hawk turned wide circles over the valley.

Deb rubbed her arms. Krys's wedding would be tomorrow afternoon, and her mother was making the cake right now. The good weather looked like it would hold out another day. Dad and the boys were picking up the kegs, and she had put all the decorations in the truck for tomorrow before she left this morning. Trevor and Krys were probably packing now, going off to the Cape for a couple days after the reception. Cash would go to work at Parks and Rec on Monday, and Bob would be back at the warehouse. First thing Tuesday, Robby would fly to Georgia for marksmanship training. Deb's mind flashed to the mouse paw on the trap. She closed her eyes and shook her head sharply. No. Don't think about that. She opened her eyes on the chair where Tigger had died. The blue and white checked cushion seemed still dented with his circle. Deb bit her lip. Her body felt heavy. She sank into the wooden rocker beside it and leaned over, elbows on knees, hands clasped under her chin. What was she going to do?

A book lay open on the glass table beside the rocker. Deb blinked, focusing. A drawing of a cat walking through forest. Deb picked the book up and flipped it over to see the spine, her fingers in the open page. *Just So Stories.* Again.

She looked back at the open page, the old-book smell of dust and mildew wafting from the yellowed page. "The Cat That Walked By Himself." Deb smiled, thinking of Tigger again, her eyes welling unexpectedly.

She glanced around the paneled room, floors gleaming, carpets straight, tall windows clear and clean. She heard the men's voices in the kitchen, saw the hawk bank and turn in the sky over the golds and reds of autumn mountains. No one cared what she did right now. No one needed her to do anything. It felt strange. She slid back in the rocker, the book open in her lap. I'll read the story, she thought. "The Cat Who Walked By Himself."

A woman and man make a home in a cave: cave-people. While the man goes out to hunt and gather, the woman performs little magic spells to draw the wild creatures to her, one by one, where she tricks them into becoming her servants—the cow, the horse, the dog. But the cat is as smart as the woman and turns the game against her, tricking the woman. He is as clever as she is. The cat . . . but the cat will always walk by himself. The cat remains free. Deb smiled, in spite of herself. It was a good story. The woman is smart, tricking the animals into becoming her helpers. She gives them good reasons to be domesticated. She makes life better for them and for herself. And the cat is clever too, gaining the comforts of the hearth, the warm milk and fire, by making himself useful—protecting the grains from a mouse, making the baby laugh, purring the baby to sleep—but he never gives up his independence. "When the moon gets up and night comes, he is the Cat that walks by himself, and all places are alike to him. Then he goes out to the Wet Wild Woods or up the Wet Wild Trees or on the Wet Wild Roofs, waving his wild tail and walking by his wild lone." Deb smiled, thinking of Tigger.

The words of the story blurred and she blinked, looking up and out into the sky. Violins swelled again, the music signaling the conclusion of the ceremony. Joy. She imagined the beautiful polished woman in her white dress, the handsome groom in his tailcoat, the little children and wiener dog and bridesmaids and groomsmen under the white tent, surrounded by flowers and greens and golds of Vermont. A storybook perfect wedding. Just so.

A burst of laughter from the kitchen, deep male voices. What would Melody Westerly's life be like, Deb wondered. Would she and her new husband start a family? Did she work outside the home? Did she have a new home, a house to keep, to decorate? Would she cook for her husband? How would they live?

She laughed to herself, finger tapping the book in her lap with a thunk. Surely not in a cave, she thought. Melody Westerly wouldn't need to be clever like the woman in the story; she'd just buy what she needed.

Deb closed the book and stood to return it to its place on the shelf. As the air moved, she caught a whiff of death. The mouse, probably. Somewhere in the walls. Nothing like that smell. And suddenly she understood. Just so. Not making things perfect. Just so. Just because. Just so.

The High Priestess, a black-haired woman in a white robe, held a red silk cord above the granite stone that served as an altar, closed her eyes and lifted her face to the sky, chanting: "In all of nature, there is nothing more powerful than love, a quickening to which we are called by the goddess, the gods, by nature herself. We call on the spirits now to bless this circle, to share our joy in the infinite nature of love." Deb couldn't believe this was her daughter's wedding. Her little girl. Chubby little Krystal had grown into a woman, now holding her hand across the stone, crossing it over Trevor's.

The priestess wrapped the cord around their wrists, mumbling something. Circled by her brilliant red lips, the gap between her white front teeth was dark, a small flaw that made her gorgeous. Deb wondered if the beauty mark on her cheek was real or a dot of mascara. Bob slid his hand into hers in her lap, and their fingers laced automatically.

The priestess led the couple by the leash of red silk to face the east, where the sky was brilliant blue over the New Hampshire hills. "Blessed be by the element of air," she said, "wisdom, thought, intelligence." Deb watched Trevor's profile. He looked stoned, eyelids half-closed, a dopey grin. Krys would have to be smart enough for the both of them.

The group turned and circled south, facing the picnic shelter, where the kegs and barbecue grills were waiting, crepe paper streamers fluttering in the breeze. "Blessed be by the element of fire. Creativity, passion and energy." Deb remembered Melody Westerly and her new husband, so smooth, so cool. The bride had stopped in at the house to freshen her makeup, powdering her cheek and pasting a stray strand of hair flat, between wedding and photos. The couple had barely spoken, hardly touched each other, except when directed to do so by the photographer. The little dog had seemed the only thing alive in the pose framed on the front stair, wriggling and barking, his little feet clawing at the fragile gown until the bride had simply shoved him into Deborah's arms, then rearranged her train and her husband and her face into a perfect picture, like something in a glossy magazine. Deb had taken Jo-Jo to the kitchen where the caterers had tossed him bits of cheese and hors d'oeuvre.

The priestess turned the couple to the right again and they faced the crowd. Bob squeezed Deb's hand, and Krystal looked directly into her eyes. Deb smiled, her own eyes filling at the sight of the tears streaming down Kry's face. She bit her lip and swallowed. "Blessed be by the element of water," the priestess intoned, and Deb hiccupped, trying not to laugh. Krys grinned then, and winked at her. "Friendship, empathy, love." Yes, Deb thought. Love. Please God, give them love.

The trio turned again and stepped away, toward the pine forest this time, the north. Beyond the white lace of the wedding gown on Krys's wide back and the puffy white sleeves of the groom's shirt, the grey-green of trees and spider-webs blurred into shadows. The crowns of flowers in the couple's hair seemed the only color in the gloom. Her little girl was leaving her, Deb thought. "Blessed be by the element of earth," the goddess said. "Blessed be with health, success, fertility." Deb blinked. Grandbabies. Tears trickled from her chin. She almost laughed. Why hadn't she thought of that? Grandbabies.

Westerly had called in the middle of the night, her own wedding night, waking Deb at three. "It smells," she had said without even a hello. "The house reeks. You have to come here and fix this now."

Deb had listened with her cheek still on the pillow, staring at Bob's freckled shoulder, smelling his warmth. "I'm sorry," she had said. "about the smell." She closed her eyes. Almost time to get up for wedding day number two. She sighed. "There's nothing I can do, ma'am. Sometimes things die in the walls, but there's no way to get them out. The smell will go away on its own, eventually. Just the way it is. Nothing you can do." And then, with Westerly's voice still rising, squeaking through the receiver, Deb had ended the call and held the button until the phone shut itself down.

She watched Krystal and Trevor kiss, their wrists still bound, the fingers of their hands laced together. No tongue, thank God. Sweet even. Not perfect, no story-book picture, the bride fat, the groom stupid. But sweet. Good. Right. They held their hands near their faces, the red cord trailing to the ground. Deb felt her own hand in Bob's, the palm itching. She forced herself to let it relax, to stop pulling to get away. She didn't need to see to the reception. Someone else could. Applause broke out in the audience, and Deb heard one of the boys whistle a shrill catcall. Everyone laughed, and the priest-ess unwound the cord from the couple's wrists. "The circle is broken," she said, and threw the cord into the sky, where it seemed to snake up then settle back down with a gentle *thwump*.

When Krys and Trevor drove off in Bob's truck instead of their old T-bird, which Cash and Robby had not only decorated with shoe polish and old shoes but had removed the tires and put up on blocks in the parking lot, Deb turned to Bob with her mouth wide. "Now how are we supposed to get home?" she said. The truck's red brake-lights passed down the road and out of the park. A full moon hung low on the eastern horizon.

Bob grinned and shrugged sheepishly. "I didn't want them to get stranded out on the Cape with that old heap," he said. He took her hand. "Trust me, babe," he said, pulling her from the crowd. She heard Robby and Cash howling, "Dad! Where is he?" their fun spoiled. "Come on," Bob whispered.

When he settled the helmet on her head and snapped the strap under her chin, she grabbed his hand. "Hon," she began. "This is crazy—" The insurance company. His leg. The house. Robby. Cash . . . That goddamned dead mouse at Naulakha . . .

"Yep," he said. "Crazy, babe." He lifted her hand to his mouth and kissed it. "Come on."

The goddamned dead mouse at Naulakha. It had been so good to close her eyes into Bob's warm shoulder and go back to sleep after hanging up on Westerly. She'd dreamed of Tigger, purring. And in the morning, wedding day number two, she'd stepped right over the dead mouse on the doorstep of the Tagalong in the morning, not even thinking. She remembered it now. Of course. Tigger had left it there. Of course. Deb let Bob help her onto Cash's motorcycle, his hand on her arm, and felt the engine roar under her as he kicked the starter. She leaned against his back, her hands clasped together around his waist. It was as if they were back twenty years, before the kids, before the house, before everything. Back at the beginning again. Bob lifted his feet and the bike rolled forward down the hill toward the full moon, a bright blob behind the clouds. Not perfect; just so.

HARVEST

We never listen carefully enough to hear him. We are not so alert as he, so full at this season, so ready, but we hear him in leaves and cricket-song and feel his fullness like a moon hanging heavy in a cooling evening sky.

He watches us, the two-legged moving, like moths in morning mists hanging over the valley below. He is very still, his brown the stones and trunks of forest trees, his antlers branching into sky as if his leaves have already fallen away. We, the two-legged, will not follow him today, will not secret ourselves in trees, will not disturb the silence of leaves rustling with our explosions of fire and blood. But that season is near. His seven years have taught him the power of stillness, of closeness to us at this season. Among us, we do not see him or hear him, and if we do, we will not harvest his body but will hold our breath, becoming as motionless as he. We are one in this moment, as in that other, the moment when his body spills open for our winter stores.

Hal feels the October morning fog enclosing him, tickling droplets dampening his hair, a chill at the nape of his neck.

He rolls his head in the collar of his fleece jacket, steps off another ten paces, and jams a stake into the lawn of the Common. In the mist he sees his wife, Julie, stringing the stakes with ropes, marking off parking spots, Ashley, their five-year-old, skipping up and down the rows. His son, Will, hammers a PARKING $2 DONATION sign beside the road, the sound eerily muffled in the dense mist. Hal stands still, suddenly seeing the three—the four—of them moving like a team of ghosts on the Common, suddenly overwhelmed with love, with the feeling that they will all move on into the future as if dispersed into fog. Hal wants to hold this moment still and forever.

Then Will smacks his thumb with the hammer and yells "FUCK!" and Ashley slips and falls into the mud and Julie's head whips from one child to the other, and Hal forgets.

Hammering and a kid's yelp wake Henry Smalls, who rolls over to look at Sharon, her hair fanned across his pillow, the smooth pale freckles of her shoulders. He has no desire to ever leave this bed, hasn't gone hunting once this fall. His wife, dead all these years, had always wished for him to stay home abed late come hunting season. Henry feels a pang of regret, but he is sure that she wouldn't begrudge him this joy. It is as if all of that had to happen to him to prepare him for this . . . this what? Completeness. Something full and whole in his life, like a pumpkin. He bends to kiss Sharon's back. He hopes his wife's ghost does not mind. "Wake up," he says. "Tourists on their way to Neweden." He sees Sharon's mouth curve into a smile, her eyes still closed. The ghost in that other quiet world does not mind, he thinks, about love in this world.

Christine makes Mari sit again while she adjusts the paintings on the walls of the tent. "Up on the left," Mari says. "Think it'll rain again?"

Chris glances back. "No." Mari's belly—tight as a fruit

under the jersey shirt peeking through the gap in her coat—rolls as if monster fish are just under the surface. Another world in there. Another world right here on the edge of this world, almost ripe, almost ready to be born.

His ears and nostrils twitch, always alert. We, the two-legged, are pale, weak, slow, loud, and we have the power of harvest. He has the power of life.

Jack Crossly stretches his legs out from a picnic table, leaning back, watching the cars with blue Connecticut, New York, and Massachusetts tags line up for a spot in the lot across the road. He sips his coffee and bites into a hamburger. The sun made a brief appearance just before noon, and the high school jazz band is setting up now on the porch of the courthouse. "Good for business, I reckon," he says.

Bob Wright, still on crutches, foot up on a lawn chair, nods. "Suppose so," he says. "The wife says the big Kipling house is booked through November now."

"Good," says Jack. "Let 'em spend all that city money up here."

Bob nods. "Buy some country air and knicky-knacks."

Jack laughs. "Maybe get lost hiking up in the 'foilage.'" He grins and scratches his beard. He's seen 'em come every fall for the leaves, every winter for the skiing, every spring for the syrup, every summer for the fishing and swimming. He's seen it all. He is done with all that doing. Reckons he's earned some retired time.

Bob looks uphill into the golds and oranges of autumn. Will his son, Robby, ever see this again? His boy going to Iraq. His boy trained to kill. His boy gone.

"You hear about that seven point buck I saw up on the mountain?" Jack asks.

Bob has. Everybody has. But Jack launches into his story without waiting for a response, just as he always does.

"Biggest damn thing," he says. "Came outta fog—like that this morning—and disappeared right back into it before I could raise my gun." Jack shakes his head. "Lucky bastard." He looks up at the golden mountains. "Big as all creation, but quiet as a ghost."

"You hear that old dude?" Brandi looks up at the boy—the quarterback of the football team—whose arm she is hanging onto. She grins. Let everybody see. Let everybody— even Daddy—see that she's good enough to get any man she wants. "No way I'd a let that buck get away," the quarterback continues. "He's just a lousy hunter." Brandi pooches her lips out a little. She hopes he'll kiss her right here in the middle of the Common, right in front of the art teacher and Mr. Fellows and her own folks. That'll show them she can have it all, no matter what they think of her.

He hears the sound of our song drift up the valley, tinny and wailing as he browses the last green shoots of grass. Soon the white season will come, and he and his kin— those who live through the harvest—will gather to shelter among pines and hemlocks, bedding in fragrant needles, warmed by their collective bulk. He is full with summer and acorns for the long cold, but there is no gain without loss. If we—the hunters—are not his destiny, perhaps the harshness of winter or randomness of accident or fate. He is full as a moon, full as the universe. He is always ready.

As the tree shadows lengthen across the lawn of the Common, a breeze rustles the maple leaves, causing Lawrence to look up and around. Like someone walked over my grave, he thinks.

"Frost warning tonight." He focuses on the woman who has spoken. His daughter? He isn't sure, come to think of it. He tries to remember when she arrived. Has she always been here? His memory seems to twist around, thoughts leading him to dead-ends, then back to somewhere almost familiar. But changed. Something had been at the lettuce in the garden. The one over the septic. Deer most likely. "We'd better cover the tomatoes," the woman says.

Lawrence smiles and shrugs. The young ones always want the season to stretch a little longer. Harvest the damned tomatoes and let 'em ripen on the windowsill, he thinks, but he lets the woman—his daughter—go on yammering. He likes the sound, as full and round as the tomatoes on the vines. He is done with the garden. Let the deer have at it.

He lifts his massive crown of branches into late afternoon sun and closes his eyes, huge ears turning two directions at once. The green patches will be dry and brown soon. We will wander through his forest to take our harvest with fire and boom. The golden leaves too, will soon fall away, and silence will be gone, until it returns with the snow.

The cat named Killer sits in the orchard above the Common, watching for his own two-legs. The little one seems nearby, perhaps in the mists growing where it is darkest, where night has already come. She was an early fruit, like the apple that is bent and scarred that falls early from the tree, drawing the deer into the open for a hunter's aim.

Katie Dean sits on the steps of the courthouse alone. Jared is away at school again. Her ex-husband, ex-husband. . . . She can not yet think the words real, as if Paul has been someone else living in her life, a complete silence, a vacuum, right beside her for twenty years. Paul, her ex.

What next? Sell the house? Hit the road? All alone? She isn't a child anymore, all grown up. On the slow-but-not-dead team. What next?

•

He watches the vehicles empty from their rows, taking us with them along the black path, some southward to the flat lands, some into shelters here in Neweden. He smells frost. Snow. Thaw. Green again. Harvest. He steps into the universe of silence.

LOVE THEORY #7

M ari sucked in the sweet fall breeze—cider, leaves, earth—one hand cupping her huge belly, full with twins, watching Christine's car pass down the hill-road. "I am an artist," Mari whispered. "I am not afraid." The construction crew renovating the farmhouse would arrive soon. Not more than an hour alone, she reassured herself. Chris's car vanished behind the last of the golden leaves around the curve. The guys would yell 'Good morning!' through the plywood wall that kept the rain and dust from the three rooms not under construction, and everything would be fine. She would be fine. The babies would be fine. Chris would drive to work and return home fine. Nothing bad would happen.

Mari looked down, over the mound of her stomach. A cricket waddled across the kitchen floor. He pushed forward awkwardly, the little front legs scurrying to compensate for the strides of his oversized back legs. Winter's coming, she thought. Babies coming. "I *am* an artist," she murmured again. "Get to work." She opened the screen door, grabbed the handrail and trundled the belly of babies down the three steps and across the yard to the studio.

The painting Mari was working on, Love Theory #7, would be the last in this series. The show was scheduled to open in New York in February. Her first New York show. Her chance to break out, to be noticed. Her career seemed just about to take off, but the babies were due at Thanksgiving. I might not know much about motherhood, Mari thought, but I don't think I can paint with two newborns around. She sighed and leaned back in her chair, resting her feet on the file cabinet Chris had hauled over in front of the easel. Her ankles looked like the stumps at the edge of their neighbor's orchard, just over the fence beyond the studio. The last painting in this series. Maybe the last art I'll have time to do for months. Mari stared out at the view. The remains of the old trees looked like the short round houses of a fairy village, their younger counterparts stretching limbs to the sky, the last red fruits dangling like jewelry.

The baby on the left side—the girl, Baby A, the doc called her—woke up and jammed a foot or arm up into Mari's lungs. Baby B, the boy, woke up and shoved his butt—or at least that's what Mari thought that was—outward, as if trying to back out through her side. "Calm down you guys," she said, rubbing B's rump through her own skin. She still couldn't believe she was finally pregnant, that the pregnancy had worked, that she was about to give birth to not just one, but two babies. After three years of trying, after all that money spent on artificial insemination, after the miscarriage, they'd almost given up. And now this. Twins.

She picked up a brush and smushed it into the cerulean, twirled it around, and hesitated, marking the vision in her head on the canvas before beginning. A red spot on the edge of the white moved, a ladybug. "Fly away home," Mari said automatically, scooting her away with her pinky. "Your house is on fire . . . " She bit off the end of the rhyme. The bug whirred away.

Mari rested the hand holding her brush on her knee. How could such a light object seem so heavy? After the first daub, she knew she would lose herself in the painting, into the images, blurring everything else out into parts, colors, lines, textures, juxtapositions of objects, fragments of script—the biochemical theory of love for this one—giant noses, a bouquet in a girl's hand, honeycomb, bees. Until she had to pee again, of course. Or felt nauseous. Or until the fatigue washed over her, as it so often did these days, and she had to nap on the mattress Chris had set up in the corner, the racket from the hammers in the house too loud for sleep. Her hands would swell; she would suddenly feel the pain in her knuckles and focus in on her hand holding the brush, so puffy it looked like a cartoon of itself. Or hunger would gnaw, queasiness threatening if she didn't feed it—feed *them*—again, again, again. Pregnancy was exhausting. She hadn't realized how much effort it took to grow a human— *two* humans—from scratch. The ladybug thumped into a windowpane and began to crawl down the glass. How had she gotten inside? Why?

Mari heaved a sigh, resisting the urge to sleep. She had to finish this painting this month. She might never have time again. The painting would take her mind off her fears, too. She touched the tip of the brush to the canvas. Like putting the snorkel mask into the Caribbean during vacation last year, becoming suddenly lost in that vibrant and other underwater reef world, everything else—even the babies—vanished.

"Damn," said Jeff, on the other side of the plywood wall. "I forgot the goat cheese."

Back in the kitchen for a late lunch, Mari stood in the open door of the refrigerator, trying to feel desire for something. "Eat as much as you can," the doctor had said. "Eat anything you want." She rubbed the belly. The workmen were on their lunch break too, sitting in lawn chairs out in the new addition. Mari liked having them there where she could hear them, close enough so that she wasn't completely alone while Chris was off at work. She was scared to be alone. As October had dwindled with the evening light, she had begun to worry more and more. How much would labor hurt? What if she had to have a c-section? Would the babies be okay? Would Chris still love her body when it was flabby and scarred? Maybe they were too old to be parents. Would the children suffer for having no daddy, for being the kids of lesbians? Bile rose at the smell of something not quite fresh from the vegetable bin, and Mari stepped back and turned her head to breathe the autumn air. Women died in labor. Babies died. And what about my own work, my art? Mari blinked back the sudden pressure of the goddamn tears again. Will I be a good mother?

"Salad again, huh?" Gabe, the contractor, and Jeff and Joe, carpenters and brothers, were funny to listen to. Mari spotted a sandwich Chris must have made for her. They were counting on Gabe to drive her to the hospital if she went into labor while Chris was at work. Please, god, not too soon, she thought. Another two weeks at least. The babies would be more likely to live if they stayed inside a bit longer.

"Yeah," said Jeff. "I've got to lose ten pounds."

Mari shook her head. How could he need to diet? The guys worked nine or more hours a day, the impending birth of the babies a constant motivator. Muscles rippled in their arms and backs as they swung beams and plywood into place and hefted the nail guns and ladders. A diet seemed impossible. The sixty pounds Mari had gained with the babies—a perfect amount, the doctors said—depressed her. Almost forty, she had still run five miles every other day and done a hundred crunches every night before she had gotten pregnant. Chris had fallen in love with that body, she thought. And now . . . Mari rubbed her stomach. No abs at all in there. Limiting her food intake again after the twins were born loomed almost worse than did the labor. I'll have to look good for the opening though, she thought. New York . . . Mari shook her head. Don't think about it.

Eat. She took a turkey sandwich and glass of milk into the living room and lowered herself into the sofa.

"You don't look like you need to lose weight," Joe said on the other side.

A snort. "You ain't seen me in my skivvies."

Mari smiled, remembering working in the studio at night a year or so ago, tilting her chin up and keeping her back straight before the easel, imagining the way she looked, spot-lit and visible through the huge windows to everyone who drove down the road or happened to look up from the valley, the artist at work. That woman seemed almost lost, disappearing, swallowed.

"Stop right there," Gabe shouted, laughing. "Too much information!"

Mari chewed, grinning. They seemed to have so much fun together, these guys. Baby B kicked and twisted so that her lower belly rippled under her t-shirt and Mari rubbed him. She put down her sandwich to lift her hair and drape it over the back of the sofa. That was another thing about being pregnant that nobody told you. Her hair, already thick, had become as lush as jungle vines, a weight that tugged at the back of her head.

"I tried to get him to go to the gym with me," Joe said, "but he's too busy. He'd rather eat rabbit food."

"Heck," Jeff said, "I get plenty of work-out at work! I don't get why anybody'd take time off to do more work."

Mari closed her eyes and massaged her scalp, coaxing the impending headache to recede rather than build. She had loved the gym when they had lived in the city. When she and Chris had moved to Vermont, a half-hour away from a good indoor workout, she had missed it terribly. The focus of that hour workout, the routine of it. She and Chris had even met at the gym in Boston all those years ago. Here, she'd become a runner, a skier. An exercise opportunist. Whenever. Whatever. She rubbed the back of her neck. Maybe I should just cut my hair, she thought. It had taken five years to grow out, the whole time they'd been here in the farmhouse. I need a change. Maybe shorter will make me look thinner. Too bad she couldn't go back to that punk look she'd had when they'd been dating in Boston, half shaved, spiky, wild. That would freak her students out. Too old for that now. It wouldn't be me. Whoever that is.

"Baby A," Mari said, washing her brushes out in the kitchen sink at the end of the day, the house quiet with the workmen gone, "you need to stand on your head again. And soon."

That week's ultrasound had showed that Baby A, who was presenting—that is, closer to the cervix and who would therefore be born first—had flipped herself over. Her head was up instead of down. "Swimming in a pool might help," the doctor had said, but the nearest indoor pool was an hour away. The nurse showed Mari some rocking exercises to try to get the baby back into place. "Or maybe you can talk them into it," the nurse said. "Those old wives' tales you know . . . " Maybe a mother *could* will the fetus to cooperate, Mari thought. As scared as she was of labor, she knew she *really* didn't want to be cut open for a cesarean.

She heard Chris's car in the drive. The doctor had warned that the babies were running out of room. There wouldn't be much hope of turning again in a week or so. To the tune of "Twist and Shout," Mari started to sing. "Come-on, come-on, come-on ba-by, turn it on over; twist and squirm, twist and squirm. Come-on, come-on, come-on ba-by, flip it on over, work it on out . . . ." The babies jiggled with her rocking against the countertop. "You like singing, don't you?" she asked. Baby A kicked.

Chris came in carrying groceries. "Are they listening?" she asked. "Are they moving?"

Mari turned and stuck The Amazing Belly forward so that Chris could see the gymnastics under her t-shirt.

"Whoa!" Chris grinned and put her hand to the belly to feel. "What part do you suppose that is?"

"Elbow maybe," Mari said. She put her own hand

over Chris's. She missed the way she and Chris had been before the pregnancy. She missed Chris's body and hers together, parts matching but different. She missed just being together, alone. The way they had been equal partners working together on the farmhouse renovations. Now it seemed so divided, almost like a straight couple, the way she hauled around the belly and Chris did all the housework, the shopping, the yard-work. Mari hated feeling so useless. She hated feeling like a wife, but here it was again. Nobody's fault. "Thanks babe," she said, squeezing Chris's hand. "Thanks for doing the shopping. For doing everything."

Chris responded as she had done for months now. "Thank *you* for carrying the babies."

Mari groaned inwardly. She was sick of that. *Fuck that,* she thought. But she kept her face blank and her mouth shut. Not Chris's fault.

Mari took the next morning off from Love Theory #7, even though she knew she shouldn't, and made an apple pie for the workmen—Jeff and Joe's dad, Eddie, the electrician, and both of the plumbers, Fred and Arnold, had come with the carpenters today. She carried paper plates with steaming slices around the side of the house to the picnic table.

"Oh man," groaned Jeff. "There goes the diet."

"I'll take your piece," Joe offered. "No problem."

Gabe laughed. "You know, we'll keep working even without pie," he said to Mari.

"Just want to keep the workers happy," Mari said, passing out the plates. "And besides, I like to bake. It's apple pie season. I can't help myself."

The guys dug into their slices with plastic forks. "Oh man," said Jeff. "This is so good."

Mari lowered herself into an Adirondack chair and rested her hands on her stomach, watching them eat, enjoying the warmth of the Indian summer sun.

"Getting a lot of work done?" Gabe asked, nodding toward the studio.

"Not really," she said. "Kind of stuck, actually." She felt a tickle on her bare toe and lifted her leg into the air to see a caterpillar. "Shit." She grunted, trying to lean forward.

"Let me get it," laughed Eddie. He picked the fat brown and black fuzz from her foot and let it crawl across his palm. "Wooly bear," he said. "Whadya think, Arnold? What's she say about the winter?"

Arnold tilted his head back to examine the caterpillar through his bifocals. He'd been their plumber since they'd bought the old farmhouse, thawing pipes for them that first winter. "Well, looks cold," he said, pointing. "Black bands are purty wide." He squinted. "She says the middle'll be the worst. Deep cold in January, February, I'd say."

"Great," Mari said. "Stuck inside with newborns."

"Pipes'll probably freeze too," Arnold said, squinting. He winked at her over his glasses. "This old place keeps *me* plenty warm anyway . . . "

"You'll be retiring to Florida on these old houses some day," Gabe said, "huh?" They laughed.

Eddie held his hand to the picnic table and the caterpillar trundled onto the wood. "Have a good sleep," he said to it.

"Do they hibernate?" Jeff asked. Mari nodded, thinking of the cocoon she had hatched in a jar when she was a girl, the butterfly emerging, the way its wings had inflated and unfurled before she unscrewed the lid to watch it float away on the breeze.

Eddie nodded too. "That's what I read in the *National Geographic*. They've got something like anti-freeze in their blood. You can put them into an ice cube, thaw 'em out later and they'll still be fine, go on about their business in the spring like nothing happened." The business of eating, reproducing, making something of life, Mari thought. Like art maybe. But butterflies don't need their mommies.

"Wonder what they think about while they're frozen," Joe said. The other guys laughed. "Well," he said, blushing under his tan, "you know. Wonder if they have dreams or anything. Brain must keep working somehow even if they're frozen . . . ."

"Caterpillar dreams," Jeff scoffed. "Man . . . ."

"Isn't that what makes the difference between being dead and alive," Joe asked. "Brain working?"

Gabe shrugged. "He's got something there, Jeffy," he said. "We won't turn off your life support if your brain's still going . . . ."

Eddie cut in. "Don't it have to work in the first place?"

The others laughed again. "Saw that one coming," Gabe said.

Mari shifted in her chair, trying to get comfortable. She grunted, "Uh," without meaning to, and felt the guys become aware of her body again. They were silent for a minute.

"So," Gabe asked. "Do you miss work?" He blinked. "I mean, do you miss teaching?"

Mari smiled. He had probably heard her complaining about how people around here thought of her as just a high school teacher and not an artist, about how no one took her seriously as an artist. Those plywood walls . . . . "I do," she said. "Sometimes." She closed her eyes into the sun, listening to the faraway voices of the apple pickers in the orchard, the screech of a hawk. "I mean," she continued, "I miss the kids. I think about whether they're getting stuff done or just playing around." Mari thought about the AP students for a second and felt guilty. Was the sub helping them put together winning portfolios? And what about slutty, surly Candi in first period? Had she told the sub to watch out for her, watch out for the mood swings that swept in like weather fronts? She was just a kid, just trying to figure out who she was, or who she was going to be. "I worry about them," Mari said. "They're making sets for a drama club production, Shakespeare. Power tools and teenagers, you know."

The guys chuckled. Gabe said, "Oh, I know." He had a teen-aged son, a kid at the bigger high school down in Brattleboro. "They're dumb sometimes, for sure."

"Most of us survive," Jeff said. "Become something. Maybe not much, but something. Most of us figure it out."

Mari knew he was talking to Gabe about his kid. She'd heard him worrying about him to the others, about his lack of ambition, lack of drive, through the plywood wall. "He'd sleep all day if we'd let'im," Gabe had said.

"Yes," she replied. "I think teenagers grow into themselves. What's great about them is that they can imagine it all. They still believe they can make the world perfect. They still think they can have it all."

"You mean we can't?" Joe asked. He stopped his fork halfway to his mouth, and widened his eyes. They all laughed.

Mari thought about her days in the studio, all the time she had had to paint this last month without the drudgery of going to school, the time- and energy-suck of having to earn a living. For just this moment, she did have it all. And in a month, she'd have the babies, but what if she lost everything else? Was motherhood worth it? What would happen when her brain—already nearly consumed, like her body, by the babies—switched off, froze up? The caterpillar, a lump of brown and black, moved slowly across the table.

Back inside, Mari cleaned up the kitchen as best she could. She washed out the rolling pin and bowls and wiped down the counter, bending over to reach the faucets beyond her stomach. The apple peels and cores would have to wait for Chris to get out to the compost pile. She really couldn't help herself from baking pies in the fall. Something— maybe the working of the dough, cold with ice water for a flaky crust, or maybe the ritual of trying to peel each apple in one long curl for luck, or maybe just the comforting smell and thick lazy warmth of all that butter and sugar in her blood—calmed her, soothed her mind. She cut another small slice to take back to the studio, where Love Theory #7 awaited. The hammers rang out again, the men back to work, and Mari smiled, remembering their appreciation of the pie. One of them started whistling. Mari shook herself out of her fog. Back to work, she thought. I must get back to work.

Cramp. "Ohh-uff," she muttered aloud, grabbing her side and leaning hard against the door jam. A contraction tightened the belly. Was it Braxton Hicks? What if she was in labor? She waited, breathing through it, suddenly very tired. It stopped. Maybe just a little nap, she thought. Go to the studio for nap-time, then work. The wooly bear caterpillar can be frozen for the whole winter. In the spring, she's fine, ready to go on about her business of sewing herself into a cocoon, changing into something else. A mind inside ice.

"How do students construct identity in an online classroom where they never meet in person?" Chris asked for the zillionth time. She was on the phone with an old friend, describing her dissertation project.

Mari knew it almost by heart, at least all the catchphrases, and she raised the quilt she was stitching high enough that Chris wouldn't see her yawn. It was only seven. The sun set so early these days, time speeding up as the sun inched south, diminishing as her stomach expanded, a waxing moon.

"Well, they write their identities, of course, in the online classroom. It's the only mode of communication, the only way they can let the others know who they are. . . ." Chris was still excited about her project, and that, at least, made Mari want to care about it too. She wanted Chris to finish the dissertation, get the doctorate, keep moving. Somebody in this relationship should . . .

She bit her lip, feeling guilty. No. She got to be pregnant. That was important too, something Chris—the doctor had said her eggs were too old—couldn't have. But damn it, Chris was going to have it all—career, family—a full life with no delays.

After the miscarriage, the crush of that disappointment, that sorrow, they had both stalled in their work, the creative work. Jobs had always been the thing they did to make money; writing and painting were the work that mattered. In these last few months, during the pregnancy, first when it seemed clear that it would keep and then with the news that there would be two babies, everything had seemed back on track, the work moving on the tide of their joy, the pace of Chris's dissertation writing and Mari's painting for the New York opening frenetic with the urgency of the impending births. And the house renovation project—delayed for a whole year—had suddenly moved into action as well, Gabe nailing up the plywood walls that would divide them off from the upstairs (fine, since the doctor had forbade her from climbing them), the machines arriving to knock down the old enclosed porch with the tilting floors, to excavate stones and earth and the perennial garden for the new foundation, the concrete poured, the framing and roofing, the school-year begun and then her maternity leave. Reduced activity. Everything would change again when the babies came. But how? Mari thought of the Love/Theory series. Why couldn't she finish this last piece? She had to get it done.

Chris had started a fire in the woodstove. It heated their three rooms quickly despite the draft around the edges of the temporary plywood walls. The windows had been delivered today, and the men would install them tomorrow, enclosing the addition a little more. Then the insulation would go in, then the drywall and trim, then the floors. Arnold had roughed in the new upstairs bathroom, and Gabe said he'd get the stair landing done while Joe mudded the drywall. Mari couldn't wait to be able to see the work upstairs, the new dormer that ran the length of the two bedrooms and new bathroom. She wanted to be back in her own bedroom, newly light and airy, open to the view of fall colors on the hills, and she wanted to get to work on the babies' room, choosing the colors of the walls and arranging the cribs. But that was probably just a dream, Mari thought. It would be at least another month of work before Gabe finished. They would all live downstairs until the guys finished the work, the babies in the same crib, all four of the family in the three rooms with plywood dividers.

"So I'm tracking the references students make to themselves in the online discussions," Chris said into the phone. "Especially in ways that seem to help others see who they are in the real world outside the class." Mari thought again about her painting. How was that annunciation, those bees and hives, a communication about her? What was she telling the world?

Mari pulled the needle around the edges of the beaver shape on the baby quilt. Each square had a different animal shape. Mari had made so many of these quilts for other people, for friends, but this one would be for her own baby. For one of her babies.

"Right," said Chris. "Like they're building who they are for others to imagine."

The animals on this quilt were all from New England, animals the babies might see: a deer, a red-tailed hawk, a moose, a bear, a cricket. Mari hadn't decided what to put on the other quilt, maybe exotic animals, like lions and monkeys, or domestic animals like cows and horses and pigs. Maybe something completely different, like toy shapes or food shapes. Maybe city shapes. Would the baby with a New England animal quilt stay close to home? Would a baby covered by city shapes or exotic animals grow up to move away? Would a baby warmed under the images of farm animals become a farmer? Mari smiled. She wondered what identity she was sewing for herself.

The painting *still* wasn't right. Mari had been staring at it for an hour, her hands resting on her stomach. The sounds of hammers from the farmhouse were muffled, the guys working inside. Chris was off at the university again. Another week of waiting gone. Another last minute of painting vanished forever. I have to finish this, she thought, rubbing her stomach; the clock is ticking. What is it about this one, #7?

The painting was complex, incorporating a medieval annunciation scene, but changing the dove that is supposed to be God impregnating the Virgin into a bee stinging her, and outlined with text from Dante: "In the middle of life's journey, I found myself in a tangled forest that obscured from me the wanted way." Something was still missing. Mari always worked intuitively on a series, usually beginning with theme—love, in this case—which she researched in the library, finding for herself the ways the idea had been theorized over the ages, discovering the images from art history and contemporary culture that expressed her own, usually feminist, perspective on that theory. Sometimes she tried to make fun of the theory, like with #3, on Freud, into which she had painted a hotdog and donuts. Number 7 just wasn't yet right. She tapped the paintbrush on the glass pallet. What was missing?

"Fuck it." Mari let her paintbrush drop to the table. She looked around the studio. Crumpled paper towels blotched with paint littered the floor. Old computer print-outs, ashes from the woodstove, Styrofoam peanuts from an unpacked box of canvases, and empty plastic water bottles added to the clutter. She had to clean. The house was a disaster of sawdust and muddy boot tracks, and she couldn't do anything about that until the renovation project was finished, but at least she could tidy up the studio. Mari grabbed a broom and started to sweep, jabbing at the windowsills and edges of the baseboards. The babies were quiet inside, rocked by the rhythm. On the south wall, she tilted back a stack of blank canvases to sweep behind them. She gasped. Hundreds of ladybugs lay like little drops of blood on the grey painted floor. What the heck? Mari hesitated. What could she do? What had happened? She gave herself a shake and swept the dry husks of the bugs into the pile of dust and trash.

She rested, leaning on the broom, and looked out. Through the window, the sky was a brilliant fall blue, the leaves just past peak color. Now that it was cool, Chris started a fire in the woodstove for her in the mornings on the way to work. Mari paused, looking down into the orchard next door. Beyond the stumps, apple pickers, the Jamaicans who came each year to work for Zeke and a smattering of white kids in their twenties sporting beards and dreds, perched on ladders, bulging sacks over their shoulders, the red fruit like ornaments in the trees. The orchard was organic and Zeke had good luck recruiting pickers from the Co-op bulletin board and the vegetarian restaurant to supplement the black men who had been coming from the islands every year for decades. She herself had picked apples when they moved here after she finished grad school, looking for a place to make a home, a community where being a lesbian couple was no big deal, and where they could actually buy a house and a little land with the money Chris's grandmother had left her. They'd both done whatever work they could that year—substitute teaching, farm labor, house cleaning—to make ends meet while painting and repairing the old house and converting the barn into a studio. And then Chris had started work on her doctorate, and Mari had landed the high school teaching job, and they'd started trying to have a baby. Picking had been hard work, dawn til dusk. Mari stretched her back; the ache from carrying the twins was not that different from that she'd felt during apple picking. But at least then, she'd been able to sleep comfortably at night. The Jamaican men did most of the tree work, their thighs and backs and arms muscled hard, and she and the others had packed the big crates and hauled ladders. It wasn't the physical exhaustion that had made her quit though. It had been the yellow jackets.

They were everywhere, drawn by the sweet stickiness of bruised and bleeding fruit. And she hadn't bothered about them at first, had ignored them like everyone else. Then, her third sting in one day put her in the hospital, unable to breathe, her heart pounding, the adrenaline making her feel so much rage that she had punched the nurse who was trying to give her a sedative. "It's typical," the woman had told her later. Luckily, the nurse had ducked, avoiding most of the blow, and Chris had stepped in to hold Mari down. "The fight or flight response. Bee sting reactions trigger it, make your brain go a little haywire. Don't worry about it." Remembering, Mari felt her embarrassment all over again. She hated losing control of her emotions, her body, like that. Of course, she could have died.

One of the babies stretched, pushing into her bladder. Mari gasped with the sudden pain. "Ow," she said. Damn. She had to get to the bathroom again.

Gabe looked up from his table saw as she rounded the side of the barn. "Hey," he called. "You okay?"

Mari nodded, grimacing. "Sure." She felt like throwing up.

Gabe frowned and started over to her. "You don't look okay," he said.

"Just gotta pee," she said. She gripped the railing of the steps to the kitchen and took three deep breaths. Her belly constricted. Contraction. How many others had she had today? Should she start timing them?

Gabe's small rough hand gripped her arm under the elbow. "Let me give you a hand," he said. "Take it easy."

"It's going to hurt, isn't it?" Mari heard herself say. "The labor." Gabe helped her into the kitchen. "You were there when your boy was born, right?" She heard the note of fear in her voice, but she couldn't help it. What if something went wrong? Things did go wrong at labor, especially with multiples. Mari swallowed, trying to hold down the lump in her throat. She wanted these babies to live.

Gabe shrugged. "Yeah," he said. "But it wasn't me giving birth, you know."

Mari stopped at the door to the bathroom. "I'm not going to die, am I?" she asked.

Gabe held her gaze, not smiling or laughing, and shook his head slowly. "No," he said. "You're not going to die."

"I was an idiot," she said to Chris later, back in the studio. "He must have thought I was nuts." Her neck and cheeks burned. "Damn damn damn damn damn."

Chris massaged Mari's feet, propped in her lap. "I'm sure he understood," she said, her voice low. The guys were working late at the house, and Mari had awakened from her nap to the smells of drying leaves and frost and sounds of hammers and Chris opening the door. She had almost cried with relief. "I'm sure he doesn't think anything except that you're a pregnant lady with lots of chemicals floating around in your blood. Hormones."

"That's a crappy excuse," Mari moaned. "I hate people thinking I'm crazy. Oh shit, I am so tired of this." She laid back into the pillows. The babies fluttered in her abdomen.

"Gabe doesn't think you're crazy," Chris said. She squeezed her foot. "You're not crazy." Her voice was low and steady. "Things can go wrong, but nothing will. You'll have the babies, and the guys will finish the house, and winter will come, and we'll tuck in together, safe and warm while it snows."

"And I'll never finish my paintings," Mari said. "I just can't get this last one." She nodded toward the easel. "And the show is coming up and I'll never have time to do it after they get here." She swallowed and bit her lip. "I'll never be an artist again."

Chris took her hand. "Of course you will," she said. "It's who you are."

"Really?" Mari said. "Is it really who I am? It is now, but will it be next month? This winter? Next year?" She felt A flippering around, wriggling into B. She patted her belly, the babies. "What about them?" she asked. "Will they let me be an artist too?"

Chris pushed Mari's feet off her lap and stood up. "Yes," she said. "They know that's who their mommy is." She walked over to the window and stood beside the easel, looking at the painting. "It's great," Chris said. "I love it."

Mari watched her lover's eyes—squinting, moving around the canvas, back and forth, pausing on something, moving to consider something else, going back, reading across the text, blinking. This was the woman she loved. This was the family they had made. Chris wouldn't let her get lost. She'll keep reminding me. The work, the ideas, the joy. All of it.

"Do you think you can't finish it . . . " Chris began. Her eyes met Mari's. "Do you think you can't finish it because you need to start the next work first? You know, like I have to know what I'm going to write next before I can let go of something . . . "

Mari blinked. They had had this conversation before, over and over again throughout the ten years of their relationship. The new project had to be conceived before the old project could be completed. Why hadn't she thought of it? Mari pushed herself to her feet and walked over to stand by Chris. She leaned against her. "Maybe," she said. The dark windows seemed to frame the two of them, standing close like this in the light, The Amazing Belly protruding toward the easel. Mari thought of what they would look like to the person driving by, or to someone looking up from the valley floor. "But I can't even imagine what will be next," she said. "I don't know who I am going to be."

Chris hugged her close then, tight to her shoulder. "Oh babe," she said.

Something on the floor moved. Mari blinked. The tidy

pile of dead ladybugs, the ones she had swept together from the south wall, were scattered again, individual red dots spread out across the gray board floor. She leaned around Chris to see better. One moved, crawling away from the heap, then another fluttered a wing, and another one took a tiny step. "They're still alive," she said. "Look." She pulled away and pointed.

"Wow," Chris said. "Where'd all those ladybugs come from?"

Mari bent a little, hand on the windowsill. "I swept them up when I was cleaning earlier," she said. "They were all over the place." She watched as another one labored away from the pile of bodies, headed toward the wall. "I thought they were dead," she said.

Chris laughed. "I heard Eddie telling Gabe that the ladybugs were coming in," she said. "I didn't know what he was talking about." She knelt down beside Mari for a closer look. "They hibernate inside the walls and under the baseboards if they can find a way in," she said. Chris put her fingertip down to touch one. It climbed on. Chris held it out to Mari, the smooth round shell glinting like a ruby, the little stick legs walking deliberately across the hairs on the back of her hand. "Not dead at all," she said. "Just taking a little nap."

When they walked into the kitchen, it took Mari a minute to register the change. The doorway had been opened. Over the counter was space instead of a plywood panel. She could see into the new room. "Wow." They both stood still for a minute, staring. The black of the windows reflected Gabe and Jeff and Joe, who had stopped working when they entered, grinning back at them. The space was enormous, bigger even than she had imagined it. Chris squeezed her hand. The studs were still exposed and there was no railing at the stair, but it was a room, enclosed, a part of the house, a bigger house.

Mari felt the babies flutter low down in her womb.

Love Theory #7 could wait. She could finish it in winter, even encased in ice and snow. She would find the time. Chris would help her find the time. She'd find something new, she thought, fingers laced over her belly. Some new subject to paint, some new idea, new passion.

Gabe moved suddenly, stooping low. "Got'im," he said. He held his cupped hands to the window and opened them. The cricket inside hesitated, then sprang away, backward into the room instead of out into the night.

Mari laughed, her voice loud. The cricket scrambled under the stair despite the carpenters' chase, Joe finally sliding on his knees, Jeff lying on his back on the subfloor, laughing. Gabe shrugged at her, palms up. Chris squeezed her hand. "How about a beer, guys?" she asked.

"I been thinking about that pie all day," Arnold said.

Mari felt the babies flutter inside, an insect feeling. She thought of Love Theory #7. She thought of her next life. The cricket chirruped, loud in the big new room.

ONE-HUNDRED ONES

On the day after Brandi married Eddie at the county courthouse in the same dress she'd worn to homecoming, Lee picked them up at the apartment and drove them to Dollar General. He—she—Lee gave Brandi an envelope stuffed with $100 one-dollar bills. "To set up your new life with my son," Lee said.

Brandi tried not to think about whether she—he was a man or a woman, just like Eddie said. "She's my mom, just in a different body than when she had me." He'd told her about his mom and her transition to a man—"not my dad, just Mom in a different body"—on their first date, ice cream and a movie in town. He had just held her hand on that warm September night, didn't even try to kiss her at the door of the farmhouse when he returned her home, never mind parking or a drinking party up on the mountain. Eddie was cute that way. Sweet. It was weird to think of him knowing so much about how his mom was turning herself into a man, taking hormones, having her boobs cut off and her private parts—the place Eddie himself had come from—reconstructed into a dick. Brandi looked at the pile of dollar bills because she was afraid she'd stare at Lee.

"Thanks, Mom," Eddie said, and Brandi mumbled a thank you, still watching the bills.

"Better get started or you'll be late to work," Lee said, yanking a shopping cart from the row. "What the hell was that stupid moose doing on Main Street anyway?" He—she snorted and shook his head like a man. The cops had blocked off the road for fifteen minutes or so while the young moose had wandered through town, swaying his big head, huge wet eyes rolling, while locals and tourists alike pointed and watched. Poor thing, Brandi had thought. Moose were notoriously near-sighted, and often unpredictable; this one was probably a two-year old who had been chased off after his mother gave birth to a new calf last spring. When the Christmas lights strung over the streets clacked in the cold early winter breeze, he started, running a few yards on improbably long legs, raising his over-sized feet clumsily, like her little brothers in their basketball shoes. He'd probably been wandering all summer, too young to win a mate, alone in the mountains. At least he'd made it through hunting season. If he lived through the winter, he'd be okay—a proper bull, still alone except for the week or two of rutting, but tough enough to survive. He stood with his front legs wide on the asphalt and huffed air through his nose, a steaming cloud of breath, and looked back at the flashing blue lights of the cruiser, the twinkle of the holiday decorations and the line of humans raising cameras and cell phones to capture the moment. Brandi closed her eyes and leaned into Eddie—away from Lee—on the pickup's bench seat and wished the moose well. She had swallowed the tears that closed her throat— she would not cry—and tried to relax into her new husband's armpit.

Eddie squeezed Brandi's hand and pulled her into the dollar store behind Lee with the cart. "This will really help, Mom," he said.

Lee glanced back and grinned. "I know," she—he said.

Brandi saw that Lee's jaw was bristling; she—he needed a shave. Eddie looks a lot more like Lee now that she's a man, Brandi thought. The money, the stuff they could get at the dollar store, though, that was a woman thing. Brandi's dad would never have thought of a gift like that. And they really needed it; they had nothing.

Brandi though of Diana, the only thing Daddy had ever given her, and that was only because the calf's momma had died giving birth and Brandi had been begging for a 4-H critter to raise. It seemed so long ago—two years—that she'd stood in the stall and hugged the blood-slicked body to her own, saying "Please, Daddy. She needs me." His eyes had flickered. He'd snorted and waved his hand derisively as he'd turned. "Whatever," he'd said. Momma had told her that Daddy was going to sell Diana now, because the inseminations wouldn't take and what's the good of a dairy cow that don't give milk? But Brandi knew Daddy was just pissed off that she had gone off the farm and got married before finishing high school. One less milker and one less mucker in the barns. He might have to hire another man. The cow was really hers anyway. Daddy should give her the money. Brandi thought maybe she'd just tell him so. She felt tears threatening to spill out of her eyes. It's just the cow, she told herself. I'll miss Diana.

Lee stopped the cart in front of the dinnerware shelf. Brandi picked out eight plain white plates and four mugs. Eight bowls for cereal or soup or ice cream. Eight plain glasses. Lee smoothed a finger across each rim, checking for chips. Lee's finger was small and thin, the nails short and clean. It was a woman's hand. Brandi smiled to herself. At least they'd start with perfect stuff.

The wedding might have been closer to perfect if Momma and Daddy and her little brothers had come. Only Lee had been able to get to the courthouse. Momma had promised to come, but the snow that morning had delayed the milking and the school bus had been late and then Daddy needed her to help plow out the driveway.

They'd waited a whole week after they'd got engaged after the homecoming game, and the judge had asked if they wanted to wait until more family could make it, but Brandi knew it had to be quick, especially since Eddie wouldn't go all the way until they were married. He said he want to treat her like a real old-fashioned girl, so they'd said their "I dos" and Lee had dropped them at the apartment they'd rented. Brandi thought maybe Eddie had been a virgin, but she hadn't said anything. He'd carried her over the threshold like in the movies, and they'd fucked like bunnies all night long on the mattress they'd bought at the thrift store. Lucky she'd sneaked a sheet out of the linen closet at home when she packed her bag. At least now they'd have mugs for coffee in the morning.

Eddie held up a big dented can of Maxwell House. "We can use the can to keep loose change after we finish the coffee," he said. They were saving for a used car. His brown eyes were happy, creased at the edges, and his bangs brushed his eyelashes. The fuzz over his lip was soft and dark; he didn't even have to shave every day. Brandi smiled at him, and he blushed. Eddie didn't care about all that stuff the other boys said or that she had cow shit on her wellies. Brandi wasn't a slut or dairy queen to Eddie. And I'm not, she thought, touching his hand on the handle of the cart. He wrapped a pinky finger over hers. Not now, she thought. I've got a husband and an apartment in town. Momma and the boys can get up at five to do the mucking and the milking without me.

"Look at these," Eddie said. He held up a beer mug. "We can put them in the freezer like Dad does." Eddie's dad, Arnie, worked as a plumber. The way he looked at Lee reminded Brandi of the way Diana had looked at the bull moose who'd appeared from the woods that fall, across the pasture fence—maybe the same one as had been in town that morning—moaning and snorting at the cow, in love with the wrong kind. She felt sorry for Arnie, even though he was remarried and Eddie said he was happy. Brandi didn't think he'd gotten over Lee.

Brandi shook her head at Eddie. "Wine glasses," she said. "Way classier." She clinked a glossy pink fingernail against one so that it made a little ting like a bell.

"Nah," said Lee. "Just use the regular glasses." Brandi sighed. Lee was right. Brandi replaced the glass on the shelf. They should probably save the glasses for special too; anything that cheap would break easy. They already had four Big Gulp cups they could use everyday.

Eight forks, eight spoons, eight butter knives were a bargain at two for a dollar. Brandi picked out a plastic tablecloth printed with purple grapes and twining vines. She wanted to have the folks over—her mom and dad (if he'd come), Lee and his-her girlfriend, Eddie's dad and stepmom. Plus his stepsister, Sierra, and her new baby. The baby wouldn't need a plate or utensils, and neither would Brandi's three little brothers. The baby's father had ditched Sierra. I won't need a plate, Brandi thought; I'll be busy bringing food to the table. Spaghetti. She chucked four boxes—four for a dollar!—and eight little cans of tomato paste—eight for a dollar!—into the cart. They were up to forty-three dollars.

Brandi worked in the kitchen at the co-op after school—that was where she'd met Eddie, who was a night stocker. She'd already been a pretty good cook since the house was mostly her job on the farm, and she'd convinced her dad to let her keep the summer job on into the school year since the littlest brother had gotten old enough to work in the barns and didn't need her any more. None of them really needed her any more. She liked the cooking, but she hated the customers. All snooty and dreadlocked and stoned, spending twice as much for organic milk as regular, asking stupid questions about whether the curried tofu was gluten-free. At least she ate for free during her shifts, and Eddie could get damaged boxes and dented cans sometimes at a discount that made it cheaper than the Price Chopper.

On the next aisle, Brandi added one aluminum roasting pan, one spatula, and three wooden spoons in a package to the shopping cart. A colander to drain the spaghetti, a blue plastic bowl for salad, two purple pot holders, and two dish towels with purple stripes. When Grandma died last year, Brandi had saved three bent pots and a frying pan with only slightly scratched Teflon from her stuff in the little apartment attached to the back of the farmhouse. Those would do. Eddie got one of those plastic cones for making coffee one cup at a time. Coffee filters were two boxes for $1. They bought a box of aluminum foil, a box of plastic wrap, two rolls of paper towels, also two for $1, and a box of candles that they could stick into the empty wine bottle Brandi had saved from the night they got engaged at the top of Black Mountain after the dance. She'd only gone out with Eddie after the quarterback had dumped her. Maybe dumping her after one date was an exaggeration. She'd dated a lot in September, before Eddie.

Matches were six boxes for $1, the good wooden strike-anywhere kind, which they needed because the pilot light in the apartment stove went out sometimes. One vase for flowers. Brandi wanted to grow some marigolds on the fire escape come spring. Maybe tomatoes and peppers and lettuce. There were a few seed packets on the rack, left over from the summer stock. She selected ten packets for a dollar, hoping at least half of the seeds were still good. That would save money when she had to take time off from work. She knew she wouldn't be able to take much time off though. Good thing she worked days and Eddie nights.

Lee put a butter dish into the cart, and Brandi picked out salt and pepper shakers that looked like fat children. The only other choice was little coke bottles, and those were just too tacky.

Eddie chose one sharp serrated knife and one paring knife and handed them over to Brandi. Brandi's mother wouldn't ever give knives because a gift of knives will sever the relationship. "I won't take a chance on losing my only daughter even more than this stupid marriage has," she'd said when Brandi had asked for one from the farmhouse kitchen while packing her bags. She guessed Eddie didn't believe in that superstition. She touched the mountain-edge of the knife blade, remembering suddenly that her father had given her a gift other than Diana—a little pocketknife when she was twelve. He'd shown her to peel an apple into one long red curl one day after milking, must have been when Momma was just home from the hospital with her third brother, still stuck in the house with the newborn.

Brandi touched the edge of the knife blade and looked at Lee, standing in front of the shopping cart, laughing at something Eddie was holding. Lee's t-shirt was tight, showing off his chest and arm muscles. How did it feel to have your boobs cut off? Why would somebody choose that?

Brandi wondered if Lee had nursed Eddie. Momma hadn't breast-fed any of her four kids, though the midwife and Daddy had wanted her to. "Fucking boob-nazis," she'd said when the visiting nurse came to the farm after the middle little brother's birth. "And you—" she'd said to Daddy. "You're just cheap." She'd handed that brother and a bottle off to Brandi two weeks later to get back to the dairy. The littlest brother after him too. Brandi had cared for each of the boys for three or four years, until they were old enough to be useful or at least stay out of the way in the barn. The one that had come three years after Brandi's birth had been stillborn, and she'd started taking care of the next baby when she was seven, the one after that when she was ten, the littlest one when she was thirteen. The babies had needed her like Daddy hadn't. Just a girl, good for raising up the boys and taking care of the house. Momma was more use in the barns. And then Diana had needed her for everything.

"What about some Christmas lights?" Lee asked.

Eddie grinned and picked up a box of gold balls, striped with gold glitter. "These are nice," he said. Tacky, Brandi thought, but she nodded, ticking off another five dollars for Christmas stuff. They could borrow Lee's truck to go up to the woods to cut a tree. At least it would be something besides the mattress on the floor and the card table with plastic chairs in the apartment. She stood for a minute, staring at a molded plastic crèche. The blue of the Madonna's robe was a little off-kilter, splattered where her face should have been. A cow's nose poked out of the stable.

Brandi missed Diana's soft prickly cow muzzle chew-chew-chewing, her side warm against her back as they had laid in the pasture that fall. Across the fence, the stupid bull moose moaned and stomped in the shade, his long face and huge brown eyes moony, lost, lonely. Diana had paid the wild suitor little attention, just watching him, chewing. Brandi wished she could have been more like the cow, but when the boys—football players, soccer players, farm-boys, whoever—had smiled at her, wanted to touch her, wanted to be with her, said they loved her . . . well. She had felt less alone. She had known what to do. Anything to keep them close a little longer.

She missed Diana more than she missed her little brothers. They'd grown up to be like Daddy, no use for girls, left her to join in the chores, the milking at five every morning, the dreary warm smells of the barn. They'd become smelly and loud, lazy about housekeeping, superior. Those afternoons after school with Diana in the meadow had been stolen, special. Diana had been her own project. She'd fed the little calf with a bottle, kept her clean and dry and warm. Took two blue ribbons in the county fair. And after every insemination, Brandi had laid her head on Diana's belly, lying quiet in the meadow, watching the moose in the shadows, waiting to feel something move. What would that be like?

Lee and Eddie veered into the hardware aisle for duct tape, a screwdriver, whatever their last one-dollars might buy. Brandi heard their voices, both deep, but somehow more intimate than men usually were. Eddie needed her. He saw her different than the others did; her reflection in his brown eyes had been blurred when he hoisted her up and over the threshold. It didn't matter though. Brandi would be who he wanted her to be. He needed her.

Brandi stopped, her hand on a package of washcloths. The aisle smelled of baby powder. She slid her hand under her coat to her belly. It was still flat. Another month, she figured. Maybe this one would need her longer, starting like this, inside her body. Her own body. She'd do anything for it already. But the time off work . . .

The baby bottle slipped into her breast-pocket easily. It would not be one of the one-hundred ones.

CATAMOUNT

We dream him, imagine him, create him from mud and smoke and time. Without the thought of him, the mystery of him, the possibility of him, life has no depth, no hope, no beyond.

He hears our call, sweeter than the howl of the coyote pack, which will come later, after the thaw, from the open place around which we have made our dens, a square we have ringed with white lights in sacks, imagining safety in this longest night. He is legend: sacred good and evil, hunter and hunted, mystery, romance, the past that walks invisible among us, hidden always in the undergrowth, just up there, catalogued in the color of the tawny overhang of stone. His carol—for that is what our communal cry on this longest cold night is meant to be—is the clatter of one stone in the brook, one branch muffled by drying ferns, one paw sinking in early snow. He watches our shadows thrown long on the snow, listens to the voice we raise through the muffling snow. The low purr in his breast joins the voices far below.

Jack Crossly, standing a little outside the circle of singing Newedeners, feels a chill down his nape, as if a snowflake has worked its way under his muffler and coat to melt there. As if someone has walked across his grave. As if he is being watched by some predator in the forest. He hunches and digs his fists deeper into his pockets. Katherine up there singing about the Christ-child, the baby in a barn, with the others, glances back at him and scowls. The candles light faces in long wavering golds. His wife wants him to join in this nonsense every year, and every year he comes on down to the Common for the tree-lighting, the soup and bread supper, the socializing. But damned if he'll sing. Mama'd always told him what a awful voice he had. And now it's gone all rusty from disuse. Eighty years of not singing'll do that.

Something up in the hills, in the dark mountains that ring the village, maybe the earth and rocks themselves, watches. Jack feels it. Maybe God, whatever that is. Maybe ghosts, all those gone on before. Come for the singing, the soup, the bread. Jack snorts to himself. Maybe come for him.

Lee marvels in his new low, chest-rumbling song. It is as if it has always lived inside him, even when he was a woman, and has just awakened, a secret thing that is beautiful, that sings of joy to the world, now out into the world. It sings his old songs as new songs. It is changed, like he is changed, but it is also the same, as he is the same. He watches his new daughter-in-law, Brandi, squinting at the sheets of music, the words of the song. That girl has not known much joy, Lee thinks. He hopes his son will help her to feel joy. That Brandi will bring joy to him. But Lee knows that joy is another secret thing, creeping along the pathways within all along. Some know to watch for its footprints, to listen for the purring or growling in another voice that is also, somehow, one's own voice. Maybe all of their voices. Lee thinks that maybe the voices within and the voices out here—individual selves, multiple personalities, two-spirits, the calls of the wild—are all one, a chorus, anyway. The voice within rises up even stronger: let heaven and angels sing.

The infant in Christine's arms, swaddled in footy pajamas, a turquoise snowsuit, blankets and her own wool coat, feels warm against her heart, a worm, a chrysalis, vulnerable to whatever it is that lurks up there in the darkness, comforted and safe here in the circle of candlelight, the square of luminaries, the song of neighbors. Chris has never felt so tired, or so happy so deep inside. She and Mari haven't slept more than a few hours at a stretch since the twins were born at Thanksgiving—so exhausted that Chris had hallucinated a large golden animal fading into the trees on the mountain from her view at the window as she rocked and sang to the baby who was crying at 5 A.M. this morning—but this is their favorite of Neweden traditions—lighting the pagan tree while singing the Christian story of miraculous virgin birth, sharing bread and soup and voice—and she had insisted they venture out. She looks at Mari, who holds the other infant within her own coat, the dark circles under her eyes accentuated by the wavering light of candles, wetness shining in her eyes as she sings about the deep sleep of Bethlehem. This miracle is older than the Jesus story, Chris thinks. Science, in vitro, has made the miracle of virgin birth—all birth of life—no less miraculous. She bumps her shoulder against Mari's, who looks up to meet her eyes. They smile. Chris feels tears welling in her eyes. This miracle is older than all of them; it is the story of everything.

He lifts his head into the night, scenting the air. Beyond the fresh of snow, our smells are of wood-smoke and baking grains. He is full and sleepy with fullness of fresh kill, buried now in hemlocks, and with the dark of this season. We raise our call again below, thin and whole, a part, as he is part, of the long night and the time of growing and the time of longest day and the time of harvest. We do not see him, but, as we know the seasons, we know him. He is part of us.

"Oh Little Town of Bethlehem" is Robby's favorite of the carols, but as they began to sing it, he discovers nothing comes from his throat. He will be near Bethlehem in two weeks, in Iraq, in the desert, in war. Robby closes his eyes. He smells the wood-smoke and the candle-smoke and the baking bread in the Union Hall, and his mother's faint aromas of bleach and shampoo, and hemlock and pine and the crisp wet of snow. Home.

He sees the brown of desert sand in his mind. It will be the color of the catamount they'd studied in Vermont history, the one stuffed and mounted at the historical society museum. Last one killed at the turn of the century, they said, though some claim to still see one now and then. The man with the rifle across his knees in the old black-and-white photo, the lion lifeless on the ground before him. Robby is a good shot, but he's only killed once, a doe on youth hunters' day when he was twelve. The warm buckskin under his hand. The dead thing once so beautiful and alive. The liquid brown eyes fogging over. How can I ever kill a man?

"In thy deep and dreamless sleep, the silent stars go by." Robby opens his eyes to look up, knowing that the sky is hidden by clouds, that snowflakes will dampen his cheeks. And they do. One melts in his eyelashes. He tries to join in the song, watching the lights of the tree and candles illuminate the faces of everyone he's ever known, but his chest will not release his voice. He manages a whisper at "shineth, an everlasting light," but can not finish, "The hopes and fears of all the years are met in thee tonight."

Maddy holds tight to Jared's hand. The dark is so dark here in the country. The city is never like this. She had liked Neweden in the summer, but this is a different kind of visit home for the winter break with the boyfriend. All these traditions. It is cute, but maybe a little too cute. Too perfect. Still, as she glances around at the people in the circle, singing—God, could you get more cheesy?—"Better watch out, better not cry, better not shout, I'm telling you why," they seem awfully happy. Real, even though their whole lives were like a big cliché. Like they aren't performing something out of a Norman Rockwell painting but actually believe this is life. Like it is real.

"He sees you when you're sleeping," is more like it for her. Always someone watching, lurking. Surely they can feel that. That thing out there in the darkness, in the woods.

Jared had taken her cross-country skiing that morning and had showed her a footprint in the snow, like a big cat's paw. "Catamount," he'd said. "A mountain lion or Canadian lynx anyway." Then he'd laughed at the shock on her face. "Kidding!" he'd said. "Just a dog, probably." She'd retaliated with a fistful of snow down his pants. The footprint had been bigger than any dog's though.

Maddy shivers and snuggles closer to Jared. At least we're safe here in town, she thinks. Nothing can get us here. Nothing but that jolly old elf, Santa, anyway.

Ashley sings the Santa Claus song as loud as she can. If he is watching her right now, he'll be impressed. She'd been good good good all week. Not a single mistake. She hadn't spilled her juice. She'd brought the laundry to the kitchen the first time Daddy told her to. And she had just ignored her big brother, Will, when he changed the channel on the TV He'll be lucky to get anything from Santa. Will didn't even believe in Santa! Mom says that as long as you believe in him, he exists. And Ashley believes! She's going to get everything on her list, except maybe the pony. Everything is real. Even stuff like Santa and fairies and god and monsters that kill chickens in the night are real. Just cause you can't see it didn't make it not so. Air is real. Why not Santa Claus? Why not everything?

His tail thumps the rock, twitching in his sleep. He dreams of small furred creatures, of fish and birds and us, the two-legs. He hunts, he watches, he sings a low voice licking the tawny fur of a female in his visions. His stories are in the granite and the clear streams and the tall pines. He is the dark and the white ghost of fog. He is woven into us even as we move from the Common toward the Union Hall.

Vicky feels the weight of hands upon her shoulders, patting her back and arms, touching her cheek, circling her waist though her coat in the darkness though Hal is in the city for his end-of-year review. Her neighbors, her friends, her community—the whole world, it seems—touches her. The candles flicker, bending in the air of movement toward soup and bread and warmth. Her dead baby, Angela, is here too, in a way. She is in those hands. She is in the smell of winter air. She is a creature that floats through the forest, insubstantial, invisible, without form, like grief and hope and betrayal and love. And just as real.

Lawrence pats the shoulder of the girl who lost her child. He would like to tell her that children are never truly lost, that they are all one. He would like to think that she feels his touch, his presence, and that too of the child, Angela, who is there with him and with his wife and with all the others. Light and dark, they are all energy moving around and about each other. They are all, part of all.

Sharon knows the catamount is up there, watching them all. Watching over them. She has seen him, clear as day, in the treeless swath where the power-lines march up and over the mountain into the next valley. She'd been snowshoeing up the unplowed road called Steep Way toward the ruined settlement site of Oldeden at the top, her daily exercise now that the snow had come, and there he was, sitting on a boulder a hundred yards away, watching her. Her heart speeded up, but she made herself stand still, breathing hard to catch her breath, the sweat she'd worked up chilling at her back. The creature is not a myth. He is real. He is long and brown, alert but unfazed by her appearance, as if he expects her. No. As if he simply knows she is there even if she has not known of him.

He watched her. She watched him. Finally, he blinked and looked off into the woods. He glanced at her once more, then stood and jumped lazily, effortlessly, across the clearing and vanished.

Sharon feels him now, listening to the silence and low murmurs of the others, moving into the arch of gold spilling from the open doors of the Union Hall. He is above them somewhere in the darkness, watching, or perhaps, moving with them into light.

FROST HEAVES

Jack finally had a good excuse for not tending to the winter chores, Katherine thought. Being dead and all. As she had done for nearly fifty years of marriage, with no help from him, she kept the bird feeders filled, the sidewalk shoveled, the dirt road plowed, and the wood stove chocked full and hot. She watched goldfinches, chickadees, and woodpeckers squabbling for seed and suet through rippled glass etched with frost, the window sills crowded with her collection of dusty birds' nests. Twigs dislodged from them and littered the floor. *National Geographics* and seed catalogues piled up. The farmhouse too seemed to wait for spring, muffled in snow. Sometimes Katherine found her mouth open, words collecting in the hollow, and would snap her teeth together, jaw creaking. She would not be one of those old women who talked to herself, though what would be the difference? Jack hadn't listened when he'd been here. Jack was waiting, too. As she watched the birds, she thought of him, in the freezer of Seth Markinson's Funeral Home in town. Waiting for the thaw.

She had waited for Jack to come home from the war, waited for him to move out of his mother's house—this house, from which he had never moved, until now. A snort of her laughter burst into the empty room. She shook her head and took a sip from her coffee cup. She had waited for Jack all those years ago to marry her and have children, which he finally did. Then she had waited for him to come home from work, from the tavern, from the diner, from the volunteer fire station, the Eagles, the V.F.W., from hunting camp or the ice fishing shanty. She had waited for him to retire. She had waited for him to take her on the long-postponed honeymoon to Europe, or even Disney World. She had waited for him to visit their children, their grandchildren, in Phoenix, in San Francisco, in Tampa. Her waiting had made no difference.

Katherine rubbed her forehead, where a dull ache was beginning. Too much caffeine, she supposed. Her tongue whisked against her teeth and a little *tsk* escaped. She had waited for Jack all her life, it seemed. And now she had to wait until the ground finally thawed to bury him in the family plot. Just like Jack Crossly to die in January.

The funeral had been on a frigid evening, and the turnout had been good despite the cold. Jack's buddies from the V.F.W. and the Eagles Club came with their wives. Katherine's friends from the perennial swappers group brought flowers. The church women prepared food. Nicky, their youngest and still single, flew up from Tampa, to stay for two weeks. Cecilia, the oldest, came all the way from Phoenix with her husband, Mark, and the three children, including one from his first marriage. Richard—her middle child—had left his wife, pregnant and unable to fly, at home in San Diego with their toddler for the five days. Reverend Willette said kind things about Jack, and about Katherine herself, sitting shoulder to shoulder with her grown children, her strong sons and daughter and their fine families. "Jack," he said, "has gone home to his Lord, to a warm sunny day of eternal life in heaven." And Katherine caught herself thinking ill of the dead. Would Jack want to be in a place where there was no good excuse to sit with his buddies around a wood stove playing poker in an ice fishing shanty or at the neon-lighted bar in the early dark of winter? She doubted it. But maybe he *was* gone to a better place with God.

During the service Nicky had taken her hand and stifled a sob, poor boy. He would miss his father most, Katherine thought, just as he always had. He had come late in life, when she thought she was finished with childbearing, partly because of her age but mostly because Jack had begun to turn away from her, crawling into their bed in the wee hours, smelling of beer and passing out facing the wall. Or most nights just sleeping in front of the television in the living room. She had tried touching him and kissing him passionately. She read some of those books that were so popular in the 70's about how to keep the sex alive in a marriage, but by then it had been too long. They were too old. It was as if he had shoved a boulder over his heart and hidden away those few bits of himself that he had shared with her now and then in the early years. Nicky came when they were in their forties, after the last time Jack had ever touched her like that. Katherine patted Nicky's hand. He held a tissue to his eyes.

Richard and Cecilia were already teenagers when Nicky was born. Of the three, Nicky had seemed the most lonely for his father, perhaps because he had no siblings at home after Richard left for college and Cecilia got mixed up with that boy. But Jack had been no more interested in Nicky than his older children—nor in her, Katherine supposed. She squeezed Nicky's hand, wishing again that Jack had just once taken the boy off to hunting camp or for one of those endless days in the ice fishing shanty with his pals without her nagging him to do it. How did Nick remember those days, she wondered. How did he remember his dad? She wanted to ask him, but she wouldn't like the answer. Poor Nicky, now a thirty-three-year-old man with grotesque muscles, no girlfriends she could detect and a job in a fitness center—whatever that was—seemed aimless and frivolous. Jack should have showed an interest in the boy. He should have shown him how to be a man. She had tried to make up for Jack's inattention, for his absence, but a mother can only do so much.

Katherine caught Cecilia and Richard on her right exchanging a look. Probably a comment on Nick's crying. The two of them had always seemed so confident, so strong. They had been a team even in childhood, only ten months apart, first Cecilia helping the younger Richard, then, in adolescence, Richard becoming the protector of his sister. There had been little room for Nick, the baby. And Katherine in turn had had little extra time for them too, sleep-deprived as she was, rocking a colicky newborn at forty. No wonder Cecilia had gotten involved with that boy. Katherine prayed that God would forgive her her faults and failures as a mother. She had done the best she could. Maybe Cecelia's eye-roll was just a response to Reverend Willette. "Jack Crossly will be remembered as a giving man," he asserted, "a man who walked close to God in all he did." Katherine swallowed and blinked, trying to work up some tears for the sake of appearances.

January dragged into February, the days beginning and ending in a darkness broken only by the hoof-hoof barking of owls. Each day stretched the light a minute or three longer at dawn and dusk. Seed catalogs crowded the *National Geographic* in the mailbox, but Katherine couldn't make herself plan for planting, for trying new strains of tomatoes or new lettuces. Gardening season seemed so far away this year, the cold so complete and the earth so iron-hard, still buried under feet of snow. She flipped through an article on Mozambique rather than read the magazine through as was her habit, and she didn't bother to snip any articles on places she thought she might like someday to see. The old office filing cabinet in the unheated parlor where she paid bills was too stuffed already with clippings about the travels she had imagined. In the seed catalog, she turned down the corner of a page not to remind herself of a broccoli or a dahlia, but to mark the passage of minutes. She sipped coffee from the pot she kept going all day.

She stopped often to look at the feeders. The yellow of the goldfinches glowed against the gray skies. Red Hot Poker this year, she thought, in the front flower bed by the walk. Maybe some Snow in Summer in the window boxes. She could see the file cabinet through the glass door to the front room. It seemed heavy, the dust on it thick. She could almost feel the paper maps and articles fossilizing in the cold. Mount Kilimanjaro, the Great Wall of China, the Silk Road, the Appalachian Trail, the Circumnavigation of the Earth, the White Cliffs of Dover.

This winter's days were not so different from any other. Jack would be ice fishing if he were still alive, huddling in his plywood shanty over a hole in the lake, warmed by the little heater, the Wild Turkey, and the poker-talk of his buddies. She would be here alone, in his mother's house, scanning the catalogs and watching the birds, stoking the wood stove and shoveling the walks, waiting for the sound of Jack's truck in the drive, and for spring. Maybe she should do something different this summer. Maybe no garden at all. Maybe she should leave, finally travel.

"Come to Tampa for the winter," Nicky had said, sitting here at the kitchen table after the funeral. "You'll be warm. You need a change of scene."

"Or Phoenix," Cecilia said, careful not to look at Mark, her husband. "We have a room just waiting for you. And a swimming pool. And the children would love to have you there after school. *I* would love to have you there." Mark, to his credit, didn't move.

But Katherine knew what it was like to live with a mother-in-law. She noticed that Richard wisely kept silent. Her daughter meant well, but Katherine had hated those first two years of her own marriage, living with old Mrs. Crossly—she still thought of Jack's mother that way—taking care of the old woman while she slowly died, as a good daughter-in-law should, never mind that she had two babies in diapers. And Nicky's little apartment . . . well, no, that would never do. He said he needed her, but he didn't. He needed her money maybe, but not her. This house, the Crossly place, was hers now, finally, and she wanted to feel it around her in that new way. Maybe she'd have that awful old chicken coop knocked down in the spring. Maybe she'd have the peeling white clapboards painted a color other than white green or even blue. Maybe she'd grow sunflowers along the fence-row. Old Mrs. Crossly had hated sunflowers, and Jack mowed them down the year Katherine had planted them. "Mama wouldn't want it," he'd said, even though she was dead. Katherine watched as a nest on the windowsill shed a few wisps of straw and motes of dust. Her blue stoneware coffee mug clunked loud on the table. She reached for the seed catalog. Sunflowers. Definitely sunflowers.

Gravy Laval called on a Thursday afternoon in early February. "Katy," he yelled. Katherine held the receiver away from her ear. Gravy was a bit deaf and assumed that the whole world needed a higher volume. "How'ya doin', hon?" he asked. He was always too familiar.

"Just fine, Graves Laval," she said, her eye settling on the file cabinet in the parlor. How had that drawer slid open? "And you?" The tilt of the floor, she decided. Gravity.

Gravy laughed. "Oh, good, good," he said. "Keepin' busy doin' nothin', don'cha know."

Katherine knew. Just like Jack, Gravy divided his time in winter between fishing, hunting, and drinking, the first activities always including the third. What did he want with her? "I never thanked you for giving the eulogy, Graves," she said. "I'm sure Jack would have liked it."

Gravy had shouted out fish stories and drinking stories from the pulpit, and had surprised everyone, including Katherine, by ending with a poem. "Jack used to recite this on those long afternoons down to the pond, all'a us huddled 'round the hole and the heater," Gravy had said. "He said he'd like it read at his funeral." Katherine remembered the odd sensation of her jaw falling. She remembered Cecelia's raised eyebrows. She had had no idea that Jack ever thought about dying, much less that he knew any poetry. The poem was Frost's "The Road Less Traveled."

Gravy finally got around to the point of his phone call. "Just don't wantcha to forget that Jack's shanty's still on the pond," he said. "When the ice starts to thin, the Fish'n Wildlife'll be postin' notes."

Katherine sighed. Just like Jack to go off and leave chores undone, a mess for her to clean up. She touched the soft web of brown grass inside a nest on the windowsill. The hardened mud shell cracked and the whole thing disintegrated into a heap of dirt. One more thing to clean up. "Tell me what I need to do, Graves," she said.

Six weeks after Jack's passing, on the first day the temperatures broke the freezing mark, a flock of cedar waxwings arrived. They chirred and squabbled in the crab-apple tree, methodically cleaning the dried fruits from bare branches, starting up in a flutter each time Katherine came out the door to fetch wood, then settling back down like living decoration, their black masks and bright yellow tail feathers brilliant beside the red beads of apples and the blue winter sky. The roof dripped under the sun, long icicles cracking off and the snowpack zipping off the metal roof to whump onto the drifts below.

On the third day of the snowmelt, Katherine started up the old pick-up truck and eased down the driveway, glad she'd had Nicky lock the hubs into four-wheel-drive before he left. The cold had her arthritis flaring up. She'd read that on the new trucks you could switch over to 4x4 with the flick of a switch inside the cab even while driving. Jack had refused to buy anything new. The roofs of three rusty hulks of parts trucks, the same model as the one that worked, poked through the snow behind the barn.

This year, she decided as she drove out, she wouldn't mow or spray Round-Up back there. Let the poison ivy and Virginia creeper and honeysuckle vines grow, and parts for the truck be damned.

The dirt road down the mountain was treacherous, the mud still frozen but skinned thinly with melted water. At least the town trucks had been out ahead of her, spreading gravel and salt, something for a little traction. At the end of the stone wall that marked the Crossly land, Katherine stopped and shifted the truck into park to keep the engine running and the heater going while she scooted across the seat, rolled down the window and reached into the mailbox. Bills, the new *National Geographic* with a feature titled "On the Brink of Extinction." A map fell out onto the seat. She sat still for a minute, smelling the air and listening to the little breeze clacking the birch trees together. She noted a tiny nest about six feet up in the sugar bush beside the road. It was cup-shaped, a hummingbird nest, she thought. She didn't have one like that in her collection. Could she reach it ? Maybe so, if she could climb the snowbank pushed up by the plows. Next time out, she'd bring some nippers to cut the branches.

Bootprints marked where someone had gone up and through the opening in the wall into the Crossly family cemetery. Maybe Seth Markinson or one of his boys from the funeral home had been by, checking on the location for Jack after the thaw. The snowpack was still knee-deep, crusted with a layer of gleaming ice from the last nor'easter. Likely they'd have at least a few more big storms before spring truly arrived in April, but this little plateau got good south light, the view down the valley to the white steeples of town wide and bright. The snow would melt early here. She could already see old Mrs. Crossly's gravestone protruding through the white, like a gray bridge, the arch too perfect against the wildness of the sugar bush and snow-draped hemlocks. The footprints continued past it to the far stone wall, and there sat Sam Fellows in the sun, scribbling on a pad. He looked up and waved.

Katherine set the parking brake, left the engine running, and eased herself down from the pickup. A map from the *National Geographic* fell into the road, and she stooped to rescue it, dripping with mud and ice crystals. Sam stood and started over, sinking into the snow with each wide step. "Morning Miz Crossly," he called. "How are you?"

Katherine stopped at the snow bank, the hand with the map resting on the warm hood of the truck, and waved back. "Doin' fine, Samuel. And yourself?"

He kept walking as he called back across the snow, "Well, thank you." Sam was not a young man, though Katherine remembered minding him as a baby, just after Jack had come home from the war, when she had still been giddy with the thrill of their engagement and before it had become clear that old Mrs. Crossly did not want to lose her son to another woman just yet. Why Sam must be nearly sixty, she realized. Such a sad life. Gone to the bad war in Vietnam and come home, like so many of the boys, bearded and quiet. A few years later he married Lucy, that hippie girl from New York, in the orchard at his grandfather's place. She remembered holding Nicky in her arms, she and the baby both crying. Weddings—the way the young people looked so fresh and confident—always pushed a chunk of bile and pain up into her throat. A year or so after that, Richard had been Sam's student in History at the high school, the same year the wife, Lucy, had gone missing. Sam had found her; she'd hanged herself from an apple tree in that same orchard.

"What are you up to out here in the cold, Sam?" Katherine called.

He half-slid down the snowbank, just under the hummingbird nest, and stood by the truck, stomping his boots to make the snow fall off his wool trousers. "Working, Miz Crossly," he said. "Working." He wiped the hoarfrost from his mustache with a finger and grinned. "I'm documenting all the cemeteries in the county, making a list of repairs needed. The state gave me a little grant money, and in the summer I'll have a bunch of Y.C.C. kids working for me."

Katherine smiled. Sam had taught history at the high school since the '60's, and everybody knew about his graveyard interests. "Good for you," she said. She nodded toward the Crossly plot. "How's she look?" she asked.

"Oh fine," Sam said, consulting his little pad, "near as I can tell with the snow anyway. I reckon we'll at least come by to right that stone that's askew." He pointed to the tall column that marked Jack's grandfather's grave and grinned. "Every spring after the thaw my pap used to say he was harvestin' stones. Frost heaves, you know."

Katherine laughed at the old joke. Then she made her mouth serious. "Well," she said, "we'll be putting Jack in there soon as it's warm enough."

Sam nodded and put his hand on her shoulder. "Yep," he said. "I'll come for the burial, Mrs. Crossly," he said. "You be sure and let me know when. It can be a hard time. Harder than the funeral even."

Katherine looked up at the nest again to avoid his gaze, blinking, remembering that his wife, Lucy, had died in the winter too. The woman had been buried in the Fellows family plot up above the orchard, and Sam too had probably had to wait til spring.

When Nicky and Cecilia urged her to leave Vermont for the winter, Katherine had used Jack as her excuse. "I can't leave your father here like that," she'd said. "Not yet at rest." But she knew he was at rest, even in the freezer at Markinson's, as much at rest as he'd ever been or ever would be. "It just wouldn't be right," she'd told them. Unfinished business. Though he never finished anything else, she'd make sure this last thing got done right. She hadn't left him in all these years because God wouldn't have wanted it; divorce just wasn't done, not in her family or in his. And she damned sure wasn't leaving him now, not yet. She loved him, though he was a hard man to love, and he had loved her, after his fashion. They were husband and wife, joined by God in the church, and that was as it should be. Til death do us part.

"The pipes will freeze," she'd said to her children. "And the goldfinches . . . " The goldfinches, in particular, needed her to keep the feeders full. She had lured them with thistle seeds into staying north for the winter, so she had to be diligent in checking and refilling the plastic tubes at the windows, nearly every other day. They would die if she didn't keep feeding them now.

"I don't like leaving you here alone, Mama," Nicky had said, finally packing his bags to return to Florida. "What if something happens?"

Indeed, Katherine had thought. What if something happens? That was what she had needed Jack Crossly for: to come home eventually and find her dead or injured or stuck in the snow. But he had died, not her, and she had kept from falling and breaking a hip all these years already, and could wrap the chains around a tree to pull herself out of a ditch just fine. Nothing had happened in all these years of waiting; why should it now?

When she finally reached the paved highway at the bottom of the gravel road, Katherine's fingers ached from gripping the steering wheel. She'd left Sam at his truck at the foot of the mountain, then turned down the highway toward town. About two miles toward Brattleboro, the Village of Neweden road crew—Kip Hathaway and his son, Kip Junior—looked up from the hand-painted board they were affixing below a speed limit sign and waved as she passed. The dip and bump in the asphalt, just where it appeared about this time every year, confirmed the warning they were posting: Frost Heaves. Katherine slowed, of course, the Saab with the Connecticut plates riding her bumper be damned. The old pick-up rocked and creaked without any damage to the springs, or so she hoped. The Saab roared past her, crossing the yellow line of the curve, and shot ahead. Jack would've cussed'em out or worse, chased them toward the Interstate, but Katherine just wished them a busted tailpipe at the next frost heave or a patch of black ice on a curve. "What's your hurry?" she muttered. She'd had enough wildlife jump out into the road—deer, mostly, but twice moose and once a big bobcat—to know you needed to keep alert and within the speed limit. Now the thaw had begun, the critters would be moving down from the hills.

When she reached town, Katherine was gratified to see the Saab stopped in the long line of cars at the first traffic light. See, she thought as she passed the little red car and turned into the parking lot of Markinson's, hurrying never really gets you ahead.

The waitress at Sally's on Main Street had light blue hair that stuck out every which way, a ring in her upper lip and another in her eyebrow. "Hi," she said, brightly. "Something to drink?"

"Coffee," Katherine replied, picking up the menu so she wouldn't have to look at the girl's perforated face or at the large brown envelope she had gotten at the funeral home now resting next to the salt and pepper shakers.

"Be right back," the girl said, and Katherine saw that she wore bright yellow tights under cut-off Army pants with black boots. Youngsters. Katherine shook her head. Back when Cecilia had waited tables here, the girls had had to wear uniforms, blue dresses with white aprons. Katherine remembered finding the note in the pocket of one while sorting laundry. It was from Bitsie Whitehouse—Cecilia's best friend—written in a teenaged girl's looping cursive. She waited up for Cecilia that long evening after putting Nicky to bed, and she remembered her daughter's admission that yes, she was pregnant, and yes, that boy with the ponytail from California was the father, and that yes, she was going to get rid of it. Katherine remembered that waiting room in Albany, the tiny high windows and green tile floors, and Nicky, a terrible-two, refusing to stay put in a chair. Katherine remembered the way a young girl came in the door, stomping her feet and blowing on her hands, and stopped in her tracks at the sight of the little boy staring up at her, thumb in his mouth.

The blue-haired waitress slid a cup of coffee onto Katherine's table and held her pen over her pad. "Ready to order?" she asked.

Katherine glanced at the Specials board over the counter. "I'll have a bowl of the soup," she said. "And bread." The girl nodded and took the menu away. The lumpy brown envelope seemed to move in her peripheral vision with the imperceptible pace of a glacier. Katherine shook herself. Foolish to be spooked by such stuff. She picked it up and pried open the metal clasp, then dumped the contents out on the table. Jack's *personal effects,* Seth Markinson had called them. Jack's body had gone to the funeral home from the fishing shanty where he'd been pronounced dead of a heart attack, and these were the things in his pockets. A pen knife made from a deer's hoof Jack's grandfather had owned. She would give that to Richard, the first-born son. A pocket watch that had been stopped for forty years, a casualty of the war in the Pacific, by the salt of the sea. Katherine still couldn't imagine Jack on a ship, on the ocean, coiling ropes and hoisting anchors. How could a Vermont farm boy—logger, snow plow driver, volunteer fireman, pulp mill laborer—also be a sailor? It hadn't fit, though that was the thing she had fallen for when she was fifteen, his white uniform with the jaunty cap, and the romance of loving a man away at war. Nicky should have the watch, she decided. Maybe he could get it fixed. Three dollar bills, two quarters, and a penny. Not enough for a man to have in his pockets, Katherine thought. He should have had more. She looked down the length of the diner toward the front windows. She thought of Cecilia dozing in the car after their trip to Albany, and Nicky bouncing on the backseat. She thought of Richard when she confronted him years later with his sister's disappearance: "Leave her alone, Mama. She's fine. We can take care of ourselves." Maybe they *all* should have had more.

The waitress stood at the end of the counter talking with a young man whose hair was matted into thick cords. His thick sweater looked foreign, like one of those sold by the Guatemalan immigrants in the farmer's market. At least he was clean-shaven. "I like waiting tables some," the girl said. "It's like a great thing to do while you're taking a break from real life, you know, going to college or having a career or being like a productive member of society. But the standing around, you know—Shit. Bor-ring."

The boy nodded sagely. "So why not get on with it?" he asked. "Go somewhere."

The girl shrugged. "I don't know. Get on with what, is the question, I guess. Go where?" The cook dinged a bell, and the waitress started over to pick up Katherine's order. "It's not a bad job in the meantime," she said.

Katherine pushed Jack's personal effects to the side to make room for her soup and let her hand linger on his thick brown leather wallet. She slid her thumb into the fold, swelling half-open with all the junk he carried. Cecilia used to call it a filing cabinet. "How can you bear to sit on that?" Katherine remembered exclaiming to Jack.

The waitress put the steaming soup in front of her, a thick chunk of bread on the side. Katherine flipped open the billfold. In a plastic case, she found school photos of Cecilia, Richard, and Nicky, three each of the older two, chronicling their growth from first to sixth grades to high school, and only one of Nick, when he was about ten. Old Mrs. Crossly scowled out from a black and white taken near the time of her death, her hands gripping the porch railing tightly, chickens in the yard. The only photo of Katherine was tiny, a snapshot of her at fifteen, just before Jack had left for the Navy. She remembered giving him the picture, shy and embarrassed and also excited, feeling daring, because she was wearing only a swimsuit in the photo and had posed like a film star, hip thrust out and her lipstick-painted mouth in a pout. Who had she been? Where had that girl gone?

Katherine dipped her spoon into the split pea soup. The color was beautiful, the color of spring, and she felt the warmth of it travel down her throat. She counted six-teen gas station receipts dating back three years. There were folded flyers from a volunteer fire department ben-efit barbecue and the V.F.W. annual community service awards banquet. Inside one soft sleeve, she thought she felt a twig that turned out to be a small red feather, a cardinal's probably. Jack had never seemed to notice her bird feeders, except to complain about how much money she spent on seed. Where had he picked this up? Why had he kept it? Katherine brushed her lips with the feather and laid it on the table beside her coffee cup.

The wallet held fifteen business cards from tractor sales-men and antique dealers. On the back of several, in Jack's familiar block print, were notes and numbers, prices or sizes of items he was considering. In the section for money, Katherine found a copy of the poem Gravy had read at the funeral, a page torn from a book, yellowed tape holding it together at the folds. She re-read the last stanzas.

Oh, I kept the first for another day!
Yet knowing how way leads on to way,
I doubted if I should ever come back.

I shall be telling this with a sigh
Somewhere ages and ages hence:
Two roads diverged in a wood, and I—
I took the one less traveled by,
And that has made all the difference.

Why this poem? Katherine fingered the smooth tape on the page. Jack's life had been ordinary, plain, as plain as hers. Did he regret his choices? She clanked her spoon against the bowl and sat straighter. What right had he to regret? She was the one who had made the sacrifices. She had traveled his road, the ordinary road. She had done what was expected of her. She had tended to his mother. She had raised his children up right, had taken care of all of them, of his house, his mother's house. She cooked and cleaned for him, made a home for him. She stayed with him even after he turned away from her. She never complained. She did what was right, had she not? What had he lacked for? What did Jack Crosly think he had missed? Katherine stared down at the green soup, watching as chunk of ham broke the surface. Her stomach turned. She pushed the bowl away.

"Everything okay?" Katherine looked up, startled, at the girl with the blue hair. "Soup okay?" she asked. Katherine blinked. The girl waved the coffee pot she was holding. "Would you like a refill?"

Katherine nodded.

"Oh, Frost," the girl said, pouring. "You know that's the most-loved poem in America. I mean, that's the poem most Americans say is their favorite." She grinned when Katherine met her eyes. "Ironic, huh?"

By the time Gravy and his grandson loaded the ice fishing shanty into the bed of Katherine's pick-up and tied it down, the sun had been completely extinguished, first by clouds, then by snow and ice, and finally by complete darkness. Katherine fumed, driving back up the highway toward Neweden, white ghosts swirling in her headlights. She should have known better than to expect Graves Laval to be on time. She had paid her bill and left Jack's $3.51 on the table at the diner for the blue-haired waitress at exactly 2 P.M. and pulled off the highway beside the frozen pond at 2:30, just after Gravy's grandson was due out of school. She sat there for over an hour before the pair turned up, and when they finally got the shack to shore, Gravy said,

Frost Heaves

"Maybe ya oughta wait out the storm," and offered to put her up in his spare room. But Katherine was no fool. Gravy knew how she'd taken care of Jack all those years, and she bet he was just tired of doing his own cooking and laundry. She wasn't going to be stuck with another old man to care for in this life. Gravy probably took his time getting the shack loaded on purpose.

The owl came out of total darkness, swooping low into her headlights, and Katherine gasped and ducked in reflex. It was snowy white and huge, wings and tail feathers spread, talons reaching for some small creature on the other side of the road. A wingtip brushed her windshield. Katherine pumped the brake, but it didn't matter. The bird had already disappeared into the darkness. She remembered to breathe again. Her heart pounded, rushing warmth into her chest. The truck rolled slowly forward, setting into a straight line, not skidding or sliding on the slick road. Lucky owl, she thought, probably a male, hunting to feed his mate, already nested in the dark woods above. She would never have been able to stop in time, and she would never have forgiven herself if she had killed him. Still warm and a little queasy with adrenaline, Katherine didn't remember the frost heave until it was too late. She hit the dip and the bump at her regular speed of forty-five miles per hour. The truck clunked.

She had nearly forgotten the ice shanty behind her in the pickup bed. Maybe it had begun to rock when she swerved to miss the owl. Maybe the ropes had slipped, Graves Laval and his grandson having not taken the proper care in tying them. Maybe she hit the bump too fast. Whatever the reason, at the frost heave, the tall plywood ice shanty behind her screeched against the metal side of the truck and tumbled, with a satisfying crunch, into the snowbank on the roadside.

The storm had been a big one, dumping two feet of heavy wet snow overnight, the morning sky a deep blue and everything dripping in the bright sun. Katherine stood at the window, watching the fluttering goldfinches jockey for perches as she sipped coffee. Great clumps of snow whumped to the ground. Katherine thought about the ice shanty, a pile of twigs, kindling on the side of the road, surely now buried by the storm and snowplows. She'd stopped, her flashers illuminating the snowy road, and got out to look, but there had been nothing to do for the little house. She was alone on a February night, a seven-ty-year-old woman, no traffic, no movement. She might have waited for someone to come along—Kip and Kip Junior were likely out in the plows—but Jack's shanty was broken, all akilter, worthless. She remembered the sound of the laugh that snorted from her nose into the night, a short huff under the rumble of the truck engine, the *shush* of the snow falling. She'd been surprised by the tears freezing to ice pellets on her cheeks. "God damn you, Jack!" she'd yelled into the white silence.

Jack needed me to wait, Katherine thought now. He needed me here, waiting. That's how he loved me. *Why?* Why did she wait? Katherine thought of him waiting now in the freezer at Markinson's. At peace. The wings of the owl had been so wide and white in her windshield, and she had made a little sound, *Ahh.* At least she hadn't hit the owl, hadn't killed it. Crazy old woman, yelling into the darkness, alone.

Katherine remembered Jack at the window, watching the feeders, just as she was doing now, not more than a month before he died. He had not known she was there, behind him, having just washed his breakfast dishes. A shadow rushed the window, scattering the finches, but Jack had not moved. A red-tail hawk snatched a bird as it fluttered up from the ground below the feeder under the eaves, one of the soft mourning doves. Katherine remembered the gray wing feathers spread wide, small against the background of the hawk's white and black speckled chest and russet banded tail. She remembered how the moment swelled, expanding time like a flame spreading out from twigs into the whole box of the wood stove. She remembered Jack's face in profile, his gray eyes steely, unblinking, observing. It was lovely, and it was horrible. He hadn't moved. The hawk flapped backwards, up again, and disappeared over the roof. Granite rose within her chest as she watched him, wanting him to be angry, to go for his shotgun, to do something, to say something. But Jack had just stood there, resignation on his brow.

Katherine touched her lips with cool fingers. That morning the birds had returned, one by one, to the feeders, plucking seeds from the little holes in the tubes, clinging to the suet cages, scuffling on the snowy ground. She had kept the feeders filled all winter. Jack sighed once, then turned from the window. He went off to the ice shanty to fish. To drink. To recite poems, of all things. She remembered thinking, *stupid*. The birds. Already forgetting.

The white owl had brushed the glass of windshield with his feather tips last night, as if trying to touch her. She could have killed him, changed the lives of his mate and their young forever. But she hadn't. He disappeared into the woods, the undergrowth, and Jack's shanty had tipped out of the truck to be buried by snow. The female would not have waited for the husband to return, not for long.

Katherine's chest expanded, and she felt the thickening of tears again in her eyes. Her lungs expanded, mud pushing against her chest, perhaps her heart beating, "No," she said aloud. She grabbed a tissue from the box and blew her nose with a snort that was loud and wet in the empty house. She wanted, suddenly, to clear the house of dust and cobwebs, to wash windows and scrub cabinets and closets, though it was nowhere near time for spring cleaning. Jack's clothes needed to be packed for the church's used goods store. Things needed to be gone through and got rid of. Space needed to be cleared. Wood floors scrubbed and waxed. Walls painted fresh. "Yes," she said aloud, the words echoing from the plaster walls and wood floors, "I need to . . . "

Katherine let the words hang in the air. She sat her cup down on the windowsill with a thunk that knocked a bird's nest to the floor, where it shattered into a heap of sticks. She smiled, remembering the hummingbird nest over the mailbox, imagining herself trying to climb a snowbank with clippers to get it. Absurd. And for what?

Gathering seed catalogs into a pile in her arms, Katherine opened the glass door to the front room and stepped into the cold air. In the parlor wood stove, she made a little pile of the birds' nests from the window sills, dry and twiggy, in the ashes. They flamed up quickly at the spark of the match, smoking a little. She added pages from the seed catalogs. While the logs crackled, warming the room, she brought Jack's wallet in and pulled out the picture of herself at fifteen, the girl in the swimsuit with life sparkling in her eyes, daring in her pose, hip thrust out. With that girl watching, Katherine opened the drawer of her filing cabinet and pulled out a pile of maps. Time to get on with it. Mount Kilimanjaro, the Great Wall of China, the Silk Road, the Appalachian Trail, the Circumnavigation of the Earth, the White Cliffs of Dover. She spread open On the Brink of Extinction, the blue and green planet and bright creatures blotted with mud from the road. Little gravel rocks clattered to the floor. "Okay," she said, "Let's go."